Copyright © 2024 Elliot Eaton

All rights reserved.

ISBN: 9798877953147

JOSEPH JADE PUBLICATIONS

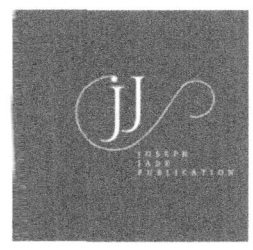

CONTENTS

CHAPTER ONE Connecting the Worlds	2
CHAPTER TWO The Fox's Debt	16
CHAPTER THREE Mr 'Bullet' Brown	30
CHAPTER FOUR The beautiful south	44
CHAPTER FIVE Terry's Hub	57
CHAPTER SIX Horror Storie's	70
CHAPTER SEVEN John Corbett	84
CHAPTER EIGHT Casemore Gold	98
CHAPTER NINE The Deadly Meeting	112
CHAPTER TEN The Superintendent	125
CHAPTER ELEVEN Captain Spike	137

CHAPTER TWELVE Whitwall Harbour Royalty	147
CHAPTER THIRTEEN The Burning Funeral	157
CHAPTER FOURTEEN The Council	166
CHAPTER FIFTEEN The Lost Initials	177
CHAPTER SIXTEEN Miss Gold	187
CHAPTER SEVENTEEN Guilty Without Trial	198
CHAPTER EIGHTEEN Unexpected Reunion	209
CHAPTER NINETEEN The Kingdom Portal	220
CHAPTER TWENTY The Secret Weapon	231
CHAPTER TWENTY-ONE Somewhere In-between	241
CHAPTER TWENTY-TWO Just Use Your Imagination	252

ACKNOWLEDGMENTS

There are too many people to acknowledge for just a paragraph before the story begins. However, as many of the elements of this story are taken from real-life situations I should mention a few.

I started my working life at 'The Bulls Head' which was referred to by my uncle as 'The Black Bull' most of the time. The staff there (including my now wife) or other establishments influenced many situations that although I would never work in a pub again, give me fond memories.

Yes, I am a Leicester City fan which had to be snook into at least one of my novels.

The original idea for this story began with me being off work ill from regular surgeries and whilst contemplating a lot of things at home unable to do a lot, let's just say my imagination went wild. If at the time I had the know how I would have written a dozen stories. When I started to look back at that time which was dark and scary in its own way, this story has come together and has been such an amazing way of putting a difficult past into something enjoyable for hopefully more than just me.

And now an acknowledgement that has led the way in the story. It all begins with a man called Terry. Named after my grandad, who I have spent many years, especially my younger years, listening to stories, and jokes, coming up with movie ideas for rides at Disney World and even designing our own rides. I know if anything inspired me to finish this book and use my imagination it is him.

So, to everybody, I thank you! And I hope you enjoy reading this as much as I have writing it and remember never be afraid or be told you are too old to use your imagination.

Chapter one

Connecting The Worlds

In nineteen forty London, films were slow. Nobody had the space or money to do anything. An orphan who lost his parents during the ongoing world war, couldn't stop imagining stories and worlds in his mind. His name was Terry, and it was his job that he gave himself to entertain the younger kids at the orphanage with stories. Stories that he had made up about adventures in the forests, fighting for gold in the desert and being the first to board a mission to the furthest stars.

One Tuesday morning he woke up in his dirty dark room, still in his old trousers from the night before. His shirt was far too small and dirty, and his long dark brown hair finished off his look of someone who the world would always look down on. Tuesdays were special days for him. It meant that the local filmmaker, Mr Bridges was in the Havelock Studio, and if anybody would help it would be him. Terry had never met Mr Bridges; he had seen him in the newspaper and read that he was at the studio on a

Tuesday. Mr Bridges was the chairman at Havelock Studio who had recently announced that two new films were being shot at the studios. Amid the destruction of the war Terry knew that if he could convince him how good his stories were maybe, just maybe, he would help him.

Terry had made his way to the dining hall of the orphanage. It was about as dark as his bedroom; the walls were as grey and depressed as the women who helped serve the food to the kids. The kids at Grants Orphanage ranged from four years old to eighteen where they were then told to get jobs and fend for themselves.

'Here he is look, dirty Terry!' shouted a tall ginger-haired boy from the end of the table called Gary. 'What stories are you going to tell us today? Loser.'

Terry had heard this many times. Over time he learned to block all sound that came from Gary's mouth. It was funny to watch his ugly face as a mute, as he ignored him with a smile. After Terry had picked his choices of breakfast, which ranged from porridge to oat flakes. He then, disappointed as per usual, found a seat far away from all the others. He had thought of another story during the night and mentally thanked Gary for reminding him of it because it made a very good dream.

'Terry, where are you going?' said a soft voice from behind him.
Terry panicked and tried to talk but all that came out were small bits of porridge, missing a very attractive girl standing in front of him,

'Oh.. er... Charlotte.' he managed to say after finally swallowing too much porridge making him choke.

'Are you going to the studio again?' asked Charlotte.

'Ye, would you like to come?'

He stopped and looked at the walls. He had never asked anyone to keep him company, but nobody had ever asked to come along.

Charlotte was a very pretty, timid girl with long blonde hair that felL past her shoulder, framing her shiny blue eyes.

'Yes I would, I always love hearing your stories,' she said.

'My stories?' he replied immediately, when has she heard his stories?

It wasn't until he saw the recognisable large red bow in her hair that was holding it out of her face. He saw her the last time he told the young children the tale of Broderick the Brave Adventurer. She stood at the back of the room listening, as he knelt in front of the children, telling his tale. He could remember turning red and getting hot as he caught sight of her.

'There's no Broderick the Brave in this one,' said Terry.

'That's OK, I want to hear new stories and sitting in with the babies makes me feel a little awkward.'

This is incredible he thought. Nobody could ever understand why Charlotte spent time with Terry.

The workers at the orphanage let you go out and explore when you turn sixteen. This is provided they didn't get anybody complaining about your behaviour. Gary and his gang spent more time at the orphanage as the police showed up most of the time after they had ventured out. Terry, went to the same place every time, Havelock Studio. Charlotte was a little younger than Terry, she was only fourteen. This meant he had to sneak her out without any of the staff seeing. This proved very simple as the staff were not that interested in what they got up to out of the grounds,

'Ah hello,' Charlotte said to a man who stood next to the gate. 'I wonder if you could help me get to the hospital wing as I have rather hurt my knee,'

'Alright missy,' he said. 'Follow me,'

Terry walked past the man without incident, as he walked back towards the house. Charlotte then turned and ran following Terry out of the gate, across the road and into the woods.

'How far is it?, asked Charlotte,

'Not far, I normally walk straight down the road but if we stay in the woods, they won't see you. That's if they're looking for you that is,'

Charlotte didn't know whether she was offended or not so frowned back at Terry, who didn't catch the look or intent.

'The woods scare me, Terry,' said Charlotte.

'Scare you?' gasped Terry. 'They are just inspirational; how can you not walk through the trees and have your imagination run wild?'

Terry swung from branches and kicked up leaves in a small dance.

'Half of my stories came to me walking through woods,'

Terry reached for Charlotte's arm and ran up hills and over rocks until the trees opened and the horizon was in front of them.

'Terry it's beautiful.'

Charlotte stood to gaze over the fields of cows and sheep.

'I grew up here. I think,' said Terry unsure, as they finally reached the town of Havelock.

'It's amazing, I never left my father's house and as soon as the war broke I moved from orphanage to orphanage,' said Charlotte.

The town of Havelock was only small, the buildings were not symmetrical in any way. Windows were wonky on the fronts and the pathways were narrow leaving little room for the traffic of people trying to get about. The Studio was on the main road, which had recently been constructed for cars to get around yet the town was still inaccessible other than on foot.

They made their way down the long drive towards the big brown wooden doors of the studio. Charlotte looked a little disappointed.

'What were you expecting, pearly gates, celebrities?' Teased Terry. 'Mr Bridges will be here I know it,'

They opened the door and stepped into a small entrance room with a desk in the middle and two doors behind it.

'Where is everyone?' Whispered Charlotte.

Terry rang a small bell that sat on the desk and waited for Mr Bridges to welcome him.

One of the doors finally opened,

'Oh, hello dears.' Said a plump woman squeezing her way behind the desk sounding like she had run a hundred metres. 'And how can I help you both?'

'Err, hello there. I would like to see Mr Bridges please,' Asked Terry proudly.

'Oh right, err he isn't seeing anyone at the moment, he is extremely busy,' she said. 'Can I ask why you want to see him?'

'Sure I have ideas for films,'

'Leave them with me and I will pass them on to him,' the lady interrupted very sharply.

'Ah well I haven't written them down, they are in my head, but I can tell him as they go along,' said Terry.

'Young man you can't put in film ideas without a script, manuscript or something I'm afraid… Mr Bridges!' she squirmed.

Mr Bridges bundled out the door with boxes and a briefcase under his arm, knocking Terry and Charlotte to the floor.

'Mrs Doors, err… please lock up on your way out and err… leave the keys under the big rock will you, I'll see you soon,' he then kicked the front door and left.

'Well children I believe were closed,' said Mrs Doors shooing them both out of the door.

'But wait plea…' but it was too late, the door slammed shut and Terry heard the brass lock click.

Terry never did make his film. When he turned eighteen, he managed to get a job at the local motor factory, as an assistant to a ageing scientist. Nobody could understand what this scientist did or even said most of the time. Terry made a special connection with him and continued to work with him for many years. He was well paid in his job which helped him get a house in the local area. Even pay for a nice wedding for him and Charlotte who had been inseparable ever since their days at the orphanage.

Terry and Charlotte had a boy and a girl who looked identical to their parents when they were younger. At thirty-six years old Terry, who had given up on his storytelling days, started to have dreams once again. Strange dreams took him away from his present time and place and into another world. The scientist, whom Terry had worked with was now retired, but he still visited from time to time.

'Frank, how old are you now?' asked Terry.

'Ninety-three years old my boy and still going,' replied Frank.

'There is something I want you to have, Trevor!' said Frank,

'Terry,' corrected Terry,

'Come with me,'

Terry followed Frank into what seemed to be a never-ending corridor. Frank stopped and pulled out a key ring with over twenty long brass keys. After trying at least half of the keys, the door unlocked,

'Come on, Tom,'

'It's err... Terry, I only worked with you for like ten years!'

Terry rolled his eyes and followed Frank into the room. They entered a small room and in front of them was a podium in the middle with a box on top. Frank unclipped it to reveal a battery-shaped item inside.

'What is it?' asked Terry.

'This is my new power supply prototype, I have been working on it for many years now, and it is for you,'

'For me?' said Terry, taken aback.

'Yes, now Trevor,' Terry ignored the name this time. 'All those years of working together you inspired me to create this. Your stories you told me all the time and your dreams of being able to tell them, well this will allow you to do it in real life. I won't be able to continue with it or move it, I need you to find a home for it and build it,' Frank pointed to a pile of boxes to the side of the room.

'But how does it work?' asked Terry.

'The instructions are in the boxes, take it I'm too old to carry on,' said Frank,

Terry thanked Frank, filled his small car with the boxes and left to return home. He would never see Frank again. Terry searched his house for a place to build Frank's invention but his house was not big enough. He needed floor space and with two kids that was nearly impossible. He racked his brain to where it could go, and then it hit him. Why did he not think of this before? He jumped in his car and then found himself parked outside an abandoned building. It was the old Havelock Studio. Half of it had been torn down but the entrance hadn't changed since he visited as a child as it was listed and considered a part of the history of Havelock.

Terry stepped inside, and in front of him stood the same desk that he and Charlotte had had a run-in with Mrs Doors all them years ago. Behind the desk were the two doors, Terry decided to go through the one on the right which he saw Mr Bridges storm out of. As he entered, he went down a couple of steps and he was in a huge space, it was like a warehouse.

'Wow' he gasped, 'This must be where they filmed everything,'

The room smelt old and damp. Branches were growing through small gaps in the windows. It was dark as any power must have been cut off long ago which put dark shadows in each corner.

'This is perfect!'

Terry excitedly ran back to his car and started to empty the boxes into the room.

'Connect the step to base A,' he mumbled as he read the instructions trying his best to connect the pieces left by Frank.

'Clip the red wire to the trans, err... whatever that says,'

Several hours passed and finally, the machine was completed.

Four long black metal arms bowed over the top of the base and wires sprawled across the floor around it.

'Only one thing for it then,' he said, as he approached the control panel lifted the cap and flicked a small red switch. Nothing happened. He flicked it again, and again until he lost his patience and kicked it, 'Aagghh!' he yelled holding onto his toes.

He must have missed something, he thought. He looked back over to the boxes and saw what he needed. The small box that Frank had shown him sat under empty cardboard boxes. Terry opened it picked up the battery from inside and inserted it where the not-so-clear instructions told him to. Underneath the battery was a bracelet, it had a black strap and a gold round front. After putting it on he approached the panel again, braced himself and flicked the switch. Sparks flew around the machine, blue light flashed making Terry duck away then smoke filled the room. But then, once it settled, Terry could see that the machine was on.

Terry realised he still didn't know how to use it. He found the instructions and continued reading,

'Once the machine is on, picture your world like you are there. Close your eyes, your senses gone, no other living world will compare,' Terry rhymed. 'Wow, Frank was a poet, and I didn't know it, ha!'

Once Terry had composed himself again he stepped onto the base of the machine. He closed his eyes and started his mind going wild to his most recent story. At first, nothing happened, but in his story, he was pushing his way through a forest looking for a lost golden statue of a tiger.

'Wait no not that one!' he said shaking his head. He closed his eyes again. Now he was sitting in the cockpit of a spaceship entering a battle against some grotesque grey alien race.

'No, no, no!' he gasped. 'Too risky I don't want someone to try and kill me, well not yet.'

For the third time he closed his eyes again and this time he was standing outside a temple in the desert. Smoke once again filled the room, it swallowed Terry at once. He opened his eyes, he could feel the heat on his face, and the sand rolled off his hands.

'It worked!' he shouted jumping as much as he could while trying to keep balance, 'Frank you are a genius, although…'

He paused and looked around curiously,

'How do I get back now?'

He remembered the bracelet. The bracelet lit up with a white circle with a star in the middle of it, he touched it gently. Smoke once again bellowed out from around him and when he opened his eyes again, he was back in the studio.

A couple of weeks later, Terry and Charlotte had saved the money together to buy the old studio and had transformed it. finally, it looked like it did during its prime. Nobody who lived in Havelock knew why of course, or what they had renovated for, not knowing what it held inside.

'Charlotte!' Terry called, 'bring the kids down!'

It was their daughter's eighth birthday and her parents had something quite amazing planned for her. Emma loved Terry's stories, more than her older brother George did which automatically made Terry tell her more. Her favourite stories were scary stories, which was quite ironic because her birthday was October thirty-first, Halloween. Terry wanted to make this Halloween one to remember for the whole family. So he and Charlotte decorated what Terry now called the hub, with cobwebs all over the walls, and pumpkins with faces carved into them. Some were funny, some just pure evil and they all dressed up in typical Halloween costumes. Emma was dressed in her favourite cartoon character who was part werewolf part vampire and looked purely terrifying.

'Terry, before we go in are you sure it's completely safe?' Charlotte asked him after taking him to the side, out of the kids' earshot.

'Dear,' replied Terry softly, 'if any of this was dangerous do you think I would do it? besides how many mountain trolls have you seen me throw down mountains before in real life? They are twice my size, height and width, It's my story we will be fine,'

Charlotte was surprisingly reassured by Terry. Together, they have travelled to many places that have come to Terry's mind. Some romantic, some not so romantic and they have had to fight off beasts who, like Terry had said are creatures in real life who eat them for supper.

'OK folks, it's time,, announced Terry as they all joined him on the base of the machine. 'Hold on to me tight, close your eyes,'

They did as he told them to and Terry then closed his and counted, 'three, two, one,' smoke filled the room and they were gone.

'Where are we Dad?' asked George, rather nervously.

'We're in the forest son,' replied Terry.

It was so dark they could barely see their hands in front of them.

The tree tops stopped any light reflecting from the moon like a canopy. A thick layer of fog covered the floor of the forest.

'It smells like sewage!' shouted Emma, 'why did you bring us here, Dad?'

'Because Emma, you have heard every story I have ever told, so I needed a new story, a different story that you wouldn't know,'

'So you thought a forest bog, nice one Terry,' said Charlotte, with a little sarcasm but partly meaning it.

'Follow me, we must be close,' Terry said as they led them on,

'Ah ha, here we are!' All their shoes kept sticking to the swampy floor. They neared the edge of the forest and in front of them stood an old derelict building. The windows were cracked, all the walls discoloured to a mouldy grey and vines had taken over surrounding most of the area.

'Dad I'm scared,' said Emma, clinging onto Charlotte.

'It's fine sweetheart,' Charlotte reassured her.

'Aaahhwooooowh!' a cry came from out of the forest, Terry turned round as the others clung to each other in fear.

'Brilliant!' said Terry, very excitedly, until he turned to see the others terrified. 'Oh right come on then let's go!'

He led them up the steps to the front door which he shoved with his elbow until it flung open.

'Home sweet home,' he joked.

The other passed him into a grand main hall, which had marble staircases and paintings of noble members of a family.

'Wow!' said Charlotte impressed, 'If you can create this in your imagination, why can't you build me a house like this?'

'One day my love, you will have everything you deserve,' Terry replied kissing her on the cheek. 'come then explorers, watch the cobwebs, and moving knights in armour, we have a campfire to get to,'

The kids followed him out through the back of the house onto a patio area that, like the rest of the house looked overgrown and damaged beyond repair.

'We can't sit out here,' said Emma, 'the werewolf will get us,'

'Emma darling, trust me you will be fine,' said Terry as he lit the campfire. Then handed out drinks out of a flask that Charlotte was carrying in her rucksack. 'Happy birthday Emma!'

After they played some games and Terry told a few stories, the kids started to tire.

'I think it's time to go home, Terry,' said Charlotte as Emma was lying on her knees trying her best to stay awake.

'Yes, of course, let's just...' CRASH!, the window upstairs smashed into little pieces, as little shards of glass fell to the floor.

'Daddy, what is that?' screamed Emma.

'I don't know,' replied Terry. 'Look, stay here, we need to get back to the forest to get back home so before we all go through the house again. I will go and have a look around OK?' Terry got up a started walking towards the house.

'aaawhhoooooowwhh!' cried out again. Terry stopped for a minute but then carried on into the house.

The stairs creaked with every step he took, and cobwebs clung to his face. He carried on up to the window that shattered.

'No one here sees!' he shouted out to the others, but they weren't there. The dying embers of the fire lit an empty area where they were all sitting. 'I told them to wait for me,' he grumbled. He turned and headed back down the creaky stairs expecting to find them at the bottom. He turned the corner and a blue fog floated past him, he could make out a face within the fog, one that he recognised but couldn't think why.

'Charlotte!' he shouted, starting to run around the house, 'George! Emma!'

His heart was now beating faster and faster. The hairs on his arms started to harden feeling like little knives were poking him in his skin. He flew out the front door hoping they were there waiting for him, he continued back into the forest,

'Charlotte!' he screamed again but in silence.

He was now in the dark forest where they started. He heard whimpers.

'Emma? Is that you?' he whispered and approached carefully where he heard the sound, and before him, a werewolf stood. Blood dripped from his teeth, veins protruding from his brown, muscly body.

'no!' he said terrified.

Terry looked at his bracelet which remained completely blank so he shook his arm and poked it repeatedly, but nothing happened. He turned to face the house and at the doorway were Charlotte, George and Emma held by the figure which was once blue mist giving out an evil crackle.

Terry tried to run to get to them but then his bracelet lit up and smoke rose from around him,

'no, not now.' he pleaded but before he could get to the end of the forest he was gone.

Chapter Two

The Fox's Debt

'Five, four, three, two, one, happy new year!' roared around the Black Bull pub, Two thousand and Twenty was finally upon the people of Havelock. The Black Bull is a very traditional British pub, set in the countryside. The smell of freshly baked pies and chips flooded the bar, on most days but today is different. New Year's Eve and finally the pub is full.

'Happy New Year Len,' said a drunk greying man over the bar.

'All the best Barry, shall I call you a taxi?' Asked Len.

'No, no Len, I can walk today thank you,'

Len is the landlord, he's a well-respected man in the village. A kind well-mannered licensee. His tall thin figure stands him out from the crowd, but it gives him a huge advantage as he can see over everybody.

'Len!' Shouted a middle-aged blonde-haired woman, trying to pour three pints of lager at once. 'Where is Kai?

I'm running out of glasses, what do you want me to pour drinks into soup bowls?'

'I will find him Jen,' replied Len.

Jen or Jenny is Lens' wife and long-term publican partner who has followed him around to different pubs across the country. Chasing Len's dream to build some sort of catering empire. Unfortunately, they are yet to run a successful pub.

'Come on Kai, you here to work,' said Len pushing a smaller version of himself through a swinging door.

'Dad, stop it I don't want to work New Year's Eve. It's past midnight let me see my friends,' said Kai, as he started placing pint glasses into trays ready for the glass washer.

'You have been hiding all night, and for that, you can do the breakfast shift as well!' snapped Len, making Kai slam glasses down harder into the trays. No one ever wants to do the late shift and then breakfast, especially after New Year's Eve.

'Well it's been a successful new year, Jen don't you think?' asked Len. 'The till is full a nearly empty cellar and I only had to kick one person out. Oh, and Tony being Tony but that's the norm, but all in all a success,'

'Len, a good new year will not make up for a year of poor sales,' Jen said knocking him back down to earth with a huge bang. Lens's face did look like he had fallen from a great height and landed on his head. 'These sales will fix the oven, but we still have microwaves sitting in the corner out of use,'

Lens's mood never picked up again after that. He always imagined having a bustling pub but it just never worked. Flashes of red and green lit up the pub as fireworks continued outside,

'come on, let's watch the finale and get locked up,' said Jen as she led Len outside.

'I'll clean up,' shouted Kai sarcastically, as he continued to pick up glasses that were sprawled out over tables and sideboards around the pub. The Black Bull always produces cheaper drinks on New Year's which gets the crowd but the celebration moves into town after midnight. This leaves the pub like a ghost town once midnight has passed.

'Happy New Year Dennis,' Kai said to the last remaining customer sitting in the corner by himself. He didn't get a vocal reply, more of a nod and a raised finger that was resting on his walking stick.

'I'm gonna have to kick you out soon Den I'm afraid,' Kai said picking up the empties on Dennis's table.

'This beer tastes like vinegar!' he spat.

'Well, you've drunk them haven't you, why didn't you tell on the first one?' Kai replied, getting a grunt in return.

'Now I have got to walk past the loony at the old studio. Sparks and banging all the time coming from there, smoke was billowing from a loose tile the other day!' moaned Dennis as he got up pushing on his walking stick,

'Well walk quickly past there then Dennis,' said Kai.

'With this bloody thing, you young'uns don't know you bloody born,'

He left and Kai took a sigh of relief. He followed Dennis out of the front door to double-check the garden which consisted of a few picnic benches and flower pots dotted here and there. Usually, there were glasses left outside by smokers,

'See I told you, look,' Dennis shouted, not knowing Kai was there, but he was right. A cloud of smoke plumed in the distance. Flashes of green and yellow lit the night sky like a fireworks display.

'All the bloody time,' Dennis continued, but to Kais' relief, it was more of an echo as he turned the corner out of sight.

Kai locked the door and returned to the bar where his parents had returned.
'Successful night then Dad?' Said Kai, as he poured himself a pint of lager,
'Not enough for you to help yourself,' Len replied tiredly,
'Too late,' said Kai under his breath,
'Remember you're on breakfast,' said Len dropping his face into his hands and rubbing his eyes, 'he better be up!'
'I will do breakfast,' said Jen.
'No, he can, you and me are having a lie in. We have done alright tonight I'm happy, tired, but happy,'
Len wrapped his arms around Jen and they headed upstairs to their flat. Kai walked around the pub with his lager locking all the doors and windows. He turned off the bandits and other game machines and finally, he locked the exit from the kitchen.
'Bloody kitchen staff, dirty bleeders, couldn't clean up if their lives depended on it!'
Usually, Kai would make sure the kitchen was clean and tidy. But it's a known fact no auditor will be out on New Year's Day, so instead he left a note for them to find the next morning.

This kitchen is a joke, clean it up or no tips for this week,
learn to mop the floor,
lots of love Kai.

Kai managed to wake up and open the restaurant for breakfast considering he only managed about four hours of sleep. Until Dennis arrived and informed him he had put tea in the coffee flask and coffee in the tea.

'Can you not read?' said Dennis. 'seriously, it's going downhill in this place!'

'OK Den,' said Kai rolling his eyes as he walked away with the flasks.

'Thanks for the note Kai, You're the boss now then yeah?' said a small round chef,

'no Dean my dad is, although a food safety course may well be needed chief.'

Dean was a middle-aged man who had a shaved round head and long whiskers coming from each nostril.

'Don't wind me up Kai, it's too early for your nonsense, there is nothing wrong with my cleaning or standards,'

'OK Dean,' Kai walked past him pointing towards splats of ketchup and BBQ sauce that looked like they had been on his white jacket for most of the week.

After fixing Dennis with his coffee and full English breakfast, he sat down with a laptop to have a coffee of his own.
'Morning Kai, put the kettle on duck,' said a pretty young brunette, speed walking through the entrance.

'Morning Laura, how are we?' Kai responded to Laura who is the Black Bulls regular breakfast waitress.

'I'm OK thank you, all the better to be here,'
Kai looked up at Laura with confusion, as she sat down with him after helping herself to a coffee.

'Yeah right, my head is killing me and I just want my bed,'

'You had a good night then?' asked Kai trying to concentrate on the laptop,

'Not really, Havelock would be so much better if it wasn't full of absolute…'

'Your coffee is all gone!' Dennis interrupted.

'It can't be I just filled it' said Kai quietly to Laura,

'Let's have a look Den,' she picked up the flask held the button down and filled up his mug.

'rubbish things,' grumbled Dennis as he headed back to his table.

'So are we busy today then Kai?' asked Laura.

'Usual rabble, oh and a party of twelve for breakfast,' replied Kai. 'we better warn Dean, bless him,'

'get ready for the rampage,' said Laura as she walked towards the kitchen.

Kai started moving a couple of tables together ready for the big group when he heard a Smash! Come from the kitchen.

'What was it this time?' asked Kai, as Laura left the kitchen.

'The egg pan along with three eggs still frying as it hit the wall,' laughed Laura, 'he is ridiculous, stresses over nothing,'

'He's a drama queen Laura you know that,'

'Well, he wants to put his dummy back in!' Spat Laura.

Laura picked up a hand full of cutlery to lay out the table booked for the party. They were placed right next to a Christmas tree decorated with gold and red baubles, with thick red tinsel curling from top to bottom. One thing about the Fox family was when they did something they did it properly.

'when doing something, make it perfect,' Len always used to say, especially to Kai when he had school projects and other homework. His parents were perfectionists as shown by the decorations of the pub.

By lunchtime, the restaurant hadn't filled up at all. New Year's Day wasn't always busy as the assumption is that people are hungover. If they did have a busy spell then the conversation is always 'Why are they out?' or, 'Surely they are over the driving limit?' but what the staff mean is, 'Get out of our pub we want an easy day.'

'So what you up to later Kai?' Laura asked him as he looked miserable at the welcome station. 'Working I suppose?'

'Not a chance,' said Kai. 'I'm watching the super foxes, in a bit, we will beat Chelsea this time I promise you!'

Laura not at all football-minded, nodded along and of course, Kai meant Leicester City whom he had supported all his life.

'What about you?'

'Nothing, James is out with his mates so I suppose I'll be all alone,'

It was a known fact that Laura and her boyfriend James had no interest in each other. They had nothing in common and nobody understood why they were together. So, she joined him looking miserable.

'It's my birthday!' A young boy shouted as he burst through the doors.

Kai and Laura rolled their eyes and pretended not to notice.

They left Mandy, a bubbly middle-aged woman to deal with the over-excited child. She only just reached five feet in height but had an extra foot added on with her curly blond hair.

'You didn't say it was a kids' party!' Laura moaned as eight young children bundled in after the birthday boy,

'Well Mandy, loves it we won't need to do anything,' said Kai walking towards the bar, 'you may even get some tips this week,'

'That'll be a first, it's so quiet, even for New Year's Day," said Laura,

'I know Mum and Dad are stressing about it, they haven't admitted it but I know they are. I just hope they're not getting into a mess like last time.'

'Why what happened?'

'Well, we had to sell nearly everything to pay off debts and then my nan died so my mum got left some cash from her will so decided to give it another go…'

'Ah, so you managed to open up on time then Kai?' Asked Len appearing from behind them, 'Now you can help Dean because Scott has called in sick,'

'What? Dad, there's like twenty people in here, twelve of them are one party.' Kai protested,

'Just go Kai, then at two o'clock you can finish,'

Kai stormed away slamming the kitchen door. Nobody enjoys helping Dean. It ends in arguments every time, all because he can't handle any kind of pressure in the kitchen. Also, Kai is a perfectionist when it comes to the kitchen and Dean just isn't up to his standards in cooking and cleaning.

'I need peas!' Shouted Dean in his usual demanding way,

'Dean, there is mate!' Kai replied. 'chill out man, you have like three tickets on!' Dean ignored Kai and just shook his head in his usual miserable way.

Thankfully for Kai, two o'clock came around very quickly and he made a quick getaway only to be stopped by Laura,

'Oh you off now then Kai?' she said standing in front of him,

'Laura, yes I am, cheesecake please Johnny' he said trying to avoid Laura.

Johnny is the pot wash and desert chef, he is a small gaunt man who is a little odd compared to many other team members,

'I need a ticket Kai,' said Johnny in his squeaky annoying voice,

'I put it through a second ago!'

'No ticket, no desert Kai!' Johnny stood his ground,

'I took the ticket off and threw it in the bin,' Kai lied. 'Laura you saw me right?' Kai winked.

'yea definitely, Johnny just do the damn desert!'

Kai stood and waited as Johnny finally placed a coffee cheesecake on the side for him to take away,

'Thank you,' Kai shouted as he walked away, 'it gets him every time,' he joked to himself.

On his way upstairs to their flat, he overheard raised voices in the office,

'Twenty-five thousand pounds Len, where are we going to find that money?' He heard which sounded very much like his mum,

'Jen, I don't know I, I could get a loan?' Answered Len,

'Len, that won't solve anything, we will still owe the money to somebody. Perhaps we should just quit now and sell up, at least we should get back enough to get us a house,'

'What about our jobs?'

'We can get new jobs, Len if we leave it too long it will be too late. I'm going to visit the estate agents tomorrow and get the pub up for sale,' Jen's voice wobbled a bit she was getting upset, 'Perhaps we could go and work for a brewery and manage a pub, then we won't worry about the debts?' said Jen,

'Work for them? They are corrupt Jen, they don't care about the staff and their well-being, it's all about the money,'

Kai started feeling guilty about helping himself to a desert and not paying his way as his parents would say. He decided to scarper before his parents realised he had been listening to their conversation, his fears had now come to be. They were in debt again and Kai knew exactly what that meant.

Kai heard Jen walk up the stairs around eight o'clock which is closing time for New Year's Day. At first, he didn't want to mention what he overheard but he liked Havelock. He had made friends there an. d didn't want to move anywhere again to find a new pub, so he decided to talk to her.

'Mum, we're going to be moving again aren't we?' he said as Jen came into the lounge and sat down with a coffee,

'what do you mean? We're not going anywhere why?' Jen asked,

'I heard you and Dad arguing, in the office earlier. I know you are in debt again,'

A short silence followed before Jen thought about the best reply to not get upset but also be as honest as she could,

'You're not stupid Kai, It's obvious something isn't working here. The pub is haemorrhaging money, equipment, food, drink, and incompetent staff,' Kai agreed with that. 'We don't want to move Kai but if we don't start making money we won't have any choice,' Said Jen before gulping her coffee,

'What about dad? what does he want?' asked Kai,

'To stay, he still thinks this place is a gold mine waiting to find its potential, well I'm still waiting,'

'Where is dad?' Kai had been waiting for his dad to walk in during the conversation at some point.

'He's gone out, to clear his head. We argued in the office, which you heard I suppose. Then he left, he'll be back, I just hope he isn't doing anything stupid, as this is your father after all,'

Kai agreed again, his dad was known for his brass decision-making as he didn't always think things through. He wasn't a stupid man, Len was very intelligent. He could easily join in on debates on TV and answer every question on a quiz show. Only Kai wishes he thought about his decisions and more importantly what impact they have on his family and his mum.

Kai lay in the following morning as he had a day off. He didn't sleep very well as he was subconsciously listening out for his dad to turn back up. It turned out it wouldn't have mattered as Len announced his return by accidentally setting off the pub's security alarm. The alarm was so loud it could easily wake the neighbourhood up never mind Kai and his mum. He didn't hear any arguments when he got back so maybe his mum ignored his return and fell back to sleep. Any suggestion that she slept through the alarm would be ridiculous. To be fair to Len he got up again first thing and opened up for breakfast. The walls and floors aren't very thick so you can hear every bang and shout from downstairs, usually from the kitchen if Dean is working.

Kai wanted to speak to his dad so decided to go and have his morning hot drink at the bar. He knew Laura was working so it wouldn't be so awkward when he was busy as he could talk to her. Living upstairs has its positives but the negatives can sometimes outweigh them, especially if you're the manager's son,

'Oi, you!' Kai turned round to see Dennis limping up to him, 'that meal last night, rubbish,'

'Really? Oh dear,' said Kai as politely as he could. The boundaries of the way you can talk to customers are pushed to the limits when Dennis is concerned. 'Maybe tonight's will be better,' Kai knew the meal wouldn't have been bad it's just Dennis, well being Dennis,

'Better? well, your chef needs to learn to cook potatoes, and peas! They were like bloody bullets!' Dennis went on.

Kai nodded and then ignored him luckily Laura came round the bar so he could order his coffee with her, prompting Dennis to head back to his table.

'Never happy that one,' said Kai as Laura placed the coffee in front of him, as she knew what he liked.

'Blimey Kai you paying?' Laura was shocked as she held her hand out for Kai to drop some pound coins into,

'Yeah well, I thought I better start paying my way,' he admitted taking sips, 'I only came down to see you and Dad, I forgot I would get an ear bashing from Den!'

'It has been the worst today, some woman kicked off at your dad first thing,'

'Why what happened?" asked Kai,

'Not a lot, your dad was calm. The woman just wants the world but doesn't want to pay for it, typical of the world today really, they feel they are entitled to something.'

As the morning went on the restaurant although busy, felt quiet. Until a long beeping echoed through the building,

'ah ha it's here,' Len rejoiced striding towards the front door, 'round the back please fellas,'

'What he's ordered?' Laura asked Kai,

'I don't know.' wandered Kai. He followed his dad around the back of the restaurant and watched a brand-new oven and microwaves being carried into the kitchen,

'Come on Kai, you're a strong lad, come help these men out will you,' Len shouted waving his arm above his head excitedly. Kai helped lift the old greasy oven out of the back door and into the back of the lorry,

'Now then Kai, top of the range this one, look eight rings, eight! And these microwaves, well newest models in the industry, it'll cook a chicken in a minute and a half!'

'Brilliant dad, does mum know you have brought all this?'

'Yes, yes not to worry,"' Len said as Jen walked out the back door,

'Len? Where are these from?' Jen asked with a thunderous tone,

'Havelock catering, look side of the lorry,' Kai laughed but in return, he got a scolding gaze,

'If you're both done come with me!' Jen walked with a purpose back and Kai followed behind leaving Len to sign the paperwork.

'I don't know what to say, Len, after what we talked about last night!' Jen was furious. She had locked them all inside the office which felt no bigger than a broom cupboard. 'How did you pay for that?' she looked around meeting eyes with Kai,

'Mum I have nothing to do with this, I'm completely innocent, wrong place wrong time,'

'You got another loan haven't you!' this wasn't a question,

I, err... yes,' admitted Len taking a seat at the desk,

'How much?'

'Jen...'

'How Much!?' screamed Jen, her face turned bright red, and she looked in slow motion. Len didn't leave Jen's gaze for what felt like minutes, 'thirty thousand,' Len said finally,

'Thirty thousand pounds? wow,' Jen placed her head in her hands, 'Len what were you thinking? how can we afford this?'

'I have already paid our debts and brought the equipment, Jen we will be OK. We just need to pay every month,' Len pleaded with Jen for her understanding but it didn't seem to come,

'Where did you get the loan from?' asked Jen,

'Look don't worry about the loan, leave that to me, darling trust me,'

'Sounds ominous,' said Kai, 'and Where is the money for the repayments coming from? You pay the staff and are left with nothing for yourselves. I don't want to leave but I don't want to go running from bailiffs. I'd rather you admit that it hasn't worked and we try something new like Mum said,'

'No, we can do this, I have new ideas, we're not far off from making the place a success,' said Len,

'Please I need you both,'

'Well we're not going anywhere, are we mum?' Kai said before leaving the office and heading back into to restaurant. The dread had already filled Kai of what the future may hold for him and his family. The memories of leaving friendship groups, schools and ex-girlfriends. A new mentality kicked in with Kai vowing that he would not let that happen for him or his parents. He tried to think of ways that he could help, maybe doing extra shifts or volunteering his time. After thinking that, he saw Dennis again and dealing with him for free was definitely out of the question.

Chapter Three

Mr "Bullet" Brown

Three weeks had now passed since Len had taken out a loan and Kai had seen the true situation they were in as a family. They kept the debt issues to themselves making sure other staff members didn't feel the pressure of the debt to make sure panic didn't ensue. Kai thought he was covering it up well. He took on extra shifts and agreed on a salary with his parents that saved them money but also was what he felt he could live. Although he didn't make this public, a member of staff was taken off each shift to save money. This didn't hit the team too hard as the beginning of the year was notoriously quiet so work was slow. One team member who had started acting a little strange around Kai was Laura. She hadn't lost any shifts but was friendly with other team members who had and Kai started getting very paranoid that a clique was being formed. Kai set up breakfast like any usual morning and Laura was the first team member in, heading straight for the coffee machine as per usual.

'Morning Kai,' she said helping herself to a latte, 'here again? Where's Lottie? I thought she did Thursday mornings?'

Kai started his new work arrangement with a positive attitude. He was helping his parents out but as time went on and a lot of questioning from other members of the team his positivity fell dramatically,

'She has been moved to Friday morning; you have to put up with me,' he groaned.

This negative sense he was giving off wasn't how he felt he was coming across. He felt he was being normal Kai. But he knew the team were talking and accusing him of benefitting from being the manager's son and getting more shifts than the other people.

'I know what you thinking Laura and no it isn't to get me more money,' said Kai.

He tried to defuse the thought in Laura's mind but what he didn't realise was Laura was the one team member who could see what was going on,

'Kai you don't need to explain yourself to me,' said Laura while passing Kai a hot latte in his favourite fox mug. 'You're not yourself at the moment and I can tell there is something up. Not to mention the restaurant not taking the money! I have worked here long enough to see what's happening Kai,'

Kai didn't respond, other the scrunching his face up a little when Laura had finished talking,

'Right, come with me tonight to the Hare and Hounds on the other side of Havelock. My treat, you need cheering up a bit,' Kai looked up at her and agreed he could do with a blowout.

The evening came around very quickly for Kai, but when he thought about it his shifts with Laura always did go quickly which was down to her company. The Hare and Hounds pub is a very old-fashioned pub hidden away within the town, which could be mistaken for an end-terraced house. Inside had a typical smell of a pub. Stale beer, snacks and smoke that had blown in from the back door where the regular smokers stood.

'Two lagers please, Steve,' Laura asked the barman, who was a greying man with a very stern face,

'Five, sixty please,' Steve said back after placing the pints on the bar. They found space on a sofa in the corner, where it was a bit dark and gloomy. The pool table sat in the middle of the room with two kids trying to play, one of whom could barely reach over the table.

'Come on then, what's getting to you,' Laura asked.

'It's my parents I suppose, my dad hasn't told anyone where he got this loan from,' said Kai.

'Why's that a problem though Kai? Their adults, they're allowed to take a loan out,'

'Remember what I was telling you the other day, about the financial difficulties they have had in the past. They have not got the credit rating to allow them to just come home with a loan,'

'So what? He took a bad credit loan? people always do that,'

'With a guarantor, who would they use to guarantee a payment plan? there is nobody,"

'Well, your pub is worth money so maybe they used that as a guarantee,'

'Well I don't know what's worse, risk losing the house and business, or...'

'Or what?' replied Laura quickly,

'Or loaning from a shark or someone we don't trust. This is my dad we're talking about here, he doesn't know the difference between a good deal and a scam,'

Laura sat back down at the table after returning from the bar with two more beers,

'I'm sure they know what they are doing, have a bit of faith, Kai,'

The two drinks were soon gone and the conversation to Kais' relief moved on to other things. Such as the run-down appearance of the Hare and Hounds and why people would come here when to Kais' parents credit the Black Bull is so much more appealing.

'Thank you, for today Laura,' said Kai placing his empty glass down, 'it was much needed,'

'I could tell!' chuckled Laura. 'Tell you what, the fair is in town this week why don't we go?'

'Together?'

'Yes together, Kai,' said Laura,

'As in, a date?'

'Oh Kai, you're bloody hard work sometimes, il see you tomorrow,' Laura then got up, wrapped her arms around Kai then left the pub.

This gave Kai a couple of minutes to contemplate what had just happened. He had worked with Laura for a while now, but he never saw her as relationship material. She is kind and helpful and they have gotten on well since day one.

'She left you mate?' said an old man at the table next to Kai,

'You should go after her, don't let these good women go so easily. They don't come around that often,' Kai felt a little uncomfortable with this, so he saw it as a good reason to leave. He politely nodded at the man and left.

The rest of the week felt quite good for Kai as he worried there would be a slight awkwardness between him and Laura, but there wasn't. Nothing was mentioned about the trip to the Hare and Hounds or the fair until five o'clock Saturday evening when Laura knocked on the door to the flat. Kai opened the door enthusiastically forgetting he was trying to play the situation as smoothly as he could. When Kai first saw Laura standing through the opened door, he almost didn't recognise her. She wore black leather trousers and a zebra-striped top, a contrasting difference to the uniform he was used to.

Their taxi dropped them off at the temporary fencing that closed the road down the High Street,

'Of all the years I have lived in Havelock, this is the first time I have been to the Fair,' said Kai as they walked down the High Street. Hundreds of people were crowding around the different rides. The Havelock Statutes was an annual fair that came to the town at the same time every year. It created the same havoc for commuters who use the main road to get to work. The fair consists of the same lineup every year except for the odd new ride that they would add so people keep coming back. The clubs and pubs down the High Street always made the most of the extra visitors with the fair, meaning beer can be sold out on the streets.

Kai finally plucked up the courage to ride a tornado, which spins you around, while your seats also span the other way. Laura was a thrill seeker, she made it her mission to ride each one, although after the tornado, Kai was feeling very nauseous.

'Come on Kai, look it's the fear fall! Let's go!'

'That doesn't sound good' Kai grumbled as he let Laura grab his hand and pull him from the curb to join the queue. The fear fall was this year's new addition to the fair. Once seated, it lifted you to way above the buildings, held you there for what felt like an age and then dropped you back down. Kai survived the fear fall but managed to talk Laura into getting some food and sitting back at one of the benches that edged the high street.

After finishing his food that he didn't enjoy but as he was at a fair it was acceptable to eat. Laura went to find some toilets which left Kai alone when a man sat next to him. He looked as though he was in his forties, his hair was very messy and his clothes looked very old,

'I love this fair you know,' he said to Kai. 'Oh yes come every year, nineteen thirty it started you know, yes very enjoyable,'

Kai politely nodded but went back to screwing up his napkins that held his greasy fair burger.

'The Fear Fall, I saw you on it, was it good?' the man asked Kai,

'Er yes I suppose, not a fan of thrill rides really,'

Kai wasn't sure whether he knew this man, had he served him at the Black Bull? He didn't recognise him anyway. The man then started dancing to the music in his seat, making Kai slide slightly over as far as he could,

'God Laura, where are you?' He whispered to himself, as he knew he couldn't go wandering because she would never find him in all these people.

'Ah yes, this music takes me back you know, in ballrooms back in the day. This is the only time I come out to town, the fair.' said the man,

'It looks like it, err… I mean really? wow,' Kai squirmed at what he just said out loud and wished the floor opened up and swallowed him,

'I know somewhere where that can happen you know not great though,'

'What can happen?' Kai asked confused,

'The floor, open up and swallow you whole, nasty things under there though, I wouldn't recommend it,'

'I...I didn't mean...'

'It's fine, it's amazing what people are thinking you know. Can you see those two bouncers over there? They haven't taken their eyes off us since we sat down, what do you think they are thinking?'

Kai shrugged.

'I can't tell either, curious... she fancies you,' the man said as Kai looked in at a group of girls walking past,

'Found a friend Kai?' said Laura. 'How are you, Mr Toone?' Laura asked the man,

'Yes, very well missy,' replied Mr Toone,

'Every year he's at this fair Kai, a bit of a mascot aren't you Mr Toone?' said Laura as if she were talking to a toddler. Mr Toone nodded,

'I will see you both very soon,' said Mr Toone as he got up and left them,

'That was the strangest experience I have ever had,' said Kai.

'With Mr Toone? Yeah, he's a bit odd, he doesn't look a day over forty yet talks like he's been around for decades,'

'Yeah, Noticed that,' Kai added but decided not to talk about the mind-reading part,

'Come on, there's so many places we need to go and then I have managed to get us VIP at the Heart.'

Kai couldn't shake the memory of Mr Toones' conversation, which Laura noticed as he looked very distracted and less conversational. Later that night he found himself at the bar of the Heart ordering himself a beer before entering the VIP area. One of the girls who walked past him during his conversation with Mr Toone waited next to him,

'Two vodka and cokes please,' she asked the barman, and when she looked over at Kai, he gave her a subtle smile. She rolled her eyes took her drinks and left. Maybe it's all nonsense, he thought because that wasn't a reaction of someone who fancied him. Kai was a little relieved and decided Mr Toone was just a crazy man who made stuff up for conversation and it was just a fluke that he knew what he was thinking.

As Kai woke up the following morning he had a spring in his step. He knew he hadn't drunk too much to be hungover but just enough to feel good. Which was unusual as Sunday mornings started to become a bit depressing as it involved an update from his parents on the performance of the pub.

'Not a bad week this week folks,' Len started, as he stood in the office with Kai and Jen. 'It's the best we have had since we have been here,'

'Oh good,' replied Kai as he knew the quicker the pub started performing the sooner his routine would return to normal

'Yes, yes it is, however, Easter is coming up and I believe we should make the most of it,'

'In what way Dad?' Kai knew he was about to hear a wild idea from his dad again,

'Well it's a Bank Holiday, the weather is better so what better thing to do than a special event,' said Len as Kai rolled his eyes.

'Now Kai I know what you thinking and yes it involves more work but you won't do all the work alone,'

'I'm doing it?' Kai shouted louder than he meant causing Jen to throw him a stern look 'I...I mean I'm doing it?' he repeated in a much softer tone, 'Who with?'

There was a knock on the door,

'Ah Laura come in,' said Len as Laura poked her head around the door,

'As I can see you two are getting on so well, who better to become a team and smash the perfect Bank Holiday event,' Kai looked at Laura and shook his head.

'It will be fine Kai, we can do this together,' Laura said as they walked to the entrance of the pub.

'I'm sure we can Laura but I don't know what to do,' Before he could finish Laura grabbed his hand and pulled him out of the pub and round the corner of the car park.

'Now forget about that for a minute we will sort it,' She paused for a minute not realising she still had her hand on Kai's. 'Erm, last night, you enjoyed it right?' she asked still holding Kai's hand,

'Yeah of course why?' replied Kai. 'Well I have been meaning to ask you for a while but with you spending so much time working and with your parents recently it's been hard to talk to you,' said Laura getting more confident and tightening her grip on Kais' hand. Kai came to realise what Laura was trying to say and without replying he leaned in and kissed her.

'Good job I felt the same,' Kai said as he pulled away,

'Are we now?'

'Boyfriend and Girlfriend?' Kai joked finishing Laura's sentence,

'Sure, we should give it a go,' Laura gave him another kiss, and then as they separated a car pulled into the car park behind them,

'Oh it's Kate, I got to go, we will catch up later yeah?' said Laura gradually stepping backwards toward the car,

'Yeah, I'll see you,' said Kai as Laura smiled at him got in the car and left.

Kai managed to agree with his parents for a few days of the following week to be able to work on his event and more importantly, spend time with Laura. The news of them now being together was meant to be secret although acting normal around the other team members was difficult. It soon got out and was then common knowledge, even to his parents which, although awkward at first soon became easy to live with.

Kai and Laura met at the pub one Wednesday evening to discuss the suggestions for possible ideas for the event. The ideas didn't come easily. When at work they didn't act like a couple so that wasn't the problem, what was the problem was that they didn't know how to organise an event. The hours went on and they didn't have much written down,

'We're really bad at this,' said Laura,

'Yeah, good job it's a couple of weeks away and not this weekend,' Kai joked,

'I'm going to go home Kai, and I'll sleep on it,' said Laura as she saw Len about to lock the door. She gave him a little kiss and left.

'What a smart pub,' a voice echoed from the other side of the restaurant.

'Were closed pal,' said Kai as he headed to the other door to lock it,

'Not yet you're not son, I want to look around!'

In the corner of the room sat a man scowling at Kai. He had a white shirt on with the sleeves rolled up to his elbows revealing a dragon on each arm crawling down his wrists. A dark stubble dressed chiselled jaw and his long black hair held up in a ponytail.

Kai looked around for his father to back him up a little, but he was nowhere to be seen,

'Seriously now, we're closed. You're going to have to leave,' Kai repeated nervously as the man was very intimidating,

'Your father here?' the man asked as he ran a sharp claw between his fingers. 'I assume you're Kai? Lens son?' the man's beady eyes looked directly into Kais in a way he couldn't escape from,

'Yeah he is,' Kai said slowly, returning the gaze,

'Be a good lad then and fetch him for me, and a pint of bitter would be lovely, thanks, the man said as he sat on the sofa in the bar area.

'Wait who are you? and how do you know my dad?' asked Kai,

'Mr Brown, I'm a business associate of your parents, trust me he knows who I am, now,' Mr Brown got himself comfortable on the sofa, 'How about that drink?'

Kai nodded at the man and headed behind the bar to find Len who seemed to have just disappeared. It didn't take long to find him, however, as after going into the office Len was sat in the chair bouncing his head on the desk,

'Dad, what are you doing?' asked Kai, which made Len spin around with a nice red patch on his forehead,

'Nothing son what's up?' Len asked casually,

'Well I have a feeling I will be asking you the same question soon,' said Kai, 'Why did you hide when this Mr Brown walked in?'

'No reason!' said Len immediately,

Kai did not buy this at all and gave his dad a stern, unimpressed look,

'OK, OK!' Len spat before Kai could raise his voice, 'his name is Mr Brown, he is the man I took the loan from,'

'You didn't get it from a bank or any other half-reliable source! Dad, you could not meet a more stereotypical crook if you imagined it.' Kai's voice got louder as he went on,

'Shh… Kai please,' Len pleaded, 'go get the man a drink and I will deal with him OK,' Kai shook his head and went back to the bar. Kai was a confident barman, but he had never poured a drink with more nerves than he had with this one. It was worse than the first drink he poured for Dennis.

'I thought you had left,' said Mr Brown as Kai brought the drink over and placed it on a beer mat he had also picked up from the bar. 'I trust your father will be joining us shortly?'

Fortunately, Len walked around from the bar meaning Kai didn't have to answer. There was an awkward silence as Len sat opposite Mr Brown who was smiling, creating a chilling expression.

'Kai pour me a lager would you,' said Len leaning over towards Kai,

'No, no, there is no need Len,' Said Mr Brown after taking a final large gulp of his drink and placing his glass gently down on the table. 'why don't you show me around my new pub?'

'What?!' Kai shouted, 'What do you mean your pub? Dad?'

'Mr Brown, that's not what we agreed,' Len questioned with a wobbly voice, 'only if I don't pay, you get my pub,' Kai looked at Len in astonishment. 'Now Kai, loans need collateral and the pub is all we have,'

'Yes Dad the pub is all we have, and you now handing it to someone as collateral!? does mum know about this?' Kai couldn't believe what he was hearing. His home and workplace are not at serious risk of being handed to this crook.

'Kai please!' Len once again pleaded, 'she doesn't need to know about this, we made our first payment and we are on track there is no reason for you to be here!' he shouted towards Mr Brown, who then proceeded to stand up pushing the table over, towering above both Len and Kai,

'Don't forget where you stand Mr Fox,' Mr Brown threatened, pushing his dragon claw into Len's chest. 'one wrong move from you, your son or your wife and this little pub that you call your home, will be mine, and I can assure you sir, you will no longer call it home.'

Len and Kai sat down on the same chair gazing into the eyes of Mr Brown, who unbuttoned his shirt to to show a matt black revolver tucked away in a holster.

'I didn't pick up the name Bullet Brown for the way I smiled at people Mr Fox. I pick my investments very, very carefully,' Mr Brown started to walk away from the table but stopped and looked back at the pair still sharing a chair, 'I believe a punishment is when you can understand the deal that we are involved in,'

Len looked petrified. What punishment could be worse than having this man standing in front of you flashing his gun? 'your payment this month, doubled, and if you fail to pay it, we'll I might just move in upstairs with you,' Mr Brown laughed and turned towards the exit. 'Good evening Mr Fox and Little Fox,'

'Little Fox, how dare he!' Kai muttered,

'Go and tell him then Kai, to his face,' moaned Len, 'I'm done, ruined, wait until your mother finds out about this,'

'She doesn't need to find out dad, just don't pay me this month and give it to Brown it's fine,'

'Kai you don't get it, this is how it is going to be now, what have I done? again!' Len started to sob.

Kai stepped away from Len to go and lock the door Mr Brown had left through and a figure caught his attention in the window.

'Hello? who now?' Kai asked himself, but after opening the door to look out, there was nobody to be seen. He was sure he recognised the face, that of Mr Toone he met at the fair. 'I must be going mad,'

Kai continued to lock the door and returned to a sobbing Len.

'Dad it will be fine, okay, I told you what we will do and we'll just take it one month at a time,'

'Who were you talking to out there?' Len asked, 'Is Mr Brown still there?'

'No Dad, he's gone,' Kai reassured Len. 'I thought I saw someone, but it's my mind playing tricks on me… that's all, must be tired.' Len nodded to Kai in agreement that it was time to go upstairs to get some rest and somehow sleep without letting Jen know about what had happened.

Chapter Four

The Beautiful South

A week had passed and thankfully for Kai his mum had no idea about the visit of Mr Brown. This did not calm their nerves when she was around. The pub was once again very busy which helped the time go by very quickly and of course the quicker the days, the quicker pay day came. Until Kai remembers he promised to work for free to help pay Bullet.

'He can't be that much trouble, can he?' asked Kai, as Laura sat opposite,

'Kai, why didn't you ring me? I would have helped you,' said Laura trying to work around Kai as he stood in her way of getting cutlery. Kai waited at the waitress station for her to return,

'But he had a gun Laura! why would I call you into that situation?'

'Because I would have helped Kai… move,' Laura shoved him to the side so she could get in the cupboard. 'Look to answer your question, yes Mr Bullet' Brown is that much trouble and you would not stand a chance if you even tried standing up to him. I can't believe he was by himself, he obviously doesn't think you and your cad are up too much... now do some bloody work," Laura said continuing to do her job around Kai.

Kai continued to pester Laura for most of the day about Bullet, which became very annoying for her,

'So what do I do about him?' Kai said when he caught up with Laura behind the bar,

'I don't know Kai, what makes you think I can get you out of this?' Laura replied,

'Well, you wanted me to call you when he was here and in fact how do you know so much about him?' Kai asked making Laura stop in front of him, pausing before answering,

'He caused a few issues for my family once before, but that was years ago. Kai it's going to be fine. Pay him like you said you would it will be fine,' said Laura as she turned back to the till, but once again she froze to the spot.

'Laura? What is it?' Kai asked, turning his head to look into Laura's eyes which were transfixed to the screen on the till.

'It's him Kai...' Laura said with a wobble to her voice, pointing to the till,

'Who?' Kai asked following her eyes, 'oh him,'

'I can't...' Laura said as she pushed past Kai and dashed through the door to the back of the house area. Kai looked harder to read the message on the screen properly, it read,

Seven hundred and fifty pounds for Friday or the Black Bull will have a new landlord

Kai took his phone out and took a picture of it before deleting the message,

'Kai,' a waitress shouted from a till point in the restaurant, 'my screen just crashed!' Kai picked up the pub phone and headed over to take a look.

'Dad, I need you to see something,' Kai said down the phone as he was tapping the screen which wasn't doing anything. Moments later Len appeared in the restaurant behind Kai,

'You called son?'

'The tills have crashed and shut down all at once!'

'Well reboot them then,'

'No Dad, I think there's more to it than that,' Kai pleaded,

'Just reboot it and it will be fine, come on,' said Len rashly,

'Dad just wait,' Len then moved Kai aside, opened the cupboard below and rebooted the whole system. Almost immediately the till screens all reappeared in working order,

'There we go,' Len mumbled as he marched away. Kai followed with determination but didn't catch him until they were in the office,

'Dad you need to look at this,' Kai said raising his voice,

'Kai stop I'm too busy and have far too much on my mind for this,'

'Just look,'

Kai pushed his phone into Lens' hands showing the picture he took of Mr Brown's message,

'Seven hundred and fifty? Kai, when did this appear?' Fear covered Lens from head to toe,

'I took the picture and closed the message, and then the whole system crashed,'

'That's impossible, he can't do that,' Len said shaking his head,

'Wait you still don't believe me it's there in front of you,'' Kai shouted,

'No, no I believe you Kai, it's just how and why?' Len handed the phone back to Kai and let his head fall into his hands leaving the room quiet for some time before Kai broke it,

'I think it's more than the money Dad,'

'What do you mean?' Len asked, raising his head to Kai,

'He wants this pub, I don't know why, but he's pushing this way too hard for it to be just about the money,' Lens's head fell back into his hands. 'Loan or not, he would have been here at some point, we've just given him the opportunity, showed vulnerability and he took it.'

Kai headed back into the restaurant to help clear up after the lunchtime rush asking himself two questions. Why does Mr Brown want this pub? Also, one that worries him more than it should with everything considered, what does Laura know and how does she know about Mr Bullet Brown?

The following morning, the whole family were working the dreaded breakfast shift. It was a Friday and it was very quiet which Kai didn't like. A busy restaurant keeps his parents busy but when there was no work they argued and discussed issues in their life, which now included a loan that somehow needed paying back. Kai knew that his mum didn't know about Mr Brown yet so at least that discussion wasn't happening, yet. One other thing was on Kais' mind, Laura. He hadn't heard from her since they last spoke about Mr Brown and his message started to appear on the till system. Brown spooked her more than Kai could ever know why. None of his messages had been replied to and his calls were ignored, or so it would seem.

'I hope you're cancelling Easter Dad?' Kai said to Len as he approached,

'What? When we need the money, are you mad?' said Len, not impressed with the suggestions Kai had made,

'Dad I haven't heard from Laura for ages, she's not answering my calls or replying to my texts,'

'Lovers tiff?' Len Joked,

'Dad once again you missing the bigger picture. She had a run-in with Brown before and that message scared her, and you want me to chase her about an Easter Bank Holiday?'

'No!' said Len sharply, 'I asked you to sort it, so sort it!'

'You haven't told Mum yet have you?' Kai said trying to move the pressure back to his dad away from his mind,

'No… that I will sort, she doesn't need to worry about it,' assured Len, as they watched a customer head to the bar,

'You gonna get that?' Kai asked his dad,

'Nah your mum will sort it,' Len said turning away,

'You're gonna wind her up, and something bad is going happen to us,'

'LEN!' screamed Jen's voice from behind the bar,

'You're in trouble,' the customer whispered as he walked back with his coffee. Len and Kai shared a look and casually walked towards the bar,

'What is this?' said Jen turning as white as a ghost. The same message had appeared but this time a mug shot of Mr Brown was next to the message,

'How is he doing this?' Said Len under his breath,

'He! Who is he?' Jen's voice echoed around the bar, making Len usher them both into the office, 'Len I can't do this anymore, this is about that bloody loan isn't it!'

'Jen…'

'Yes mum it is,' Kai interrupted, 'I can't do it, Dad, just tell her or I will,'

Len sat in the office chair with a thud and let his hands catch his face which had become a regular position for him over the last few months,

'Okay, his name is Mr Brown,'

'Bullet! Mr Bullet Brown,' Kai corrected,

'Mr Bullet Brown then, he is who I got the loan from and it would seem he is trying to get more back from us than just the money,'

'You mean the pub? He can have it, why endanger our family for this place?' Jen shouted,

'We have put so much time and money in this place we can't just run,' said Len trying his best to reassure,

'I can run,' Jen added,

'Wait… no… you can't, we're a family we need to fight this together, we will get through this,'

'How many times do we have to get through something until we can live a safe, normal life, Len,'

'Jen if we run, we can't pay him back so he will chase us, I know I have made a mistake taking that loan from him and I'm sorry. I didn't know what he was like,'

'So the bouncers on either side of the desk didn't give it away then?'

'How do you know about the bouncers?'

'Oh My God Dad, it was a guess, but wow, that is unbelievable,'

Len had his head back in his hands as Kai had to turn away in part amazement and some disbelief. He wasn't exactly shocked by what his dad had done, he is very trusting even with the wrong people.

Jen left the office and went up to the flat, stomping every step she made going up the stairs,

'Kai!' Len shouted after Kai had gone back to the restaurant.

'Those eggs were hard and crispy, disgusting they were!' Dennis grumbled to Kai as he walked around the bar,

'Cheers Den, see you at the usual time tonight for you dry fish and bullet peas!' Kai shot back.

Dennis gave Kai a loud grunt and headed out. Luckily for Kai, the breakfast rush ended earlier than usual so the restaurant was now empty of customers but full of dirty plates and glasses. His parents were nowhere to be seen so he began the task of clearing up on his own ready for a dinner service.

'Lock the doors son and put this up,' Len said handing Jack a paper sign, which read,

> Due to unforeseen circumstances
> we have had to close

Sorry for the inconvenience this may have caused.

'Your mum is talking to your aunty Mel,' said Len,

'Aunty Mel! I told you something bad would happen to us,' Kai shouted, he wasn't exactly on talking terms with his aunty Mel,

'Besides she won't want to see me,' Kai said turning back to the door with a roll of tape, 'can't you remember the hosepipe thing?'

During the summer last year, Kai and Mel's son Sam were having a water fight on a summer evening. Kai grabbed the hosepipe and aimed at Mel who continued to slide down the garden hitting her freshly laid flowers and ornaments, destroying them.

'Oh Kai that was years ago, I'm sure it will be forgotten and forgiven,'

'Dad, you can't forget and forgive, you either forget or forgive, which she has done neither,'

'Yes, but Kai when you send her a Christmas card with a garden gnome broken into pieces on the front she's hardly going to forget is she?'

'What? It's funny,' Kai laughed, which brought a smile to Len's face as he wasn't fond of Mel, especially the idea of staying with her.

Later in the afternoon, Kai opened the door to his bedroom finding packed suitcases on the landing,

'Mum! What is this?' Kai shouted,

'We are moving to Southampton with my sister,' said Jen, struggling to lift another case from her room,

'No, you're serious about this?' Kai questioned, thinking it was another crazy idea that his dad was just making up,

'Yes we are so get your bags packed, we're leaving this evening,'

'I'm not going mum, I'm happy here, we can't just run away,' said Kai still standing in his doorway staring at the amount of cases Jen was brought out of her room. The atmosphere changed as suddenly realised Kai was serious about not wanting to leave,

'You can't stay here Kai, it's not safe,' Jen pleaded with Kai to understand what she was trying to do, but Kai was determined also to stand his ground,

'I'm not going, I'm good at my job so I'll find another,'

'Where are you going to stay? Here? Alone? It is not safe Kai!' Jen's temper rose,

'I will stay with Laura!' Kai snapped back, making Jen stop for a second,

'Do not drag Laura into this. If you care about her you will stay away and not get her involved, you will get her hurt,'

'What about Aunty Mel? We will go to family if we run, he's probably expecting it already, no?' Kai grabbed his coat off his bed, 'I'm out of here, if you want to go, then go! I'm staying, I need some fresh air,' Kai left before his parents could stop him and slammed the door behind him.

It had become dark very quickly, he thought, although he didn't realise that he had been walking around outside by himself for a couple of hours now. At the time of leaving, he didn't have a plan, he just went in one direction and kept going. If he followed the main road far enough it eventually circles back to the Black Bull. But it had become clear to Kai that he had turned off at some point because he didn't recognise anything around him. The town of Havelock isn't that big, and he thought he knew it well considering how long he had been there. His next plan was to head to Laura's, but he still wasn't sure how to get to her house from home, not alone in the middle of nowhere. The roads became very dark. Kai couldn't see past the bushes that grew on either side of the road, leaving him with tunnel vision only in the direction the road went.

'This is stupid, what am I doing?' he said to himself, pulling out his phone. He found Laura's number and tried to call, but like his other attempts, it went to voice mail.

He eventually came up to a signpost which read 'Havelock' and then underneath said 'Town centre'. Relief came across Kai as he could find his way home at least from the town centre. It would be a long walk as he had no cash for a taxi, but that didn't bother him.

Further up that road, he came across a building he had never seen before. It was dark and surrounded by trees so what little light was around cast a shadow over it.

'Studio entrance?' whispered Kai as he pulled a branch and fallen leaves of an old sign, he didn't know of any studios nearby Havelock. A loud shout of pain echoed from the building startling Kai and then several flashes of light lit up the inside. It went quiet and Kai couldn't decide whether he should investigate inside or leave pretending he didn't see or hear anything, he decided to go check it out,

'Your mum just called me,' a voice called from behind him. He stopped and looked as he recognised the voice, 'What are you doing?' asked Laura,

'Laura!' Said Kai, heading away from the studio door and back to the road where she was standing, 'What are you doing out here?'

'I have just dropped a friend off in Havelock and I like to come this way home. Then your mum called me so I thought I would look out for you, I didn't expect to find you here though,'

'I needed some time to myself, wait, you answered a call from my mum? What about my calls' Kai scoffed, 'I've been trying to call you since the day you finished work,'

'I know, I know, there's a lot I need to tell you. Something I didn't ever feel I needed to tell you until I saw Mr Brown's face on the computer,' said Laura, feeling a little awkward. 'I don't know how to start,' Laura paused and looked at Kai waiting for a reaction, but only receiving a short shake of his head, 'OK, your mum told me about you moving to Southampton,'

'I'm not moving to Southampton,' Kai interrupted,

'She told me that too, you are in danger here Kai, all of you,' said Laura, after sitting at an old bench a few yards down the road,

'I'm not running Laura,' Kai persisted, 'if Brown wants the pub, he can have it,'

'He wants the money Kai. Yes it seems he has an interest in the pub but thirty thousand pounds is a lot of money that he will want back. He won't just leave you alone,'

Kai looked around, trying to make sense of the thoughts that were appearing and disappearing quicker than he could process them,

'I know I don't have time but I need to think about this properly. Why did you panic when you saw Mr Brown's picture?' Kai asked Laura who looked down knowing this question was coming,

'I'm an orphan, Kai,'

There was a pause,

'An orphan?' said Kai, not really knowing how to respond,

'When I was younger Mr Brown threatened my family who chose not to run. I must have been eight or nine, I can still remember the morning I came downstairs, my breakfast was on the table waiting for me as normal. What was different was my parents, they were being over polite. I didn't think anything of it at the time but looking back now, they were scared for the future and my safety. Anyway, I went to school, and my dad dropped me off as he normally did. He kissed me as he did every morning because he knew I would have a meltdown if he didn't,' Laura gave a small laugh at that part, still holding back tears. 'I had a normal day at school, until we queued up at the door waiting for our parents to pick us up and, they never came to get me,' she couldn't hold the emotion back. Tears rolled down her face, all Kai could do was look her in her eyes and listen,

'I had overheard an argument my parents had days before and it was all about Mr Brown. I didn't know who he was, or what he looked like. I heard a brief description once but that was all. When the police asked me if there might be any reason why they weren't there or what might have happened to them, I was too scared to tell them. I didn't say anything, they could have been saved that day but I didn't help them, and I wish, I had,'

'Laura, you can't blame yourself for that, you were eight years old,' Kai said as he went to hold around her,

'I know, Kai, but you can still help your parents, go with them and get to safety. Yes, he may try and find you, but you might just slip away and you will be safe. Don't leave it until it's too late and they are gone because Mr Brown won't care for what he might do.'

'How come you stayed here, even though you know Mr Brown could appear at any time?' Kai asked,

'I don't know, I suppose I always hoped my parents would reappear, as they were never found, dead or alive,'

'Well I will tell my parents to go and we will go out and find your parents, together,' Kai suggested. His enthusiasm died as Laura's reaction wasn't as he hoped it would be,

'Kai, that's sweet. But it's too late for my family, it's been too long. I don't think I would recognise them now, but your parents will not go without you, please do the right thing,' Kai nodded as they embraced. Laura held Kai tightly thinking this was the last time she may see him.

Their moment was interrupted by another loud bang and flashes of light coming from the studio behind them.

'What is going on in there!' Kai shouted stepping in front of Laura, as smoke poured out of the window filling the air with the smell of melting plastic.

'Kai I think we should go,' said Laura pulling on his sleeve,

'Yeah, I think you're right,' They turned away as more sparks flew out of the building like fireworks lighting up the road,

'It must be young kids, playing with fireworks. They might get hurt,' Kai stepped back towards the studio, pulling away from Laura who was clinging to his sleeve,

'Kai we don't need to get involved, it's their own damn fault if they get hurt, let's go!' Laura managed to pull Kai away and he then gave up and walked with her to her car,

'They must have been in there for a while then. I wonder if they knew we were there?' said Kai, Laura shrugged her shoulders and remained silent for the remainder of the car journey back to the Black Bull.

As Kai stepped out of the car he placed his hand on Laura's and squeezed,

'Thank you, Laura, for everything,'

'As soon as you get wherever you are going text me please, we don't need to be strangers,' Kai gave Laura a smile in return and walked towards the pub.

Kai noticed his parents' car was still sitting in the car park a little relieved. He took a deep breath and entered the pub. It was dark and quiet. At the top of the stairs where all his mum's suitcases still sat on the landing in his way. The smell of pizza was strong in the flat. Jen hated the pizza from the restaurant and wouldn't eat if she didn't have to, so clearly she decided to stay here and eat waiting for him to get home. Kai ignored any signs and went into his bedroom and decided he would talk to his parents in the morning about the decision he had made. Sleep however did not come to him easily, for a long time his eyes were focused on a silver suitcase sitting on the floor of his bedroom,

'You win mum,' Kai said to himself as he opened his wardrobe and started packing his clothes into his case. He had a lot of clothes so picking just so many was going to be very difficult, not to mention the rest of his belongings. His case filled very quickly and he zipped it up before he could question his decisions and headed back to bed. Two photos on his bedside table caught his attention. One of his parents from the last family holiday they had taken, a caravan in Great Yarmouth, which was owned by his aunt Mel. Kai didn't enjoy those holidays, the British weather was always typically bad. The entertainment was poor and worse of all, they had to use what spending money they had on air fresheners to remove the smell of wet dogs from the caravan. If they were lucky, on the last day they could wake up to a fresh smell, but the family time as a kid was amazing. The other photo was taken a couple of weeks ago, of him and Laura at the Havelock fair. They hadn't been together long but it felt right to him to be with her and to just leave was going to be a lot harder than he thought. After he held the picture for over a minute, he placed it face down, lay on his bed, turned over and said to himself,

'A new life in Southampton, the beautiful south.'

Chapter Five

Terry's Hub

The next morning, the sun beamed through a small gap in the curtains waking Kai up as it lined up perfectly with his eyes. Kai looked at the time on his phone as he fell asleep expecting to be woken up by his parents ushering him to pack and leave for Southampton. The pub was quiet however, so he took his time to get up and then made his way out onto the landing. To his surprise, his parents' bags were still packed and ready sitting outside their bedroom,

'Mum? Dad?' Kai shouted, no answer. He edged their bedroom door open slightly to see whether they were asleep but the bed was empty and still made to its usual pristine fashion.

'They never stay out overnight?' Kai grumbled to himself. His curiosity about the situation started to get the better of him. Especially after looking out his bedroom window and noticing that their car was still in the same spot as when he came in last night.

After a quick search around the restaurant to no avail, he finished in the office where he found Len's car key and decided to take his search on the road. Kai did pass his driving test and managed to convince his dad to put him on the insurance for his car but never got the chance to drive it so now was his chance. But of course, leaving in the morning would never be that easy, without a visit from Den,

'Why is this pub not open?' Den shouted across the car park at Kai who nearly got to the car and thought he got away with it. Kai paused to think about this position as he probably wouldn't see that man again, so could he say what he felt? Ultimately he decided to continue to be polite,

'Er... gas leak Den,' he shouted,

'A gas leak!' Den barked, Kai instantly regretted that decision, why did he say a gas leak? 'why wasn't I informed? I live next door you know!'

'I am quite aware of that Den,' Kai replied calmly,

'Well then you should have sent me a letter, telling me about the situation, I could sue you!'

Kai's patience was weaning very quickly,

'OK I will write to you Den, I will send it second class, expect it in two working days,' Kai said with a growing smile,

'Two working days! my house could have blown up by that point, with me inside!'

'Ideal,' Kai said louder than he intended, 'Look, I have warned you. Maybe you should go stay with your amazing son you keep telling me about and we will let you know when it's safe to return. Just post your son's address through the letterbox,'

Den scurried back around to his house looking the pub up and down several times before actually leaving. Kai was now hoping for the pub to blow up so he didn't have to read that address. Either way, that may have just gotten rid of him or worse case he will be Mr Brown's problem if he does take the pub off them.

As Kai left the car park he had to think for a couple of minutes where to start looking for his parents. He tried calling them several times, but no answer. He tried calling Laura, no answer. He decided to head into town and just scout the area as they had often walked there together. But the more Kai thought about it and the further into town he got, it was not often after all. Has he run out of ideas of where they could be already? He had only just started his search. Kai pulled into a space in the car park of Jollies, a small supermarket his mum liked to use instead of the big popular ones. He felt awkward now, people watching wasn't his favourite thing to do not alone looking for someone hoping they may just turn up.

A buzz started coming from inside his car, it was his phone. After the last failed call to Laura he through on the back seat and now found himself scurrying around to find it.

'Hello,' he said, answering it in time, he didn't get a chance to look at the name of the caller.

'Hello… Kai?'

'Laura, where are you?' Kai asked breathlessly,

'At home, what's up? You sound like you have run a marathon,'

'Er… yeah you know just ran round the block, clear my head,' he lied. That sounded better than being tired out from rushing to find his phone in the backseat of his parent's car,

'Oh ok, so what's up?' Laura asked again,

'It's my parents, have they called you again by any chance?'

'No, I haven't heard from your mum since she called the other day… Kai what's going on?' Laura started to sound impatient, and a bit nervous,

'I can't find them, they didn't come home last night,'

A prolonged silence followed, neither wanted to break it until Laura spoke,

'Come to my house, I'll text you my address,' Kai felt strangely relieved to not only hear Laura's voice but also to no longer be alone in his search.

Kai followed his sat nav to find Laura's house but after a short time, he recognised the road he was driving on. On the left-hand side was that strange building he saw the night before and once again smoke was billowing out of one of the windows. He decided to pull up and this time go and have a look. It was daylight this time, so it wasn't quite a scary scene as it was in the dark, yet, it did still have a daunting feel to it.

Kai banged on the front doors,

'Hello!' he called but nobody answered, he contemplated turning and leaving but the smoke poured off thicker and darker than before. The worst-case scenarios ran through Kais' mind as quickly as a train, what if those kids were in there again? and the fire was out of control?

'I'm going to break down the doors in five, four, three, two,' Kai stepped back and forced his shoulder into the join of the double doors. They didn't feel locked making him fall forward into a stack of wooden crates. The smoke clung to the ceiling as it was being sucked out the window like a vacuum. The room was empty, apart from what looked like junk, wooden crates, old ropes, and even old swords and bows and arrows. The smoke looked as though it was coming from a door on the back wall which was open about halfway, allowing the smoke to escape. Kai felt he had come this far, so it wouldn't make sense to not continue.

Kai pulled his jumper over his mouth and nose and entered through the billowing smoke. He could not see anything above waist height, so he went on all fours to look for anyone's feet that may be stuck or couldn't find their way out.

'Hello, anybody in here?' Kai called, but no answer. It was really quiet, with no crackles from a raging fire or overworked piece of machinery that may have overheated. Whilst he was crouched down he felt that he may have found where the smoke might be coming from. In the centre of the room, there was a huge metal base with what he guessed was some sort of control panel on the side. Of course, it was drowned in smoke but it was the clouds pouring out of whatever was above it. Kai got closer to it to see if he could shut it down to try and reduce the smoke a little so he clambered on the metal base with his right foot first. Before he could move his hands over to it, Smack, Bang, whoosh! Noises echoed around him as a rope clamped tightly around his ankle as he was dragged away from the machine. Before he knew it he was hanging upside down by his ankle in the thick smoke.

'Let me down, hello!' Kai shouted, 'Come on! Help me,'

There was no other movement or sound. As soon as he came to a stop all the bangs and the sound of moving ropes disappeared and there was silence again. Kai once again held his jumper over his face and he could keep shouting because every time he opened his mouth he took in clouds of smoke.

Minutes started to pass by, but to Kai, it felt like hours and his hopes of someone coming to save him disappeared. He had attempted to get his phone but trying to get it out of his pocket whilst hanging upside down by his ankle was a tough task. He stopped trying as he spotted it on the floor probably cracked, chipped and broken. A flash of green flew through the dense grey of the smoke and again, then a purple flash. The machine started to viciously shake, vibrating the ropes holding Kai. More multi-coloured flashes followed like lightning bolts in a storm. But then, it was quiet and calm,

'What a mess,' moaned a recognisable voice.

The sound of a few clicks came before a roar from above as fans started sucking the smoke from the room. Within a couple of seconds, the room was clear. Kai opened his eyes slowly, squinting to make sure all the smoke had gone before committing to opening them fully,

'Ahh... my boy, who had thought it,' the man said, 'Karen told me about someone crawling about but I didn't think it would be you,'

'Mr Toone?' Kai said after his vision had focused,

'You remember me then... Kai... isn't it? How are you?' Mr Toone held his hand out to Kai who looked at Mr Toone up and down,

'I'm good, err... Mr Toone, how do you fancy letting me down?'

'Oh yes, of course, Karen, release him,' Mr Toone shouted towards the machine. In a matter of seconds, Kai felt the rope loosen leaving him to drop head first onto the floor, 'ooh sorry about that Kai, that's got to be sore,'

'Did she need to drop me like that?' Said Kai rubbing his head, 'whose Karen?'

'She's a good friend of mine,'

'Well where is she then?' asked Kai as he looked around. Mr Toone was leaning up against the console of his machine tapping the control panel. It took a while for Kai to realise what Mr Toone was showing him,

'She's a computer!?' Kai shouted, followed by a whip of the ropes against the back of his legs, knocking him back to the floor.

'I should have warned you, Kai... that offends her,' Mr Toone said giving the panel one last tap, as Kai was still in a heap on the floor.

'Karen looks after the place for me whilst I'm away, she was the best thing I did a couple of years ago, keeps them kids from coming in here,'

'Karen, so does that stand for something, an acronym maybe?'

'No, she complains a lot,' Mr Toone then ducked as a rope flew over his head and then gave Kai a look to say I told you so.

'Karen controls everything in this room Kai, the machine, the ropes, the lights, even the power,'

'Wait wouldn't that shut her down if she, for another word if she were to kill the power?'

'Oh yeah, a powerful threat she has, because she knows I love her really and would be lost without her.'

Mr Toone helped Kai to his feet, placed his arm around him and started to walk around the machine. He pointed at different parts of it and how important they were to make it work.

'Where did you come from anyway, just then?' Kai asked.

'A tale for another time Kai, I don't think you would understand.'

He was right about that. Kai didn't understand.

'Do you live here Mr Toone?'

'This is my hub Kai, otherwise I live wherever I want,' Kai was still very confused about what had happened and what was in front of him, 'anyway call me Terry, Terry Toone.'

Terry started to look closer at the machine to find what was causing the amount of smoke that filled the room. Kai used this time to look at the different artefacts that hung from the ceiling and walls around him. Several different weapons were laid out on desks. Weapons he hadn't seen before, only in history books, only they were different, not from this world.

'I didn't see these before,' said Kai,

'Well smoke blinds you after all,' Terry said pulling his head from the machine and instantly diving back in.

'Where are they all from? they are odd,'

'They are very dangerous Kai, that's what they are. One of the reasons they are all here. Some I took after defeating dangerous beings and some I may have borrowed, err… without permission.'

Terry was suddenly behind Kai, making him jump as he turned.

'You? Took from dangerous what? Animals? Humans?'

'When you have seen what I have seen Kai you really wouldn't be so shocked. I have deer chase you for one minute and then stand on two legs battling with swords. I have seen dolphins racing through lava pouring down a volcano and worse of all I have seen toddlers,'

'Toddlers?' Kai asked stepping slowly away from Terry who to Kai, seemed to have gone mad,

'Yes, Toddlers! Now let me ask you this, are Toddlers human?'

'Er… yes?'

'Wrong! Ha ha, wrong you are Kai! When you see what I have seen, life will never be the same again!'

Terry ran up to the control panel of his machine and started pressing buttons frantically. Kai edged closer.

'What are you doing? And what exactly does this machine do?'

'This machine will take you places you can only dream of. Places that are in your mind, or stories you have created. This was gifted to me by an old friend. Imagination, and stories. It's what I live for and I had a dream to be a movie director or something like that, but this gives me more than that, it puts me into my stories. All these amazing items in front of you are made up of the stories that I have brought home with me. It's amazing don't you think?'

Kai stood and stared at Terry and shook his head. Terry's attention was taken by a spark coming from the panel allowing Kai to look around some more. Kai didn't admit it but was impressed by the collection but they looked like film props rather than real things.

'So all the flashes and bangs I have seen coming from this place were you using this machine?'

Terry didn't answer. A long black sword sat buried below sheets of old paper and junk. The black reflected from the lights and glimmered catching Kai's glare. He cleared away all in his way to pick the sword up and the feel of it was incredible. It was so light he could move it with ease. For a minute he forgot where he was and swung it around as if he knew what he was doing. His fun didn't last as Karen's ropes tightened around the sword, removed it from his grip and placed it gently back on the desk.

'That sword, I should not have taken,' said Terry.

'Why?'

'The world of Haven is a dangerous place and I shouldn't have gone and definitely won't be going back. The person who owns this sword would have needed this sword more than me and I took it for my collection,'

'So these worlds you create in your mind, they continue even if you are not there?'

'In Karen's memory, yes. Once I create it and visit it I then no longer control it and it sits in the memory bank,'

'Delete the memory, then this guy won't miss his sword?'

'That is true, yes, but I can't delete an individual creation. They live alongside each other. You delete one you delete them all. Back during the war, I wanted to escape to my stories and over all that time as you can imagine a lot of places have been created. That's why it smokes so much when I use it I think.'

'The war? how old are you?'

'Ninety-six this year, I know I know I don't look a day over forty. Our time doesn't exist in these worlds. It continues but our bodies don't, that's why I haven't aged like others,'

'So you can't die in there then?'

'You won't age, but you can be killed, and I have to keep returning to keep the machine safe. If this machine gets destroyed whilst I'm inside… I will cease to exist. Which is why I created Karen to protect the hub,'

'If it's struggling wipe it and start again, create a blank canvas to paint on,'

'I can't…'

Terry's enthusiastic persona faded as he slumped into his chair. The bright colour of his face drained and he tried distracting himself by picking up and moving items on his desk.

'Terry?' said Kai as he attempted to break the sudden awkwardness, 'why can't you?'

Terry got up from his chair and walked slowly around his machine and stopped at a frame hanging on the wall. He unhooked it and handed it to Kai.

'This is why,' he said solemnly,

'Wait… is this… your family?'

Terry nodded as he sat back in his chair. Kai brushed some dust off the frame and looked closely. Charlotte and Terry gleamed back at him. Both had their arms around Emma and George both dressed in Halloween costumes.

'That was the last time I saw them. Halloween… Emma's eighth birthday. I took them out for a spooky Halloween treat as they loved the scary stories that I told them. It was perfect until something came and took them from me. I have spent the last fifty years searching for the world that we visited but they have been there ever since. That is why I can't delete worlds, If the worlds still exist, I know they do… if I delete them they will be gone forever… I suppose you feel the same, with your parents being missing,'

'How do you know about my parents?'

'I am very aware of Mr Brown and what he is capable of. I have been keeping an eye on him and it brought me to you,'

'So it was you I saw at the pub!'

Kai was thrilled that he wasn't going mad that night. But an uneasy feeling started to fill the room as Terry continued.

'I have helped many people who have wanted to escape him. A lot of them reside inside my magical kingdoms as they call it. All I ask in return is to help find my family and I protect theirs,'

'So my parents are in there!'

'No… no they are not,' Terry stepped away from his machine closer to Kai, 'I tried to get to your parents, but he beat me to them. I am starting to think that he has caught on to what I have been doing which puts it all at risk. Kai, I will put the same thing to you as I have many before you. Help me find my family and I will help you find yours.'

'How? Mine are out In the real world somewhere not in some imaginary one. This is real life. Mr Brown can have our pub I don't care for that, but he wants money… real money that I don't have,'

'Kai, money is plentiful inside my kingdoms, help me and together we can help your parents.'

'You're asking me to forget about the danger my family are in to help yours first, I can't do that I don't have much time,'

'Then we must be quick… Kai we can get the money to pay off Mr Brown to save your parents and at the same time find my family,'

'You have been looking for your family for fifty years Terry, I haven't got another fifty years to save Mum and Dad! No this is insane, thank you for the offer Terry but this is something I need to do quickly. Your storybook kingdom can't help me,'

Kai headed for the door but Karen's ropes flew past him and barricaded the doors,

'Kai, think carefully about this, together we can do this, we can help each other,'

'let me out, Terry,'

'Kai please,'

Kai began to pull on the ropes, but they clung to the door frame like a metal fence. Kai franticly pulled to release them and find his way out.

'Kai she will always be stronger than you,' said Terry,

Kai stopped and grabbed the sword he had picked up earlier and hacked at the ropes splitting them, but more came to replace them,

'Kai she has more rope than you have energy and patience.'

Kai realised he was right. Terry had a look in his eyes like he was trying to guess his next move. Kai looked at the console and swung the sword towards it.

'NO!' screamed Terry.

Karen's ropes wrapped around the console, and the sharp points of the rope sped towards Kai stopping just before they made contact with his skin. Kais stopped the sword centimetres before the console.

'Kai don't do this, please,'

'Let me go.'

The sharp points started to dig into Kai. He could cut the tension within the room with the blade he held in his hand.

'If you want to leave Kai, you can. Please think about my offer.'

Kai looked at the ropes which refused to move.

'Karen, let him go,'

One point flew away from Kai's neck and started to point towards the blade Kai held against the console. He realised what she wanted so he threw the blade back onto the desk. Terry screwed his face up as the metal clanged on the desk. Kai was careful not to get scratched by Karen on his way out,

'Good luck Kai,' said Terry as the door slammed shut.

Kai sat for a moment in Len's car trying to remember what he was out and about for. The ordeal within the old studio had confused Kai and he started to question whether it took place. He checked his phone which had three missed calls from Laura.

'Oh no,' he gasped, remembering that he was meant to be going to meet her. Trying to explain what he had been through to Laura wasn't going to be easy. So her not answering the phone was a relief to him. He was sure she didn't know Terry that well to the extent he had his magical kingdoms and a computer called Karen. Or maybe she did? He was sure she didn't but he was now intrigued to hear what she had to say about it. It sounded like an odd story he would normally tell her at work to make her laugh. After a while, he pulled away watching the studio fall away into the distance. Kai rubbed his head gently nursing a headache, part from when he was dropped on it and the other living through the experience with Terry.

Chapter Six

Horror Stories

It was only a short drive from the studio to Laura's flat. Kai's previous exchange with Terry was still blowing his mind, but also amazed him. The technology that he had was incredible and Karen... well Karen was something else completely.

'Kai!' said Laura as she swung her front door open, 'where have you been.'

'You will not believe it, Laura,' said Kai preparing her for his tale, 'I was on my way here, and as I went past that old studio it was smoking as if it was burning. Do you know who owns it? Terry Toone!'

'Terry Toone? You mean Mr Toone?' asked Laura,

'Yes his name is Terry and he is ninety-six years old.'

Laura's reaction played out exactly as Kai expected, a look of disbelief.

'You need to see what he has in there Laura it is mad,' said Kai as he explained the whole ordeal, Terry's artefacts, his magical kingdoms and of course Karen.

'Hold on Kai, do you know how crazy this sounds?' Asked Laura,

Kai replied by nodding,

'He wants me to help him find his family and he will help me find mine,'

'How?' asked Laura,

'I don't know, he reckons he's helped lots of people that Brown has threatened. Maybe he has other contacts or is he trying to populate his worlds?'

'Here Kai,' Said Laura as she passed him a coffee and ham sandwich that she had learned was his favourite. Laura lived in a very modern one-bedroom flat. Very typical single girls' decor, it was very clean and well-organised.

'Kai I don't think you can turn down help at this stage. We don't know where to look, the police won't get involved with dodgy transactions. Plus Brown is clever, the police won't be able to help,'

'Terry says he can get gold in his world but I don't know. I doubt it's a currency Brown will accept,'

'We need to find out, I will come with you. In the morning we will go."

The morning came very quickly. Although Kai was still very wary of Terry, he also had a slither of enthusiasm that they were going in the right direction. Laura was up and ready before Kai had got himself out of bed, but he had woken early as his mind was fixed on his parents. He contemplated sneaking out early as getting Laura mixed up in this wasn't something Kai felt comfortable about.

'Hey Kai, are you ready,'

Kai was ready, but that didn't stop Laura from banging on her bedroom door that she let him sleep in whilst she stayed on her sofa.

'You haven't had a text or anything for your parents?' asked Laura, as they both climbed into her car,

'No.'

The conversations were short like this for the whole journey. Kai didn't know where he stood with Laura as the last time he saw her they were splitting up and he was leaving for Southampton.

As they pulled into the entry of the studio, once again smoke billowed from the side of the building.

'He must be using his machine,' said Kai, 'He told me it smokes a lot at the moment.'

'Terry!' shouted Kai as he banged his fists on the door, 'Terry, Mr Toone, Karen!'

The doors opened by themselves, allowing smoke to empty. Kai pulled his jumper over his mouth and nose and entered.

'Mr Toone?'

Flashes of green and blue lit the room up, a bang shocked Laura making her grab hold of Kai,

'Kai, what is this?'

'This is Mr Toone's hub,'

'Hub?'

'Yeah, that's what he calls it,'

Lights on the console started to flash and ropes started to swing out to protect the platform.

'Karen it's Kai, I just want to talk to Terry,'

Karen didn't stop, the ropes continued to defend Terry's hub, especially from someone who threatened it. She didn't stop until the smoke started to flash making her switch the extraction system on leaving Terry Toone standing on the platform,

'Kai!... Karen, you didn't tell me we had visitors, and Laura it's good to see you again,'

'Hi Mr Toone,' said Laura,

'I must admit Kai, you're back quicker than I thought you would be. Have you thought about my offer?,

'I have, but I need more information,

'Of course, of course you should want to know more,' Terry stopped waiting for Karen to release the ropes trapping him on the platform, 'Karen please this was unnecessary and be nice to the boy.'

Karen's ropes released Terry from the platform and caught Kai on his Face as it passed by,

'Oh Ye that was for trying to cut her ropes yesterday, she isn't very good at forgiving,'

'Mr Toone this is incredible, why have you not told me about this before?' asked Laura as she walked around inspecting the machine.

'Well, it isn't something I want to be known to the public. A lot is at stake here Laura as I'm sure Kai has told you. Now what is it you need to know?'

'You told me you had gold in your world, how can that pay Mr Brown?'

'Gold is gold Kai, I chose to avoid pounds, euros and dollars,' Terry replied, 'Look I know how to get it, it's not going to be easy, but together we can do it,'

'But what Kingdom do we need to go to?' asked Kai,

'Leave it with me, Kai, I suggest we use a current world as Karen is already struggling with the memory she is holding, but I have a couple in mind,'

'What about your family Mr Toone? How do we help to find them?' Asked Laura,

'This is what I have in Mind. We get the first payment for Mr Brown, then we look for my family. Then successful or not we go and get the rest… come with me.'

Terry opened a door at the back of the room into a huge space. In front of them sat three rows of shelving units and behind that a huge statue.

'Terry, what on earth is that?' Asked Kai,

'That Kai is the hidden Tiger called Mori. It was a treasure in one of the world's apparently but it just looks like a piece of sandstone to me, beautiful but useless,'

'How did you get it here?' asked Laura,

'Let me show you, you will need these,' said Terry as he picked up some small black bracelets, a similar size to a wristwatch, 'these will return you to the machine. Now you can only leave the world in the same position that you entered it so you must remember the location. When you are in the correct place within its parameter it will light up, you then tap it and you will return here. Whatever you are holding will return with you, so think about what you are doing... here.'

Terry handed Kai and Laura a bracelet each,

'How did you get that statue in to range of the entry area?'

'Donkeys, very strong donkeys. I wanted to bring them with me but when I went back for them they had gone,'

'So which world is your family in?' asked Kai,

'I don't know, I took them to a scary mansion surrounded by forests for Emma's birthday but I'm losing places to look for them. Every time I cover an area I get Karen to cover it in shadow so I know I have looked so all that is left now is the mansion where we started and its gardens. Fifty years of searching, and nothing,'

'So you think you can skip to different worlds then?' asked Laura,

'You shouldn't. But it would seem so. I believe there is a glitch in the system, it is old after all. But what took my family I believe to be a glitch. Which is why it can bounce from world to world,'

'But with these bracelets, you can jump from world to world?' asked Kai.

'Yes, kind of but Karen doesn't like it. Look I want to show you where I took my family, then you can decide.'

Whilst Terry sorted out the machine, Kai and Laura looked around the warehouse at of artefacts Terry had collected. Old statues and more weapons filled the space. Magic wands filled one box and laser pistols filled another.

'This is insane, I'm taking one of these,' Said Kia shoving a pistol into his pocket, 'I'm not sure about this Laura, we don't know where he will take us,'

'I trust him, Kai, he just wants his family back, just like you and... just like me,'

'But what if there is no gold and when we get in there, we find his family and we can't get back? If his family get stuck in there I'm sure we can too!'

'Then we get stuck… Kai, I'm doing this, I want to help you and I want to help Mr Toone,'

'You want to risk your life for me and Terry?'

'Kai, I haven't much else. I have my flat, my cat and you,' The lights started to flicker within the warehouse.

'Alright you two come one, I'm ready,' shouted Mr Toone, 'remember your bracelets.'

Laura handed Kai a bracelet and kept one herself as they met Terry back at the hub. Bright spotlights were beaming towards the platform in the centre of the room.

'Now I must warn both of you, eighty per cent of my stories have been horror stories, even the ones that look like they should be sweet stories,' said Terry,

'Depressing,' said Kai, making Karen whip him with some rope.

'There is a common enemy I need to tell you about. The glitch I have mentioned before created a phantom-like character who I believe took my family. I have only seen him several times in the world but that's not to say it appears again. If you see it, get back to the entry point and press your bracelet as soon as you can. Do not wait for me just get yourselves out of there, do you understand?

'Err.. yes Terry,' replied Kai,

'OK join me on the platform.'

The three of them stepped up onto the platform as light grey smoke started to rise from beneath them.

'This is madness,' Mumbled Kai under his breath.

Laura grabbed hold of Kais' hand they disappeared into the cloud of smoke. Kai watched his legs turn to dust along with Laura's. Then his waist, then his chest. He lifted his head like he was drowning and needed to take a breath before being pulled underwater. When he opened his eyes he was lying face first on a dirt and twigs. It was dark and he couldn't see anybody until hands grabbed his back and pulled him to his feet.

'Come on Kai!' chuckled Laura,

'You fell on your face too... right?'

Terry and Laura laughed at Kai as they walked out of the forest. Kai was amazed at how real everything felt to him. The leaves on the bushes had the same textures, the wind blew against him like it would in the real world. Moonlight lit an old Manor in front of them.

'This is the place then?' asked Kai,

'This is it,' Replied Terry.

They followed him up the steps to the front door. The steps were not level or straight. Cobwebs covered the pebbles and dirt surrounding them. The spiders were the size of a fist sitting atop their nests awaiting their next prey to fall into the trap.

'I think one of them could eat us you know,' Said Kai, relieving a quick slap to his chest from Laura,

'Look, above the trees,' Said Terry.

He pointed to a shadow that covered the horizon only leaving the Manor and its grounds the ability to see the real night sky.

'It's the only way to know where I have covered in my search. I decided that whoever took them wouldn't stay at the house so I started elsewhere and made my way back,'

'How big is this world?' Asked Kai,

'It consists of the Manor House, its grounds and a surrounding forest. That's all I required. If you saw it from a distance it would look like a planet but it's no bigger than, I would say, London curved around into a sphere,'

'Aaahhwoooowh!' echoed all around them,

'Oh, not these again. We should get inside.'

Terry bundled them through the front door, shut it behind them and then lifted a small floorboard and picked up a rusty long key. He placed it in the lock and twisted it to the sound of a bang.

'It's not been locked for some time I can assure you, now this way.'

They followed Terry upstairs and looked out of a back window into the old gardens.

'There look,' Terry pointed to a burnt-out campfire with four rocks surrounding it. 'that is where I last saw them. I heard a bang inside and I went to investigate it and it all went wrong from there really, they disappeared. I saw them for the last time being held by the phantom and I pressed my bracelet in the hope it would bring us all back but it took me and I haven't seen them since,'

'So it's been fifty years, but we are looking for two children and a woman in her thirties?' asked Laura,

'Yes, you are correct Laura. It's odd but that still gives me hope that when I find them I can still live a happy life with them and not miss them growing up,'

'Wait a minute,' said Kai, 'you told me that these are all stories that you thought up or created yourself right?'

'That's right,'

'Well if you are any good at storytelling there will be a beginning, middle and an end. A hero and a villain, and you put your family in the middle of that?'

Terry looked away and leaned against the window frame, he felt the same heart beating just like the day he lost his family.

'You're right of course. I put them in real danger. Many of the world's I cannot remember who the villains are or who the protagonists were. In this world, there is a glitch that we don't know much about, but the villain. The phantom is the villain which I knew but I brought my family here anyway,' A tear ran down Terry's face.

'So the Phantom isn't the glitch?' asked Laura,
Terry shook his head solemnly. Kai felt for Terry and even felt guilty about making that accusation against him.

'You must understand that the knowledge that I have of this place is much greater now than it was fifty years ago. Forty of which I have spent in here looking for them,'

'What happens if you defeat the villain?' said Laura,

'I don't know Laura, but that's the hero's job, every story has a hero and a villain,'

'So where is the hero of this story?' asked Kai.

Terry stopped to think. His fingers picked against old flaky paint that was peeling away from the wooden window frame.

'I can't remember,' said Terry., 'I have never met anybody else. I thought maybe covering all these parts in shadow may bring the hero out but that has never happened...'

Terry was interrupted by a cloud of smoke followed swiftly by a bang, and another after another. It was like bombs were being dropped by a plane over the forest.

'What is that?' cried Laura,

'I don't know, come on,' Said Kai.

Kai, Laura and Terry all ran back into the forest to find what may have caused to explosions.

'Hello!' shouted Kai,

'Kai don't, we should stay hidden until we know what it is!' said Laura,

'Your right... Terry, is there anything deeper in these forests?'

'No, just forests'

Kai led them into the forest deeper. The further they went the darker it got.

'Kai, I think we should go back... Ah!'

A call from an owl frit Laura making her once again cling to Kai's arm. A smoky fog sat just above the ground chilling the air.

'You do have more friendly stories inside that mind of yours don't you Terry?' asked Kai,

'Stories mess with emotions Kai, fear can be the more simple emotion to be able to ignore.'

Up ahead Kai spotted a small cave, naturally carved into the side of a small cliff. They carefully entered as the only light was from the torch on the back of Kai's phone. The floor was sloppy where the rain had settled within the muddy ground.

'Do you think someone has been staying here?' asked Laura,

'Possibly,' replied Kai, 'what do you think Terry? Have you seen this before?'

'No… I haven't.'

They had a closer look at the darkness of the cave. Some bags appear in the torch light. A small red backpack full of old snacks and a couple of wooden toys.

'Terry…'

Terry looked up at Laura and a smile grew slowly but short.

'That's Emma's!' He held the toys close to his chest, 'they are alive I know it,'

'There's no way they have lived here for fifty years. Does the sun ever come out?' Asked Kai,

'Not whilst I have been here, what else have you found?'

Laura pulled out a paper bag that had holes on the side where I had gotten wet and fell apart.

'TNT!'

'Where in the world have they got that from?' said Terry,

'It would explain the explosions,' said Kai,

'Wait.' said Laura, 'look there's writing on this wall, they have carved something in here… The phantom grew with power with every scream and shout from the terrified children. The house beat along with its heartbeat. The house that the phantom called home.'

'That's George and Charlotte,' said Terry as he flung the bag over his back. 'they remembered the story I told them. it's the house, bring that TNT to come on.'

The three of them ran back towards the house.

'Aaahhwoooowh!'

Three werewolves jumped down from the top of the small cliff above the cave and gave chase. They ran on all fours at twice the speed of Terry, Kai and Laura.

'Behind here quick!' shouted Terry, 'these werewolves have bad eyesight just stay still and low,'

'Werewolves have bad eyesight? Really?" asked Kai,

'What? It's all coming back to now, and the heroes had to win somehow, it's a kid's story.'

They hid quietly behind a pile of rocks just on the edge of the forest. The werewolves had bad eyesight but a heightened sense of smell making them circle the area to find the source.

'Terry, what now?' asked Laura,

'Pass me the TNT.'

Terry picked out a stick, lit it with his lighter and threw it into the middle of the werewolves making them scatter for the loud bang.

'Let's go!' said Terry.

They ran as fast as they could to get to the house, but a figure in a cape caught Terry's attention.

'Who's that there?'

'I don't know, they're heading into the house!' said Laura.

A crash and bang blew out a hole in the side of the house. It was beating and extruding as if it was taking breaths. The cloaked figure flew out of the door and landed on their back followed by the blue shimmering, misty figure of the phantom.

'There he is look,' Said Terry,

'We need to help them, they are trying to destroy the house and that will destroy the phantom! That is what the part of the story meant that they had written on the cave wall!' Said Laura,

'But what if Terry's family is still here and we blow the house up which will kill the villain or phantom? That will end the story and we don't know what will happen to the world,' said Kai.

The hero continued to try and get back to the house but the phantom repeatedly pushed them back.

'I think I know who the hero is,' said Terry, 'It's George it's always George or Emma,'

'George!' Terry said as he ran towards the phantom,

'Terry, you will need the TNT!' shouted Kai.

Terry got pushed back by the phantom.

'Come on we can do this!' said Kai.

Kai and Laura ran towards the house and planted the TNT under the stairs, which were in the middle of the house. They ran out as quickly as they could and just as the phantom looked as though he was about the defeat the hero, the house blew. Shards of wood flew away from the explosion and rained down around the property. The phantom stood still, then clenched at his chest. His transparent body shivered like it was in pain. His fist held where his heart should sit.

'We need to get Terry and leave quickly,' said Kai.

Once the house was no more, the phantom dissolved into dust. Kai and Laura ran over to Terry who had landed heavy after being thrown by the phantom. He lifted his head and saw it was a boy in a cloak.

'George! Hey George!' Shouted Terry, but before he could get up a light beamed from the sky surrounding the boy. He looked at Terry and held out a hand but before he could get up the beam took him away as if he was sucked up to the sky,

'No wait... please," Terry shouted.

It was no good he was gone. The ground around the house started to crumble. Trees and walls around the building fell into the vacuum.

'Well, I think we can see what happens when the story ends,' said Laura,

'Back to the forest, go!' shouted Kai.
They ran as quickly as they could trying to avoid where the ground was crumbling around them.

'Check your bracelets!' Shouted Terry, 'as soon as they light up, you must press it. We are nearly there!'

They entered the forest. No light appeared. They went deeper and deeper as trees fell with the rest of the world. After getting deeper in finally the bracelets lit up and simultaneously they each pressed and they started to evaporate away.

Kai opened his eyes as he lay on his back surrounded by smoke. Laura and Terry stood over him.

'How do you land on your feet every time?' he asked Laura,

'Lucky I guess,' Laura said and gave him a tight hug,

'They are alive… they are alive!' said Terry excitedly, 'that is the first time I have seen my son in fifty years! And he looks exactly as I remember,'

'So where do we start… to look for gold and your family?' asked Kai.

'They could be on any of the worlds. I know where to get gold and there are people there who can help us,'

'Help us… what like a gang?' asked Laura.

'Err… well owning gold is a funny old business. It's usually owned by unpleasant people, which makes it feel a lot better about yourself when you steal it,'

'Steal it!' gasped Laura,

'Well it doesn't grow on trees Laura and I'm not about to start digging for it either I assure you. It all comes down to how desperate are you to find your parents?'

'Let's do it,' Replied Kai,

'Excellent, and I might just be able to get some information from some folk there as well. The first world that we are visiting has some very good old friends that I believe can help us out.'

Chapter seven

John Corbett

Even though he didn't know which world he was entering, Kai decided to drive back to the pub to freshen up. Of course, Laura was in tow, for support just in case the pub was now in the hands of Mr Brown and his cronies. To his surprise, the pub was abandoned. The side door however was damaged where someone had hacked at it with what looked like an axe. It was so badly damaged that he could just push the door gently and it would open.

At the top of the stairs, his parent's suitcases were still where they had left them. Their clothes and other belongings were sprawled over the landing and down the stairs. His parent's bedroom had been ransacked. Their clothes were dragged out of wardrobes and drawers. His mother's necklaces were broken and some were missing. The mattress was sitting at an angle where they had lifted it off the bed and let it slide to the floor.

'Do you think Brown did this?' said Laura,

'Well, they can't have been looking for my parents if he has them. Unless he has some idea that they have some hidden valuables somewhere,'

'Do they?'

'Not that I know of, well not to the value he wants.'

Kai's bedroom hadn't had the same treatment as his parents. It was a mess but it didn't look as though anything was missing.

'Looks like you got away with it Kai,' said Laura,

'I don't have any valuables for them to take that's why.'

Kai picked up a picture that was wedged into the side of an old picture frame. It was of him and his parents on the day they moved into the Black Bull. He could remember it clearly. The sun was beating down and the beer garden was full to bursting point of adults enjoying a beer or glass of wine.

Kai hated the idea of working in a pub from that day. Every time the sun came out in the morning he pictured that beer garden full and the mess that would need clearing up after them.

Kai changed into a black tracksuit and left with Laura to head back to the studio.

The studio was quiet. Karen was in rest mode and Terry was nowhere to be seen.

'Terry? Are you here?' said Kai,

'In here.' Said a small voice from the back room.

Kai and Laura went into the vast warehouse to find Terry sitting on an old wooden bench up against a wall.

'Is that your daughters?' Laura asked Terry who was holding a golden furry Teddy bear.

'Ye,' He replied solemnly, 'We bought it for her seventh birthday. She only had it a year before I lost her,'

Terry held the bear close to his chest. The fur was in very good condition for a fifty-one-year-old toy.

'I miss them terribly. When I saw George, he turned to me and when he saw who I was he wanted to come to me, I know he did, but he got taken away again,'

'We will find them Terry, at least we know they're alive!' said Laura,

'We know he's alive. What if he's all alone? Fending for himself,' Said Terry,

'Maybe he has just stepped up. Knowing he needed to keep his family safe until you find them,' Said Kai.

His own family flashed through his mind ending with the picture he was holding back at the pub.

'We will find them, Terry,' Laura repeated.

Terry nodded and opened a chest that looked so old like it had been sitting under the ocean for centuries.

'I found this in a pirate adventure. George would have loved it, so I cleaned it up and stored their belongings in it from home to keep here with me,'

'That's amazing,' said Kai, 'when we find them I'm sure they will love it.'

Terry placed the bear inside the chest, gently closed the lid and stroked his hand over the old rough wooden shell of the case. Laura and Kai left Terry to himself in the back room and returned to Karen.

'Well I suppose we need to wake this up,' said Kai. He strode casually around the platform looking for an obvious way of switching the machine on.

'Should we not wait for Terry?' said Laura,

'It can't be that hard Laura, it's only a machine!'

Then instantly, lights flashed around the platform and buttons flickered on the console. Before Kai knew it once again he was hanging upside by his ankle.

'Wait! what's going on let him down!' Laura yelled,

'It's OK, it's OK,' Said Kai, 'Laura this is Karen… Karen, Laura.'

Laura stopped as she looked from Kai to the console and back to Kai.

'Charmed, so the machine is a person?'

'Well yes and no. You can let me down now Karen, gently this time please!' More ropes held on to Kai and helped lower him to his feet, 'Terry created her, she's brilliant,' said Kai winking at the console.

'Well Karen's ready to go but where do you think we're going to go? I hope it's more friendly than that haunted house,'

'Laura were going to steal gold. They won't just hand it to us and say thanks for coming,'

'I know but, werewolves? He took his family there,'

'Laura come on, if I think about other people's decision-making skills, I will soon consider my ability to make the right call and go back home.'

The door to the back room opened and Terry slid in quickly shutting the door behind him. The lights around the platform got brighter as if the star of the show had just entered the stage.

'Sorry for taking a while folks, I just had to compose myself… Now, where were we? Ahh yes the mission… right, gold! I know the perfect place to find some gold and it shouldn't be too difficult,'

'No werewolves if you don't mind Mr Toone,' Said Laura.
Kai rolled his eyes.

'Yeah, a free bank would be nice Terry.' Said Kai sarcastically,

'If only it was that simple son. Right this needs to go as smoothly as possible so we should use a preloaded world,' Karen's lights flashed in appreciation, 'so the one I have in mind is the rainforest, all we need to do is get to the abandoned temple and there is gold there you see,'

'And who's the antagonist?' Terry looked at Kai in confusion, 'yeah, evil gang leader, ugly goblin King, phantom, emperor palpa thingy… the bad guy!'

'Oh, I see… Kai yes I believe there is an oversized anaconda floating around to protect the gold.'
Laura's face turned a murky green,

'A snake? Really?' said Kai, 'and what's its motive?'

'It's motive? Kai, you're thinking far too much into this,' said Terry.

A good bad guy should always have a motive, a reason why they feel it's the right thing to do.'

The room went silent for almost a minute.

'Hmm... you're probably right, what was his motive?'

'Terry a snake cannot have a real motive. It's an animal!"\' said Kai,

'Kai, have you watched Jungle Book?' Laura asked calmly,

'No... no Laura, Kai's right. Perhaps there was a reason I never made a film, anyway, we should just have our whit about us because you never know Kai, Palpa thingy may be out there... Ha Ha!'

Kai shook his head and held Laura's hand to help her onto the platform.

'So, let's see here, no not that one, ah yes that's the spot. OK, are we ready?'

Kai and Laura nodded holding hands tightly.

'Let's go, Karen!'

The lights went out and the power slowly reduced.

'Hoblett's Forest is unavailable,' said an electronic voice,

'She can talk! Hey Karen hello,' said Kai, Karen didn't reply, 'rude,'

'Yes of course she can talk Kai, she is just a bit shy aren't we Karen?'

The lights flickered again.

'What has happened here then?' Said Terry as he inspected the console, rubbing his chin with his thin fingers,

'Terry...' said Kai, making him look up, 'ask her, nicely?'

'Oh right... yes. Karen, why is Hoblett's Forest unavailable?'

'The story is completed, the protagonist completed his goals,'

'Who was the protag- wait, who was the hero Terry?', asked Kai,

'It was George… wait,' Terry paused in realisation, 'it was Charlotte! She's alive!'

Terry punched the air like hasn't ever before, and quickly hugged Kai and Laura,

'Yes, she loved the rainforest, that was her favourite place to go. I wonder why she completed the story, she used to go in just to relax with the animals you see,'

'So where else can we go now then Terry?' asked Kai,

'Well I do have a couple of places.. hmm,'

'Perhaps one where your family are not the heroes?' suggested Laura,

'Young lady my stories were for my family, why on earth would they not be? They are my heroes,'

'There must be a couple that they were not in,' said Kai,

'Well yes suppose there are some,' said Terry as he returned to the console looking in the memory bank.

'Do you think your family knew what happened when the story was completed?' asked Laura,

'No.. well they sure do now. OK, I have two. The first option is the town of Casemore. It's a town filled with gang warfare and when there are gangs, there is gold. Or we have the beautiful coastal town of Tarsea, where there has been a murder at the Golden Coast Hotel. Why is it called the Golden Coast I hear you ask? Because… there is gold,'

'So a bank job or a who dunnit?' said Kai,

'Yes Kai, I believe Casemore would be better for you. More gold available I would think, and better company for that matter. At Tarsea, they have been solving that murder since nineteen sixty-three. I'm surprised it's still there, they are no Sherlock,'

'So… Casemore town it is then,' Said Kai, 'who's the hero?'

'it's a man called John Corbett. He's a nice fellow met him a couple of times,'

'What's the story?' Laura asked.

'The gang warfare had gotten a little out of hand, more so that the police no longer have any control over the town. It's been a while since I visited. John's girlfriend had been taken by one of the gang leaders who is starting to become quite dominant over the other gang,'

'So, John is with the other gang?' asked Kai,

'He used to be, but he left to live a normal life with his girlfriend, blah blah you know how it goes,'

'So, we need to steal the gold and get back to the exit point before John rescues his girlfriend,' said Kai,

'Karen, Casemore Town please,' said Terry.

The lights blinded them; puffs of smoke sprayed from the different parts of the machine. Kai and Laura had their eyes tightly shut waiting to be sent to another world. They felt light as if there was no gravity holding them down like they were lifting off the ground. From the tip of their toe, they started to disintegrate into little particles that were then vacuumed up into the machine.

Casemore Town was covered with a blanket of a night sky. The streets started to empty of people who headed back to their homes. Bright colours sparked within plumes of smoke down an abandoned side street, leaving Terry, Laura, and Kai as it settled.

'Oh, I thought it was it was going to be a historic town, not a modern day,' said Kai,

'I thought you would Kai, there is far more gold in the modern-day banks,'

'So where do we start?' said Laura,

'We need to find a base, somewhere to plan what our first moves should be… I know just the place follow me.'

Kai and Laura followed Terry through the town centre. They strode down the road like they were a part of a parade that had taken a wrong turn. Further on down the street, Terry took a turn down a different alleyway. It was pitch black as none of the light from any of the street lamps made it that far and there were no windows where inside light escaped.

'Terry! Where are we going?' asked Laura,

'Just down here. There is someone I need to speak to before we can find our base.'

Kai didn't think it could get any darker than it was getting the further down the alley they went.

'Where are we?' asked Kai,

'Hockey Alley. Quite a friendly place,'

'It looks it.,' said Kai.

Further down the alley, a golden light shone from around the corner. It was then clear to them that the light was coming from two huge windows that fronted a pub that seemed hidden from the rest of Casemore. Just above the windows hung a wooden sign with the face of a bull on it and the name underneath.

'The Brown Bull, really?' said Kai,

'Yes, a lively little pub. I know the landlord. Now I need you both to stay here whilst I go and see him and I will be back shortly with the address of our little hideout.'
Terry tapped Kai on the shoulder and entered the bar leaving Kai and Laura outside.

'I don't know about this Laura,' said Kai,

'About what?'

'Terry's intentions. Are we just pawns in a bigger game?'

Kai and Laura stood at the window and watched Terry approach the bar and speak to the barman, who, after a small chat led Terry into the back.

'What is he up to?' asked Laura,

As they were looking through the windows the door flung open as two men stumbled out and rolled around in a tussle.

'She was talking to me,' slurred the man sat on top of the other,

'She's my wife!' Spat the other whilst attempting a drunken punch that missed his target by a foot.

'Very friendly,' said Kai as they watched the pair continue to argue as they stumbled further down the alley. As they went out of sight, the door opened again and outstepped a very beautiful lady who gave Kai and Laura a glance and lit a cigarette,

'What are you two up to?' she asked as she blew out a breath of smoke,

'Just waiting for a friend,' said Kai, 'you may have seen him go in back with the barman,'

'Terry? Yeah, I know Terry,' she said, 'doesn't come round that often. Strange bloke, he sometimes comes and just wants to speak to the boss,'

'The boss? Who's that then?' asked Kai,

'Who's that? You guys must not be from round here?'

Kai and Laura shook their heads simultaneously.

'Johnny Corbett, do yourselves a favour, make sure you join up they will keep you safe here. This town is controlled by gangsters, you don't want to be stuck in between the two. A good man John is. Now have you seen my husband he left not long ago?'

'Oh yes, he rolled that way,' said Laura pointing to the bottom of the hill.

The lady politely nodded and started to make her way to find her husband. Shortly after Terry appeared out at the front of the pub.

'Now then let's go,' said Terry,

'So what did John say Terry?' asked Kai.

'Well we can use his – wait, how did you know I was talking to him?'

'Doesn't matter. What are you up to?' asked Kai,

'Look John can help us, and we need to keep him in our good books,'

'You mean you have picked sides,' said Laura,

'You saw what happens when the story ends, we need to get to the gold but also stop John from getting his girlfriend back and ending the story. If he finds and gets his girlfriend back and we're still trying to break out the gold we will be gonna's along with Casemore. Now come on, his place is this way,' said Terry rattling the keys that John had given him.

The walk ended with what looked like an old block of flats. Five stories of identical cement-walled flats.
'Not what I expected for a gang leader Terry,' said Kai, eyeing the building with disappointment.
'Never judge a book by its cover Kai,' said Terry as he opened and held the front door of the building for Kai and Laura to enter.
The entrance hall was also uninspiring to Kai. Very bland white walls surrounded them and even the strip lights flicked every couple of seconds.
'Fifth floor folks come on,' said Terry as he led them up the staircase.
Their every step echoed throughout the whole staircase so if anyone didn't know they were there, they do now.
'Ah room one nine eight eight,' said Terry, reading the golden numbers off the door.
He opened the door and the contrast between the outside to inside the room was incredible. An open fire was already burning, dark ruby walls surrounded modern expensive furniture.
'This is more like it Terry,' said Kai,
'Hmm… I don't like it.'
'Do we make ourselves at home? I fancy a coffee,' said Kai as he searched the cupboards, for snacks and other delights.
'How much do we trust this John Corbett, Terry?' Asked Laura,
'We can trust him, he has no reason to fear us. However, come closer both of you. At some point, we are going to have to stop this man from accomplishing his goals and it is then that we may need to fear him. Now he thinks that I'm

going to help break his girlfriend out in return for shelter for the three of us. So whilst I'm doing that you two need to break into Casemore bank,'

'And what if you find his girlfriend before we have broke out the gold?' asked Laura,

'Sabotage,' said Kai,

'Exactly, it will act as a diversion, once the gangs know what John is doing, the other gangsters will go to help and the remaining local authority also. Which leaves you little resistance, now remember these people don't know where we are from, we need to act like we are from this world,'

'OK, great,' said Kai, 'easy then, god I can't believe what we are about to do, where we are and it's all fake, make-believe,'

'Be careful Kai,' said Terry sternly, 'these stories, these kingdoms that feel fake to you, they are very real for someone else,'

'Wow, Terry… I didn't mean to offend you at all,'

'You didn't son, it's fine, just remember that though… Now let's get some sleep and be ready for tomorrow.'

Kai slept well that night and the morning soon came round. Before Kai knew it he was preparing himself to leave Corbett's apartment to break the gold from the vault of Casemore bank. As he left the bedroom where he was staying, on the other side of the door stood a tall blond figure. Kai hadn't seen this man before and wasn't sure whether to be friendly or question why he was there. Before Kai had made up his mind the man spoke.

'Ah, you must be Kai… Terry's nephew,'

Kai had to stop himself from correcting the man and play along with what he assumed must be Terry's idea of a plan.

'Ye… yes… his nephew. Who are you?'

'John Corbett, I pictured you as younger to be honest Kai, I'm surprised Terry hasn't convinced you to come along and help me,'

'Oh he did, but my sister you know… gets nervous,' said Kai,

'Oh yes, Laura is it?'

'Yes,' said Kai,

'This could get messy, so best to keep your head down,' said John, 'you need to keep your sister safe. This battle between us and the Roes' has gone on for years. Gangs they call us, were not a gang. We just protect people who they choose to pick on as the police are too afraid to stand up to them. We have had fights in the past that involved no more than half a dozen people at a time. This one feels different, they know we're coming. Since they took her they have been dangling her in front of me waiting for a reaction.' Kai was surprised at how open John was about the situation, especially how he sounded like he wasn't confident about coming out the other end.

'Who are the Roes'?' asked Kai,

'The Roes' want power, money, assets. Anything to prove they are some sort of self-governed body that can do as it pleases when it pleases. My people have fought back, Casemore Town may not be the biggest, but its people are fierce and will fight back against tyrants like Felix Roe,'

'Is it him? Who took your girlfriend?' asked Kai,

'Yes, we were just trying to free some people from the bank after it was being raided and after we had success… they took her. I took my eye off her for one second. I suppose they felt like they needed to go back with something,'

'The bank was raided? Have they recovered?'

'Yes, they didn't take anything. But security has doubled.'

Kai had straightened as stiff as a board. How good was this extra security going to be? Is this game over already?

'Well, I hope you find your girlfriend Mr Corbett,' said Kai, as if he was talking to a teacher or other senior adult,

'Well yes, I suppose it's getting time to move.'

John seemed nervous to Kai. He didn't give off an aura of going into-battle mentality. As John was about to leave Laura walked in.

'Kai I –' she stopped as she saw John,

'John this is my sister, Laura… Laura this is John Corbett,' said Kai quickly trying to give Laura a hint of what was going on before she dropped them both in it.

'Nice to meet you, Mr Corbett, your apartment is beautiful,'

'Thank you, Laura, your Kai's sister? Are you the same age?' John looked unconvinced.

'A year younger,' said Kai, there was only a year between them.

'Right… Can I ask when we return what are your intentions? Because I haven't known Terry long but long enough to know he isn't one for gang warfare. Is he up to something?' Neither of them answered him, they just shrugged their shoulders, 'very well! Keep yourselves safe, you know you can use everything or anything in the flat and hopefully, I can introduce you to my much better half by morning… Farewell.'

'He already suspects something,' said Laura,

'We need to hurry and get that gold, find Terry and get out of here,' said Kai.

They watched four cars leave the parking garage of the apartment block and head away into town. The tall turrets of the grand Casemore bank rose above the skyline, casting more darkness over the town centre which hid from the moonlight.

'I don't think I can do this Kai,' said Laura nervously. Kai continued to watch the cars which were still in sight.

'Terrys in those cars, he must be. We must do this Laura, if not for the gold, then for Terry. If John is already suspecting something, then it's already starting to get more difficult. We stick to the plan we will be ok,'

'But the gold, Terry never told us how to get it home,'

'He did though remember. The golden statue at the studio, we just need to be holding the items when leave and they come with us. Laura come on we can do this.'

Laura agreed with Kai, and they left the flat together. Kai chose not to tell Laura of the extra security as it was not going you give her the encouragement she needed.

Chapter Eight

Casemore Gold

It was a short walk from John's apartment to the Casemore bank, but for Kai and Laura the darkness of the town made it seem like a marathon. The street lamps were dim adding a gloomy feel to the walk. The streets were deserted of people creating a silent eerie atmosphere throughout. Kai dragged Laura by her arm in the direction that he believed the bank was in. Turn after turn started them both down yet another dark path.

The Casemore bank sat on the corner of the High Street. It stood out from the small shops with its unusual architecture making it look more like a cathedral rather than a bank. Gargoyle and other gothic trimming finished off a grey stone building.

'There!' said Kai as he pointed to a large window at the back of the building.

'We need to get up there?' said Laura.

The large window wasn't on the ground floor. It was at least two stories high with the ledge on the fourth floor. It was a tough climb but Kai, but he made it look easier the Laura who was struggling behind.

After helping Laura onto the sill, Kai leant onto a huge pain of glass to look what was inside. He could only see shadows of staircases circling the room leading from the ground up to the upper floors. Hanging from the ceiling was a huge chandelier which even though wasn't on at the time still shimmered in the little moonlight that hit it.

'The guards are in there,' he said, 'five of them, all with torches, and I bet there is more.'

Laura stepped up to take a look herself. As Kai did she cupped her hands around her face and leaned up to the glass.

'You can't count Kai,' said Laura sharply,

'Come off it Laura… look,'

Kai shot back up next to Laura,

'Look, one, two, three…' Kai stopped.

Six other guards had joined the others from the upper floors. Handheld torches were flashing all around as the guards walked from side to side.

'What are we going to do now?' said Laura,

'We need to carry on… come on,' said Kai.

He unclipped a small metal latch opening one of the windows and squeezed in trying to make as little noise as he could, followed closely by Laura. After a small drop from the window, they hid in the corner covered by shadows avoiding being seen by the guards.

'Look there, the front desk,' said Kai pointing at an oval desk at the front of the hall,

'The front desk? Kai, they won't leave a safe key at the front desk,'

'Do you have a better idea?'

Laura spotted a room over on the other side of the hall. It had a front of glass windows with a metallic plate on the front saying 'Office'.

'It's locked how are we going to get in?' said Kai,

'Diversion.'

She picked up a plant pot from the corner and threw it through the glass plane which shattered into millions of pieces.

'Quick Kai come on!' Said Laura pulling on Kai's arm. They ran to the other side and up a couple of staircases before they heard shouting and torchlight bouncing up the stairs from the ground floor.

'You're mental!' said Kai smiling at Laura.

They both watched as the office was being searched. The guards were all dressed in black, armed with a pistol and their torchlight.

'So what now?' said Kai.

'Do you think we can take one guard?' said Laura,

'Yeah... I guess... why?'

Laura pulled a small pistol out of her bag and shot at an office window a few floors down. Kai covered his ears as the bang of the pistol and the crashing of the glass took him by surprise.

'Woah... Laura... what?'

'Come on!' said Laura, as once again she pulled at Kai to follow her.

They charged down the steps as the guards ran down towards the noise of shattering glass. Just as Laura predicted, it left one guard standing in front of the office. Kai sneaked up on the guard grabbed him in a headlock and managed to kick his gun out of his hands. The Guard wrestled free but searched desperately for his lost gun and then his radio. Kai kicked him to the floor and held him down. The guard continued to fight back at Kai before Laura's fist flew past Kai hitting the guard in the chin with the pistol handle first nocking him clean out. Kai had to catch the guard as he fell to keep him from banging as he hit the floor.

'I will check the desk you look behind pictures for hidden safes and stuff,' said Kai.

Next to the desk was a pile of old brooms and mops that were sat inside tin buckets. Kai pushed them aside and started to rifle through the draws looking for keys or cards that would open the main vault.

'Why do I feel Terry would have been useful here,' said Laura as she continued to slide photo frames aside hoping for a hidden safe or compartment underneath,

'Maybe, there must be something in here, have you found anything?' said Ka,.

'No… nothing.'

A huge CRACK! Exploded next to them as the room started to fill with fog.

'Get down!' shouted Kai in a panic,

They both hit the floor to keep below the rising smoke around them,

'Kai quick under the desk they are coming,'

Footsteps were charging up the steps like a herd of antelope running from a hungry lion. They heard each step as they got closer to the sound of cracking glass under the feet of the incoming guards. Kai looked at Laura who had a finger on her lips and waved her hand up and down to signal Kai to stay down. A sudden feeling of failure flew through Kai's mind. He had brought Terry to a place where he would die without finding his family. Even worse he had dragged Laura with him also. Although he knew how she would react to him thinking this.

'I wanted to come. I volunteered to help.'

But that didn't help the guilt that he was taking over his body.

'You have to the count of three to show yourselves before we fire!' said a muffled voice coming from the door of the office.

'Slide your weapons out, put your hands up and we will let the authorities deal with you. If you choose to make any sudden movements we will also fire,'

Laura shook her head. They wouldn't shoot, would they? Kai thought endlessly to think of a way out of this,

'Three!'

'Kai,' said Laura in a whisper, 'they won't shoot, they're bluffing,'

Kai tried to look through a small pinhole in the back of the desk. He couldn't see anyone and the smoke had risen away out of the room.

'Laura, I think they have gone,'

'TWO!'

The belting voice made Kai curl back into the corner under the table. Laura held her pistol in her hand, making her look at it nervously. He shook his head and made her lower her hand as well as the pistol. The count from three to one seemed to last for hours. Was he doing the right thing? The authorities were useless. Terry told them that. Maybe they should take their chance with them rather than being sitting ducks.

'One!... aim for the desk,'

'Stop... stop... we're coming out,' said Kai afraid, 'Laura, slide the gun out... come on,'

'We're waiting,' said the guard.

Laura slid the gun under the back of the table which the guard caught under his foot. Slowly, they rose to their feet with their hands up staring at the guards,

'What are you kids doing in here?' said the guard,

'We have made a massive mistake,' said Kai, 'we're going to head out now and you guys can continue with your guard duties,'

'No you don't, stay behind the desk, keep your hands up.'

The guards stepped closer to Kai holding the gun centimetres from his face. Kai's heart started to pound quickly before the gun then turned to Laura.

'Who are you two?' he asked, 'I recognise you, have I seen you here before?'

'No…definitely not,' Said Laura gulping deeply,

'I have seen you two round here before, haven't I?'

'No definitely not, we haven't been here before,' said Kai,

'likely story.' The guard said under his breath as he lifted his radio to his mouth, 'k88 ring authorities, tell them we have some repeat offenders,'

The leader ordered his men to keep Kai and Laura at the desk who then cuffed them together. Kai knew this wasn't good. If John finished his goal and rescued his girlfriend they were history.

'Psst… Laura,' said Kai annoyingly, 'what should we do now? We need to get to John, we need to forget the gold. We can't save my parents if we don't exist. When the police come and take us away we run and find John and Terry,'

'And how are we going to just run away from the police Kai?'

Kai could feel the frustration growing within him. He knew Laura was right about the police but maybe there was another way. He just needed to think. Before he could think a second more the whole office window imploded. Everybody in the office was showered with glass. Bullets from machine guns peppered around the room hitting each of the guards multiple times. It happened in slow motion for Kai yet all he could do was stand as still as a statue. Bullets missed him by inches but he didn't move. The bullets stopped and there was silence. All the guards were lying on the floor dead, but why were they still standing?

'Laura… are you OK?'

'Yeah… are you?'

'Yeah.'

They both stood quiet in shock. Nobody moved around them. Were they on the good side or the bad side? Or more importantly, were the gunmen on the good side or the bad side?

Six men all dressed in green military clothing stepped through the shattered window and tossed a man to the floor. It was the leader of the guards and from behind him stepped forward a man who led them.

'What are you two doing?!' he said,

'Excuse me?' said Kai confused.

The man took his black cotton balaclava off.

'John... what are you doing here?' said Kai quickly,

'Irrelevant, why are you cuffed to that desk and not in my apartment?'

Kai didn't know whether to tell John the whole truth of why he was here. Does he tell him about the gold, Terry and Karen or maybe even his parents and Mr Brown in the real world?

'These guys kidnapped us,' said Kai pointing at the guards.

'Liar!' The leader shouted who then was kicked by John,

'Tell me the truth, and I will tell you the truth. I want to know what you up to,' said John,

'We have come for gold, my parents have been kidnapped back where we are from and we need to pay for them to be released.'

Kai looked at all the men dressed in army gear and suddenly felt small even though he knew the man in front of him. Worry now filled Kai about Terry, where is he?

'So what about you?' said Laura.

John walked about inspecting the room fixing his perfectly brushed brown hair.

'I followed you,' he said, 'I needed to know Terry's intentions and figuring out yours first seemed easier and you directed me straight here.'

John ordered one of his men to release Kai and Laura from the handcuffs, freeing them from the desk. He then continued to question them.

'So this fella who has taken your parents, who is he?'

'Oh, you wouldn't know if I told you,' said Kai,

'Try me,'

'OK… Mr Brown, or Mr Bullet Brown,'

'Bullet Brown?' said John,

Kai slowly nodded his head shocked that this name was recognisable to him.

'How do you know him?' said Laura,

'You're not the first people to come here to attempt to steal gold to pay off this Bullet Brown. Terry always seems to be involved as well. Which is why this time I wanted to know what was going on, 'so!' Continued John suddenly a lot louder, "when are you breaking this gold out?'

'Well, we're looking for a key, or a card or something,' said Kai,

'In the janitor's office?'

Kai looked around the room and to his realisation there was a lot of cleaning equipment and tools. A feeling of stupidity came over him.'

'Stupid, stupid,' said Kai banging his head against the wall, 'no wonder it was easy to get in here Laura,'

'How many bank managers trust their janitors with keys or codes to vault full of gold? Mind you what I have heard there isn't much gold left in there.'

That was fine for Kai. He just wanted to get what he could and leave as soon as he could.

'So where should we look then?' said Laura,

'For keys and cards?' said John, Laura nodded, 'we don't need keys or cards, come on.'

Kai and Laura followed John down the steps towards the basement level of the bank. It was a simple walk down there as the few guards that even attempted to intervene were simply shot by one of John's men. After going through a few doors that were broken through with ease they finally stood before a huge metal safe. The door was inches thick with a small wheel on the front to open it, only after a code had been inputted on the keypad next to it.

'So how are you going to do this then?' said Kai,

John didn't answer, only nodding towards another of his men, who walked up to the door and placed two grey pads to the side of the side.

'Armed!' The man said after pressing the red buttons on the top.

Kai was afraid this was the answer. He stepped automatically away from the vault knowing what was about to happen. He noticed Laura seemed to be more intrigued about what was going to happen. The thought of a cold pint in the Black Bull with his parents seemed perfect right now. Instead, he was waiting for some man to blow open a safe to steal gold from a world he knew didn't exist.

'Get behind me, now,' said John.

He pushed Laura and Kai behind him and slowly edged further away from the vault.

'Ready!' shouted the same man who had armed what Kai had already assumed were explosives.

'Stay behind me, and cover yourselves in this,' John passed Kai a black cloak which he through over himself and Laura and crouched behind a small wall that protruded out. Kai didn't hear a thing, only a quiet whistle in his ear as if he had gone deaf. Although his eyes were closed and he had a cloak over him, his vision went white, then yellow and quickly orange. Then, it went black. The whistle slowly died out and his hearing started to appear normal. Then he realised he must have frozen somehow as John's face suddenly appeared in front of him. His mouth was moving quickly but nothing was coming out of it. John's hands then started to repeatedly slap Kai's face, until Laura's voice rang around his head.

'Kai, Kai are you OK?'

Before he could answer her, he was yanked to his feet by John. He shook his head quickly and then began to come around to what was happening. Smoke and dust floated around the room but then Kai could see what had just happened.

'Oh my god Kai, look at that,' said Laura in amazement.

It took some time for Kai to see what was in front of him. An orange glow started to break through the cloudy room, which is when Kai saw that the heavy metal door was no longer covering the vault. The hinges were broken apart and the circular door was now lodged up against the wall heavily burnt and bent. Revealing more than thirty rectangular bars of solid gold sitting on a metal shelf alone as everyone stared in amazement.

'There's not much left,' said John, 'a lot was taken in a recent raid, but they didn't get the whole vault. I have to admit the extra security hasn't proved successful.'

Kai picked a bar up and inspected every part of it still in shock that they had it. But how does he get it back home to Bullet Brown?

'How much is this all worth?' asked Kai,

'What do mean how much is it worth? it's gold,' said John,

'Now then, Dolman get this bagged up will you.'

A black-haired, hooked-nosed man stepped forward. He had the same green combat gear on as John and the other men, but there was a difference to him. He had more of a fear factor about him. He had tattoos all down his arms of animals surrounding a viscous-looking tiger's face on his right shoulder.

'Yes, boss,' he said gruffly, chewing on some gum,

'He looks familiar,' said Kai in a whisper to Laura,

'And he does. He looks just like Terry, just younger and more fierce… do you think… no that can't work,'

'What?'

'Do you think when creating these stories he puts himself in, well a different carnation of himself?'

'And make himself a sidekick?' said Kai louder than he intended, making Dolman glance in their direction. They both nodded back nervously,

'Wait a minute,' said Kai, looking back at John, 'where is he taking that gold?'

'It can come with us, and then when my mission is complete you can take it,' said John firmly,

'But, we can't fight in your battle,'

'Then what made you think you could take on several guards and then break into the bank's vault?'

John was now inches from Kais' face,

'Well, you saw how that went,' said Kai, 'OK, OK fine... we will go with you.'

John turned back to watch Dolman filling bags with the golden bars. Laura leant into Kai to whisper in his ear,

'Kai we can't go with him, if he rescues his girlfriend there is no chance that we can get out of here, with or without the gold,'

'I know, so what else can we do? We can't overpower these lot and run back to that alley with the gold,'

'We need to find Terry. Let them keep the gold for now, He will know what to do. Just go along with it,'

Kai and Laura watched as the last bar of gold was placed in the second bag and flung onto Dolman's back. He had two backpacks now strapped to him full of gold bars but he didn't look like it was a struggle. It was as if they only had pillows in them.

Kai and Laura chose that it was wise to stick with John for now, not only for the gold but for their safety. They left the bank and its ground quickly and to Kai's relief, no backup turned up. But to nobody's surprise except for Kai and Laura the police were nowhere to be seen. The group were able to walk away from the bank down the street freely, with nobody knowing what had happened. The streets were empty but Kai thought that somebody must have heard the explosions and gunfire that had taken place within the depths of the bank.

The dark streets all looked very similar and when your knowledge of the town was small it was easy to walk around in circles. Kai and Laura hung back to the rear of the group and Laura suddenly grabbed hold of Kais' arm and dragged him off to a dark alley.

'What are you doing,' said Kai,

'Look where we are Kai,' said Laura pointing down the street.

'In an alley?'

'No! well yes … but look,' she pointed at some lit-up windows down at the bottom of the darkened path, 'this is where we appeared, let's just go and rethink our plans,'

Kai somewhat agreed with Laura's concerns, but couldn't help looking around and watching John and his men marching up the street,

'We can't just go what about Terry, and the gold?'

'Terry can look after himself I'm sure. And the gold… well we never really had it so we haven't lost it,'

'But Laura I need it we can't…'

Kai suddenly found himself pleading with Laura to stay when it was Laura pleading with him to come. Kai started asking himself questions in his mind, - 'do you need to save Terry? can I get the gold or normal money from somewhere else?' Kai instinctively looked at his bracelet for the time but just looked at a blank black screen.

'Hold on,' he said with unease, 'if this is where we appeared, why haven't our bracelets lit up?'

Laura followed suit seeing the same blank screen on hers too. She quickly tried to think for a reason or way around it but all she could do was spit out a loud breath of frustration.

'We need to find Terry and whatever happens John cannot find his girlfriend.'

'Come on you two,' said John who had stopped after seeing that they had left the group, 'now what are you up too? we have helped you now it's only fair that you help me. Now come on we're nearly there.'

The realisation had hit them that they may now have to take part in a made-up story of gang warfare.

'They could be fighting against anything Laura. Aliens, giants any kind of monsters,'

'We don't need to fight, we need to find Terry,'

Laura's tone had changed. Kai noticed that one minute she seemed terrified to the point her eyes shot a blood red, to be ready for an all-out war. They both followed on regardless and then once they turned a corner they saw what they were heading for. In front of them stood an old red-brick mansion. I looked like it had been picked up from a nice colourful town and just dropped into a small space that it had fit into perfectly. Kai looked at Laura whose mouth was so wide open her chin would soon touch the floor. John ushered them all into an abandoned cafe where to their surprise, Terry was sat with two other men. They were wearing murky green clothes, so it was an easy guess that they were a part of his team.

'Terry!' said Kai urgently,

'I'm fine, I'm completely fine... they found you then?" Kai nodded in reply and then looked around again at the men who scattered themselves around the cafe. Then again to see where John was sitting so he could talk more privately with Terry.

'They have the gold,' he whispered,

'Who?' asked Terry,

'The strong one with the backpacks,'

'Ahh.... yes Dolman, a good bloke Dolman, strong, handsome...'

'You based him on yourself didn't you Terry,' said Laura,

'Well yea... I guess I did. Anyway, John thinks his girlfriend is in that Manor, now here's the plan, we help him into the Manor, steal the gold and run off to the exit point,'

Kai and Laura send awkward glances at each other before looking back at Terry,

'It isn't working...' said Kai,

'What?' said Terry,

'We walked past the exit, and waited there to decide what to do next and the bracelet didn't light up.'

Terry grabbed Kai's arm and looked closely all around his wrist desperately to find an error or something. After a while, he let go, got up from his seat and walked away with his head in his hands.

<u>*Chapter Nine*</u>

The Deadly Meeting

'What do you think he is thinking about?' asked Kai, as they watched him standing in and small boarded-up window staring out at the night sky.

'I don't know but I can't be good,' said Laura mournfully.

Terry had a sad confused look on his face. He hadn't said a word to anybody since Kai told him about the bracelets not lighting up back at the alley. Kai was hopeful the news would be met with a simple solution or 'it happens all the time don't worry about it'. The way Terry took it was not something that inspired him or the success of this mission. John and his men stood up making Kai and Laura shoot up to follow suit. Before they could see what was going on they were pulled to a side by a flustered yet excited Terry,

'OK, I know what to do… I mean how we can still get out of here, safe and with the gold,'

'How when the bracelets aren't working?' said Kai,

'We need to stay with John, remember in the forest when we saw my son-,'

'Everybody!' shouted John interrupting Terry.

Terry stopped talking and turned tentatively towards John. Kai took a deep gulp before listening to the orders from his new leader.

'We know what is in that Manor, we know what is being held there. What they do hold there means the world to me. I thank you all for fighting with me and protecting the streets of Casemore from these thugs,' said John.
Kai felt a little awkward. He hadn't fought alongside him or risked his life for any cause. Many of John's men started to fist-pump the air and quietly chant his name.
'John, John, John.'

Kai chose not to join in, unlike Terry who tried his best to blend in but stood out even more. Dolman glared at Terry, then Laura and then his eyes sat on Kai. The glare was kind of like asking what are you up to and then don't try anything. Kai tried to break the connection several times but he was drawn back time after time. He whispered to Laura trying not to look obvious.

'Why is he staring at me?'

'I don't know,' said Laura, 'he's on to us already I can feel it, what do you think Terry?'

'John, John, Jo-'

'Terry!'
Terry turned sharply to Laura as she pulled at his top.

'Oh... err... sorry, got a bit carried away,'

'That Dolman, he's done nothing but stare at us. He knows something,' said Laura,

'We need to blend in just follow what I do and they won't know a thing,'

'I'm not chanting,' said Kai.

He received daggers from both Terry and Laura, but luckily the chanting had stopped and John was revealing his plan.

'Aaron Claxton, the Roe's most trusted man will be in the main room at the back of the Manor on the second floor. That is where I'm heading. Dolman, you can circle the ground floor with a few others… you can choose. I will wait for your signal and then I will make my way to free Tianna.'

The plan seemed simple enough. Kai even thought that they might get a pass as surely Dolman wouldn't pick them three to accompany him on such an important order. Shortly after his assumptions were realised, Dolman selected two other men and they prepared to leave. John Corbett once again stood up to address his men.

'Wait… wait a second Dolman, I need you to do something for me. Terry, you and your two friends could prove your worth and help Dolman,'

'John don't,' said Dolman in his low gruffly voice,

'Yeah, don't John,' said Kai, whispering to himself. They went quiet for some time before John continued.

'No… they need to prove themselves, you're just the man to keep them following orders.'

Kai couldn't believe it, but nor could Dolman. One thing Kai knew now was they were not going to be protected by Dolman and his men. They were more likely to kill them than protect them.

Dolmans' attitude towards the situation didn't improve during the walk towards the Manor. Every time he put his hand up to signal the group to stop he would make a sort of hissing sound towards Kai.

'What do we do now?' asked Kai irritated,

'We need to somehow ditch old Dolman and get back to John without him wondering why we're not with Dolman,' said Terry,

'He hasn't taken his eyes off us yet Terry,' said Laura.

Dolman's eyes were small and dark. When he looked at you it was like daggers were being pointed and ready to lunge towards you.

'When we're in there follow my lead. Now remember this isn't a kid's story where we can just kick him in the shin and he will drop the bags of gold into your hand,' said Terry,

'What do mean?' asked Laura,

'He means these men are probably going to die,'

'Correct Kai. Remember these people are not real, ok. They are not leaving families behind, parents and what have you. They are fictional characters to just serve a purpose,'

'What purpose?' asked Laura unapprovingly,

'My purpose I guess, I created them didn't I.'

The gates to the Manor were high black metal with sharp pointed tips. Above the gate, there was the letter C formed from the same eloquent fencing. They past the gate and headed down the side of the property, where a long perfectly manicured hedge surrounded the grounds. Dolman ducked into a small gap between two of the bushes and squeezed through with the bags of gold on his back. They found themselves on cut lawns with a driveway that could fit a dozen cars that circled a fountain in front of the Manor.

'Oii, you three!' spat Dolman, 'stay low else they will see you.'

Before Kai could get out his response two torch lights flickered around the corner of the house. They waited low to the ground until the men passed around the corner. Dolman waved his hand viciously towards them to follow them. As quick and low as they could they ran to the Manor and stopped themselves against the wall of the building. Dolman signalled to two of his men.

'Deal with them!'

They sneaked off with Terry following closely behind,

'No not you!' said Dolman as loud as he dared, but Terry ran on,

'You two stay with me,'

'No problem,' said Kai,

Dolman's lips curled at Kai who cowered against the wall.

'He could have given us a gun,' said Kai quietly,

'I don't think you would know how to use it, Kai,' said Laura,

'Yeah... when the time comes, I'll be fine,'

'You want a gun?' said Dolman, He opened the side pockets on the backpacks pulled out two pistols and threw them to Kai.

'One for you and one for the girl, and do me a favour, shoot the bad guys.' Kai nodded in shock that Dolman trusted him with a gun, 'Where's your friend and my men...we need to move come on.'

Kai and Laura hesitated but then followed Dolman, who was now alone after his two men and Terry hadn't yet returned. They circled to a small wooden door at the back of the house.

'This is where we get in, where in the name are they? if that Terry has got them killed I'm going on alone.'

Dolman banged his fist on the door to get it open but it would budge.

'Hey they will hear you, you're going to get us all killed!' said Laura,

'You have a gun now don't you, that's what you wanted?'

Dolman's voice started to get even more menacingly low the longer he was alone with Kai and Laura,

'I'm going to have to shoot through it,' said Dolman,

'You're insane!' said Kai with a wobble of panic in his voice, 'it will be a full-on war zone in there,'

'So what do you suggest then boy?'

'We wait for Terry and your men to get here,'

'They should already be here by now, we can't wait any longer.'

Dolman ignored Kais' fears, stepped away from the door and raised his gun to the brass lock. Kai and Laura covered their faces took cover behind Dolman and waited for gunshots.

'Click'

Kai rose suddenly surprised by the noise that came from the door. Dolman still had his gun risen but now pointing at the door rather than the lock. Dolman nudged Kai's arm trying to hint for him to do something.

'Your guns...get them out... both of you!' he said in a harsh whisper.

Kai and Laura did as they were told and pointed their guns at the door. Dolman held his steady as did Laura, Kai however stood as though he had just stepped out of the walk-in freezer back at the pub. His hands wobbled viscously. Another thud came from the door, drops started to roll and drip from the edge of Dolman's pointy nose and sprinkled away from Kai's shivering gun. One last click and the door swung open.

'Ah .. I thought it must be you three,'

'Terry?'

Kai had never been so happy to see Terry's face before. Terry stood aside letting them enter, but Dolman still pushed him further aside.

'Where are my men?' he moaned,

'They unfortunately struggled against the guards... to be honest... I thought they would be better than that as you picked them out personally,' said Terry winking at Kai,

'What do you mean struggled where are they?' Dolman's lips curled even more, nearly parallel to his nose. Veins started to protrude from his forehead.

'They were killed, luckily I were there to finish off the guards, they are in the pond out the back if you want to have a look,'

'I don't believe you, you wouldn't stand a chance against anybody that could defeat my men!'

'You better believe it Dolman because it happened and now you're stuck with us... your move.' said Terry his voice getting more high-pitched the more he talked.

Dolman eyed each of them individually and quickly span on his heel grabbing hold of Terry around his neck. Terry stopped immediately and gazed back into Dolman's tiny eyes.

'It sounds like you are threatening me... Terry. You're not on John's side. You said that you were here to help him if he kept these pair safe yet we found them attempting to rob a bank,' Terry took two deep gulps, his pointy Adam's apple struggling to manoeuvre around Dolman's skinny yet firm hand, 'I should finish you all off now and save him the bother, he knows you're not up to any good. Which is why he sent you with me because I can deal with you.'

Terry heard a loud click next to his left ear. Dolman had raised his gun and placed it to the side of Terry's head.

'Say goodbye, Terry!'
Click, click.

Dolman turned to look at Kai and Laura who were both holding their guns up to Dolman.

'Put him down,' said Kai menacingly.

He noticed that he no longer shuddered at the thought of holding a gun towards someone. The nerves no longer affected his ability to stay still and stay composed.

'You three will not stand a chance without me,' said Dolman through gritted teeth.

'Don't make me shoot you then,' said Kai.

Dolman released Terry and stepped backwards towards the wall, holding his hands up in the air.

'Now then... the signal,' said Terry, 'will you kindly lead the way, Dolman,'

'Why are you doing this? Why don't you just kill me?' asked Dolman.

'We're not here to kill anybody, we just want to get out of here, and John needs to win for us to do that,' said Kai.

Dolman didn't understand but chose to not ask any more questions and led them up staircase after staircase. This reminded Kai of stairwells at a hotel but much grander. They stopped as a long tall window stood before them, looking out to the ground and the town of Casemore.

'We must be on the top level,' said Laura,

'We are,' said Dolman,

'But I thought they were all on the first floor?'

Dolman sighed in irritation at the questioning.

'Yes, that is where John is going to head, we just need to get the signal out to him that it's clear for him to enter the grounds with the rest of the group.'

Dolman tried turning the black metal handle that opened a door within the huge window. To his surprise, it opened.

'You three stay there,' said Dolman as he stepped out onto a balcony and started to flash a small red laser light in the direction of Casemore Town. Shortly after Kai could see John and the others climbing over the gates and making their way into the grounds. Dolman flew past them and headed down the first staircase.

'The gold!' shouted Terry.

They followed keeping as close as they could until Dolman entered through a small dark entry just off the first floor landing. Without considering where Kai, Laura and Terry ran in after him. The was no light in the room which made them stop as soon as they had all entered.

'Wait where are we?' said Kai,

'I don't know,' Said Laura.

There wasn't a sound or any movement. They stepped forward tentatively as if not to wake a sleeping baby. Laura started to shiver and pulled tightly on her jacket to stop it from rattling along with her body. A short fog appeared in front of them every time they exhaled.

'How far down did we come down?' whispered Kai.

He didn't get an answer, apart from Terry stopping dead in front of them not allowing them to pass.

'I think we should leave,'

'What about Dolman? And the Gold?' said Kai still whispering.

Although he knew he couldn't see anything Terry automatically looked around and back to Kai.

'He's too dangerous... we're walking straight into his trap - Agghh!'

Terry suddenly fell to the floor.

'Terry!'

They couldn't see him. it was as if a black hole had opened beneath him. Fear filled them both. The air went cold, it felt like needles were poking their skin sharp side first. Muffled shouting was followed quickly by banging and rattling of wooden objects. And then the room lit up all of a sudden making Kai and Laura crouch down quickly. They had no idea who had switched the lights on, was it Dolman? Or Terry? Now they could see, they continued the search around the room they had discovered. The room was filled with crates as small as a chest and some the size of a small car. Dolman stood up from behind a crate with his arm squeezing around Terry's neck. His gun was raised at Kai and Laura causing them to react and raise theirs to meet it. They had never shot a gun so they knew a standoff would never be in their favour.

Dolman and Terry both had blood dotted over their faces. From a scuffle that preceded. Dolman's nose was bleeding and had a small gash on his head. Considering Terry was currently in a worse position he looked better of the two only sporting a bloody nose. Dolman stepped back onto the ledge of the basement.

'Let him go and we will leave you to do what you need to do,' said Kai.

'No,' said Dolman in a tired grunt, 'you know too much and have seen too much.'

The backpacks containing the gold were no longer with Dolman, they were convinced he wouldn't have the strength to carry the weight anymore.

'So you going to kill us all here are you?' asked Kai,

'That's right,' said Dolman, 'in fact, I will start with you!'

Dolman's gun pointed at Kai but before he could pull the trigger Terry struck Dolman in the chin, knocking him off balance. Dolman fell back before Kai and Laura could reach out to stop him from falling. Terry had already picked up a nearby rope and wrapped it around Dolman as he fell and left him hanging.

'Terry!' gasped Kai, 'what have you done?'

They crouched at the basement entry looking at Dolman's limp body hanging in front of them.

'We need to stick to the plan,' said Terry trying to keep himself composed, "we need to get that gold and find John and help him find his girlfriend. We can then get out of here with John when he gets taken away in that blue beam thing,'

'That's your plan?' said Kai,'

'Yea… do have a better one?'

Kai and Laura both disappointingly shook their heads at Terry.

'No seriously do you have another one? Because yeah…that is my plan,' they still stood silent, 'OK then let's go, get that gold.'

Kai and Laura flung a bag each over their shoulder and followed Terry to find John. The corridors were quiet, dark, and cold. As if it had been abandoned for many years, not like it had been lived in or at least used as a hideout. Terry had decided that it must be some sort of trap or tactic to scare them from continuing further into the house.

'This is it,' John whispered.

They crouched down outside two wooden doors with finely engraved dragons fighting.

'It's quiet in there? Is John even in there?' said Kai,

'Well, there is only one way to find out, come on let's go.'

Terry opened the doors slowly, tentatively. There was a real uncertainty about what he was going to find on the other side. Is the room empty? Has a battle already begun and ended? The room was grand. It was decorated and furnished like it belonged to the royal family. Ruby red walls with golden edges. Fancy light fittings and antique desks and cabinets. More importantly at the back of the room sitting at a desk was John. Nobody spoke, John sat patiently as if he was waiting for the school principal to give him detention.

'John?' said Terry, 'what are you doing? Where's Claxton?'

John didn't move, other than a slight twitch after hearing Terry's voice.

'He's here,' John looked out the window behind the desk he was sitting at, 'he will be back shortly, you need to leave, the way you came in. Tell Dolman...'

'He's not with us,' said Kai,

John turned his head to his right to see them in his peripherals.

'What do you mean? Where is he?'

'He err-' Kai couldn't get any words out,

'He fell behind, we just managed to get through,' said Laura,

'He fell behind, John,' said a high childish voice from behind them. Kai, Terry and Laura jumped as a tall lanky man walked past with a sharp smile on one side of his mouth as he puffed on a cigar on the other.

'John... where are all your men?' asked Kai,

'Oh, I'll answer that...' said Claxton, 'they are all on the other side of that door, I wouldn't bother shouting them though,'

Claxton let out a chilling laugh as made his way to the desk where John was sitting still staring out of the window.

'It's funny though, not one of my men has taken credit for defeating the mighty Dolman. In my experience, they would be cheering from the rooftops if achieved such a feat.'

Kai and Laura look nervously at each other, even John turned around curiously. Terry had somehow managed to merge in with the walls as the attention was on Kai and Laura.

'Well, saved me a job anyway. So John now that all your people are accounted for and we can talk peacefully, what are you trying to achieve from breaking into my home?'

'You know Claxton, don't play dumb with me,' Said John forcibly,

'Well, I heard someone mention something about a girlfriend?' Claxton's smile almost made it from ear to ear, 'I don't know about a girlfriend, I have Tianna here with me,' Claxton sat down and pressed a button under his desk, 'could you please join us?'

The room went silent, anticipation covered Kai and Laura's faces, Even Terry stepped momentarily out from the shadows of the room to get a closer look. The door on their right opened and out stepped a tall, young woman. Her skin was bronze and she had long brown hair that fell past her shoulders.

'Tianna? What are you doing with him?' said John, 'I have risked my life, my friend's life, all for you, for nothing,'

'Not for nothing,' said Tianna,

'What do you mean?' said John,

'Well I have made myself plenty of money, Aaron bet me that you wouldn't make it to us, but you proved him wrong. Is this Terry Toone? And Kai Fox and his girlfriend?'

Kai stepped away looking at Terry and back toward Tianna.

'What's going on here?' said Kai, 'how do you know my name?'

'I know a lot about you, Kai,' said Tianna brushing her glistening hair over her shoulder and standing behind John's chair. She locked eyes with Kai momentarily before Kai broke it by looking at Terry for some sort of clue about what to do next. Questions ran through Kai's head, how does she know Him? does she know him? Perhaps she is just testing him somehow. He felt all of a sudden that he wasn't ready or at all prepared for this. Never mind the guns and fighting, but now he was in trouble and had no idea how to get out of it.

'Kai?' said Terry quietly.

Kai looked at the doors and his mind was telling him to use them, but his heart reminded him who he was here with and he moved his gaze back to Tianna. However, it wasn't Tianna he saw. Standing in front of the window stood his parents. He stood silent until his mother opened her mouth but it was Laura's voice coming out.

'Kai, Kai!' she whispered,

'What is he doing, what is he doing?' A gruff voice sounds out of his vision.

It was Mr Brown. He was sitting where Aaron Claxton was sitting. It was the same desk, the same ornaments that Claxton had scattered in front of him.

'Am I going to have to call my team in boy?' said Mr Brown,

'Kai, what are you doing? you're going to get us killed, Kai!' Laura's voice got louder and more aggressive.

Both eyes of his parents stared back at him, so he turned to Mr Brown and glared at him. Now he remembered why he was here. It was him, Mr Brown. It was his fault, but why is he here now? His parents are right there, he can save them. Kai lifted his gun in front of him, aimed at Mr Brown who didn't move.

'Get in here now!' shouted Claxton,

But he couldn't see Claxton, all he could see was Mr Brown.

'Stop him!'

Kai pulled the trigger, again and then once more. His vision then went black, and now nobody stood in front of him. There was no sound, no voices, he was absent. When the colour of the room started to return, at first very cloudy but it got sharper slowly. A face appeared in front of him moving their lips but it was just noise. But before Kai could focus on the person trying to talk to him he passed out.

Chapter Ten

The Superintendent

'Kai, hey Kai, you awake?' said Laura, gently rocking him from side to side,

'Yeah, I think,' replied Kai, tentatively rubbing his forehead,

'What happened? Where am I?'

Laura helped Kai up to his feet but didn't answer him immediately. Instead, she let him look around at what everyone was doing. Terry, John and Tianna were talking in the corner. Terry wasn't involved much as he regularly looked back at Kai but quickly returned to the conversation once he made eye contact with Kai. He moved his gaze to the desk which now sat empty. He felt his fingers glide along the surface of the desk before he remembered that Claxton was no longer sitting in his chair.

'Where is Claxton?' he asked,

Laura didn't answer his question but instead threw a question back at him.

'What made you do it?'

'Do what?' asked Kai,

'Shoot him.'

Laura's words felt like they had just stabbed him in the gut. He looked around but the room didn't look like it had just witnessed a murder. There was no blood, no evidence of a struggle or fight. He did feel that it was odd how Terry, John and Tianna were talking calmly in the corner as the last he can remember John was tied up. Then the images in his mind started to return to him.

'My parents were here, and Mr Brown was sitting in this chair,' Kai said, looking at Laura hoping for a reaction that made his story make sense.

'I'm sorry Kai, but they weren't, nobody left and nobody else came into the room.'

Kai then remembered How odd it was that he saw his parents and Mr Brown yet heard other people's voices.

'Wait, I shot him, I shot Mr Brown. He was sitting in this chair,'

Laura nodded along with Kai as he continued, 'Claxton was in this chair, I shot Claxton!' Kai held on to the desk as the realisation kicked in,

'Kai it's ok, he's gone now we cleared up. You were gone for an hour,' said Laura,

'An hour, you cleaned away any blood and his body?'

'There wasn't much blood, you missed your first shot,'

Laura pointed at a small bullet hole on the desk,

'Typical,' said Kai disappointed,

'Hey, your last one hit him right here.'

She placed her finger gently between Kai's eyes and let it fall down his nose, making Kai smile finally.

'I was sure I had got Bullet,'

'If our first experience of Terry's worlds is anything to go by, I'm sure you will get your chance. To be honest, I thought you had got us killed,' said Laura,

'Well, what about Tianna? And his other men?'

Kai and Laura both looked over at the other group who were still debating but it was getting louder.

'She helped us move his body, apparently it was an act and she had been held captive by him. Either way, she and John are a good team they took out the remainder of Claxton's men. I'm not sure though Kai, I don't trust her, it seemed very real to me,'

Kai agreed although something else felt very real to him. How did he let his emotions take him so easily and now he carried a fear of it happening again? Is it this world that makes his mind so confused, it put's different people in his mind and makes him do things he knows he shouldn't? He knows Laura was right, he could have got them killed and this moment could have been very different.

'Hello folks, Kai how are we doing?' said Terry,

He bounded over with little care, almost as if he was desperate to get away from John and Tianna.

'I'm okay Terry, Laura has filled me in,'

'Well as much as I can Terry, your turn now what is she up to?'

Terry turned back to Kai waiting for an answer until it occurred to him the question was for him.

'Oh yes, well she is very much on our side from what she is saying. I recognise her you know, I don't know why,'

'And you believe her?' asked Laura,

'Believe her? Oh, well, yes I guess. She carries a gun but didn't move a muscle when Kai killed Claxton, nice move by the way Kai. However stick to the plan next time you feel like trying to get us all killed,' Kai rolled his eyes, 'anyway, the feeling at the moment is that the plan is going well and we need to keep hold of that gold and be ready for when this story ends and we move on,'

'That's still the plan then Terry?' said Kai,

'Oh yes, you don't have a better one, either of you… no? Okay, so we carry on then. Shortly we need to stay close and the light will appear and we grab hold and we will go with them,'

'OK well we don't know when that is going to happen though, what are we supposed to do?' Kai started turning red, 'stalk them until we know that the light is going to appear? And then what? Hop from world to world until the bracelet decides to start working again? Or until we find your family are we on our own then?'

'Kai!' shouted Laura, 'You can't be like that, Terry has helped to find the gold, yes he may have other motives but I'm sure in the end he knows a way to get back, right Terry?'

'Er... sure yeah,'

'You see, we're stuck here what's the point?' said Kai. He turned away and didn't want to look at the others. The frustration of seeing his parents mixed with a feeling of being stuck with no way out was too much for Kai. In the meantime, Tianna and John had left the room without anyone noticing. Kai, Laura and Terry scrambled to catch up with them without looking like three stalkers.
John and Tianna had made it to the café where they were all sitting putting together the plan. A plan that ended with John's men including Dolman, losing their lives.

The sun broke over the horizon and through the broken glass of the cafe. Kai was blinded by the glare that hit him as he opened his eyes. Once he regained his vision and his realisation of where he was and who he was with, it dawned on him that not one person had left the cafe and had fallen asleep. Kai looked for the time but he couldn't see a clock on any of the beige plastered walls around him. Terry and Laura had slept on sofas that were placed in the corner of the cafe, and John and Tianna were together on the other side.

'Terry... Terry,' said Kai nudging him a lot harder than he may have intended, making him jolt after each stab, 'Wha... what, oh Kai it's you, what do you want?' said Terry holding his forehead,

'What do I want? Look around you Terry, it's morning and we're sat in a cafe that we broke into last night.'

Terry sprung upright giving his head a rush at the same time before realising Kai was right. After he had recovered he encouraged John to get up and led the group out of the café. The streets were dark and quiet. Kai flinched at a small black cat that skipped from a wall landing between a group of metal bins crashing them to the floor.

'Bloody cats,' Kai grumbled.

He looked over the wall where the cat had appeared from a small blue flicker caught his attention. The blue flashed again and again. The fog that seemed to fill Casemore town around them lit up in a rapid sequence of blue and red lights.

'Guys, I think we need to move,' Kai ran towards the others pointing towards the flashes. They were approaching them like lightning pushing its way through a storm cloud.

'Casemore police, Let's Go!' shouted John.
He wrapped his right arm around Tianna, turning her away in the other direction as the others followed. Kai stayed at the back of the group to ensure Terry wasn't left behind. John encouraged them on, leading the way, hoping to be able to get as close to his side of the town as he could. The road was soon cut off as two police cars sped out of a side street. They skidded to a stop in front of them, blinding them with lights flashing from the top of the marked cars.

John pointed to an alley after seeing two more marked and one unmarked car catching up from behind. Laura could barely keep her balance as the tarmac was wet from a sudden rainfall when they were in Claxton's manor. She led the group now not knowing where these paths led. She stopped suddenly in front of a man who seemed to appear out of the shadows. The others stopped themselves behind her and stared into the shadowed man.

'You've done it this time Corbett,' said the figure whilst exhaling smoke past his cigarette still clamped between his lips, 'I told you to dare give me another chance to put you away, and here we are,'

'Howard Carmichael himself, who called you?' John replied, still trying to believe he was in charge of the situation,

'The bank manager, he told me his security guards are dead and the rest seriously injured,' He stopped to take a final long drag on his fag before flicking it away, 'he also told me that a substantial amount of gold had been stolen in two bags. Also, he believes you were helping two young'uns who managed to get in a bit of a mess,'

'Well, forever the hero Carmichael... you know me,' said John edging his way to the front to face Carmichael.

Carmichael sighed and looked carefully at each person pulling a sharp gaze at Terry.

'So are you going to come easy John or are we going to continue this chase you seem to want to carry on?'

'Well you only have two guns with you,' John nodded at the two policemen to Carmichael's side, 'so I like my chances.'

Howard smiled and stepped towards John, now under the dim street light revealing his well-built figure dressed in all black. He had a buzz-cut hairstyle and slightly longer brown facial hair covering obvious rough, aged skin showing that he was now in his late sixties.

'Look behind you John,' four more police officers had appeared trapping them in the alley, 'Ok then hero, what's your next move?'

John gave himself a couple of seconds to think of a response as he knew the detective had spotted the bags of gold he and Kai were carrying.

'Right,' Carmichael said impatiently, 'you have the time that it takes for me to smoke my last cigarette to give me a good alibi, and make it credible John, you've wasted enough of my time already.'

Carmichael lifted the cigarette to his lips and lit a match teasing the end of the cigarette until the smoke started rising gently. The problem is John hasn't got an alibi. The others looked away from him to the floor or casually up at the starry sky as he looked to them for an answer.

'Times running out John, I'm nearly finished,'

'Ok well…' said John trying to think on his feet but nothing came to mind, 'the Roe family, who's to say they aren't involved, that Aaron Claxton has been a pest to me for years,'

'So you wanted him gone right?' asked Carmichael still exhaling smoke.

Thirty seconds of silence then passed as John tried to read Carmichael's thoughts by looking into his dark brown eyes. He knew his next response was crucial. Did he know what had happened to Aaron Claxton and is just testing him or is he just casually pointing out the obvious? The longer John took the greater the smile grew on the detective's face. New wrinkles appeared around his mouth as his lips moved.

'I haven't killed Aaron Claxton if that's what you are getting at,' said John,

'No? John, I have been out on these streets since the call came in for the bank robbery. I have been chasing mobs like yourself and this gang you seem to have put together,' he laughed as he looked over the group standing in front of him, 'I knew the robbery must be linked between you guys and the Roes. But also I know the Roes are out of town at the moment leaving their trust in Mr Claxton to hold their turf for them. He isn't someone I would consider reliable enough to leave in charge which made me think this is the location of some sort of drama. We also got intel about your girlfriend swanning off,'

'Excuse me!' said Tianna in offence, but received a hand gesture from John to leave it alone,

'Well-' Carmichael continued amused, 'shall we end this act, Claxton is dead and I now need to prove it's you who did it, or one of the team,'

'We weren't even at his Manor, Tianna escaped,'

'Oh pull the other one Corbett, why are you here sneaking around the streets? Why is Claxton dead? And even more damning for you Corbett, Why are there corridors of Roes men and yours, dead?'

'Insurgence,' suggested John,

'Oh so Dolman got himself killed then did he? Other than yourself John, Dolman is the only other person from your gang I feel would be capable of such a feat.'

John took that as a compliment. Kai and Laura started to feel and look very anxious.

'Terry!' Said Kai as loud as he dared, whilst John and Carmichael were continuing their debate on whether he was guilty or not,

'Terry, why is nothing happening? John has rescued Tianna, surely that's the end of it?' said Kai,

'We need to be careful here, we can't create a new chapter to this story. Being caught by the police is not an ideal situation. We need to be ready, keep as close to John as we can.'

The argument continued to and throw between Carmichael and John. Tianna felt so separated from the situation that she just leaned against a wall ignoring everyone around them. Kai, Terry and Laura however were trying to get as close to John as they could, Kai was nearly now touching elbows.

'You can just give this up now Corbett, you have finally lost!' shouted Carmichael,

'You still do not have any proof, none of your men saw me in that house!' John shouted back,

'I didn't need to see any of your men or…' Carmichael stopped shouting and glared at Kai, who was now tight up to John's left side.

John turned his head to look at Kai and then to his right to see Terry doing the same.

'You ok there Terry?' asked John.

Carmichael, now very confused, ran his hand through his short greying hair. He then reached for his cigarette packet which sat in the inside pocket of his long black jacket and picked one out.

'Now I don't know what you people are playing at here,' he said clamping the cigarette in between his lips and lit it, then continued, 'your little gang has committed a crime and I will figure out what it is. Whatever it takes Corbett,' he leaned into John's face, so close that John could feel the heat leaving the burning end of Carmichael's fag, 'I will take you in!'

Carmichael looked once again to Kai and Terry who were still shoulder to shoulder and shook his head in disgust.

'We're starting a new storyline do something,' Terry said leaning back to Laura and Kai,

'What If it's about us and not the original characters? Surely that will just cancel out and perhaps confuse the system,' suggested Laura,

'Perhaps, I don't know,' said Terry,

'It was me!' Shouted Kai before Carmichael had fully turned away. This unexpected news pricked his ears. Carmichael screwed his face as he contemplated what Kai had just said. In years of being a detective and being stuck powerless between rival family gangs. He had very rarely been told to his face that someone was guilty of a crime such as this.

'What did you say, boy?'

'You heard me,'

'Kai, what are you doing?' gasped Laura, but she got no response

Terry placed his arm around Laura, he could feel the nerves and anxiety starting to set in. The possibility that the plan that he had chosen to follow may not work.

'How did a boy like you manage to kill Claxton and break further into the manor than Dolman?'

'I killed Dolman,' said Kai less confidently than he hoped, 'as well as Claxton's men. The plan was never to break in and kill, that was on me,'

Carmichael looked at John whose face had too much surprise in it that it didn't help Kai convince him.

'Cuff him!' Carmichael ordered his two officers. They leapt forward spinning Kai around and gripping his wrists as they tightened the metal cuffs. They turned Kai to face Carmichael, 'what are you doing boy? What's John promised you to take the ownership of the crime?'

'Nothing, I am to blame. Take us all in for questioning if you wish but you need to accept the truth,'

'Fine, let's go.'

Carmichael held Kai by his cuff and pulled him along away from the others,

'Kai, wait please!' screamed Laura, she fought against Terry as she pleaded with them to allow her to help Kai, but all he could do was look back at her as he slowly followed Carmichael away. Laura caught Kai's lip mouthing the words, 'go, get out.'

Terry noticed the policemen who stood at the end of the alley stopping them from leaving the way they came in were now gone.

'Wait we can't go without Kai!' said Laura as she started to hold back tears from rolling down her puffy cheeks, 'Terry please!'

'We need to go on Laura, we need to stay with John,' said Terry, desperate to keep Laura moving on with the others. He also however knew what could be in store for Kai if he were to be left behind once they had been moved on.

'Wait, Terry, wait, it's not that, sshhh…,' Laura held her hand out to Terry to stop him from talking and pulling her arm, 'can you not feel that?' she asked Terry,

They concentrated on being quiet and still as they listened for movement. From the distance, a thunderous sound started to erupt from around Casemore. The local fog changed to smoke and bursts of fire spewed from buildings that surrounded them.

'It's happening,' said Terry,

Laura left his side to chase after Kai who had been taken away by Detective Inspector Carmichael,

'Laura wait!' screamed Terry,

'What is going on Terry? I know you know,' asked John,

'Long story, do us a favour, hold on to the gold and stay with me,'

Buildings continued to fall, crashing to the floor and devastating anything that lay beneath them. Kai was still being held by the officers. They were pulling him as he battled against them, trying to get back to the others.

'Please detective, let me go, let me be with my friends,' pleaded Kai but it fell on deaf ears,

'Why? We're going to the station, all this destruction is just an accident of some sort you will see,' said Carmichael.

Carmichael was not going to let a devastating event like this get in the way of his duty. He was like all the others, Kai had realised, programmed beings taking part in a hero's story. How? Kai didn't know but now wasn't the time for him to figure it out. The coal-like clouds split finally and a blue light appeared slowly reaching the ground around John and Tianna.

'Kai! Come on ' shouted Laura,

She charged towards him jumping over bricks that had fallen and slabs that had risen dangerously into her path. Kai continued to struggle until a small stone flew past him hit one of the officers and bounced off the side of his head.

'Oi… you get back!'

'Just let him go we need to get out of here, Carmichaels gone,' said the young female officer.

Nobody else had noticed that Carmichael had snook away even a man of his size and stature. The officer released Kai who ran to meet Laura. The beam of light had surrounded John and the others. John started to lift off the floor, followed by Tianna and then Terry.

'Come on move!' shunted Terry.

Kai and Laura pushed as hard as they could. Laura hadn't ran as fast as this since her early teenage years, her body was no longer built for the exercise. The alleyway started to crumble from below them. Mini earthquakes split through the bricks one by one, chasing Kai and Laura like snakes chasing their next prey. Terry held his hand out towards them to try and encourage them to pick up more speed, they were close. The bags of gold past them up to the sky so they knew it was nearly time. John now sped up to the clouds followed by Tianna. Terry was now upside down holding his hand out as far as he could.

'Come on there's not much time!'

Kai slowed and grabbed Laura by her arms and threw her towards Terry who got hold of her hand. Laura turned desperately to find Kai who she saw leaping towards her then clamped his arms around her legs. The sight was surreal to Kai. He was getting higher and higher and the town that he briefly knew as Casemore Town was slowly disappearing. Detective Carmichael's police car could be seen falling down a newly created ravine and engulfed in flames. Arron Claxton's Manor emploded in on itself causing a ripple to glide away from it adding to the destruction.

Then, it went dark. All Kai could see was blackness. He was alone, with no Laura, Terry, John or Tianna. What was next in this extraordinary adventure? Although that was hardly what it still felt to him, it was more like an ever-growing nightmare.

Chapter Eleven

Captain Spike

Kai rose his head from a sandy bed having to brush never-ending grains out of his messy blonde hair. The sun rose over two high peaked mountains that overshadowed an old town. His eyes took a few seconds to adjust to the bright sunlight that was so different to where he had come from. He pushed himself to his feet and shouted for Laura, hoping she wasn't far away or worse in a different world.

It was another voice that shouted back, but it was not Laura.

'Kai, hey up here,'

Kai looked up to see Terry standing upon a tree branch looking out to sea

'What the hell are you doing up there?'

'Have you seen this view Kai? You really should you know,' said Terry,

He edged his way down the branch until he was low enough to jump to the floor.

'You were looking for the others weren't you,' said Kai,

'No, Laura is there and John is there,'

He pointed to Laura who was sitting in the sand a little further down the beach. John however was wandering around the trees that framed the small beach location.

'What is John doing? Wait you were looking for the money!'

Terry nodded, almost ashamed,

'Tianna is also missing,' added Terry,

'She's taken it then, I knew she was trouble. That's why John is avoiding us, or has she left him as well?'

'I don't know Kai, I don't think he is involved,'

'Involved in what?' said Laura, 'yeah, I'm still here,'

Hey, I know... Terry was just filling me in,' said Kai,

He wrapped his arm around her and pulled her in close, kissing her on her forehead.

'We need to go and speak to John, he might know where she is.'

Kai led them up the beach, walking quickly as the hot, thin sand sank under their feet. Once they got to the end of the sand and start of the tropical forest edge, they stopped. John was acting strange. He no longer looked or strode around like a highly respected gang leader, but more like someone you may have found had escaped a mental asylum. He was barefooted, his ankles and toes had cuts on them from stepping and sharp stones and twigs. His clothes made him look like he had been deserted for weeks rather than a few hours.

'What is he doing,' whispered Kai as they stood and inspected him.

'I don't know,' said Terry,

'Well, why are waiting like we don't know him? Hey John!' said Laura,

'Wait Laura because...' Terry couldn't finish before Laura had already approached John and made eye contact,

'Wait who are you guys? and where am I?' said John,

'Because he might not know us,' finished Terry finally,

'Wait you don't remember us?' asked Laura.

Terry and Kai stayed back letting Laura try to explain to the confused John,

'So you knew this was going to happen then?' asked Kai,

'It was a possibility, Kai,'

'What about us? Could we have lost all memory?'

Kai stiffened his composure towards Terry. The risk involved had suddenly multiplied in Kai's mind. He needed to help his parents but now coming here he is risking so much.

'I don't think so. I'm sure there is a programme in place to protect the system. It wipes the hero's memories so it then will only allow people who went in using Karen to come out using her. I have never seen it though, but I believe that is what is happening here,'

'So what about Tianna? Do you think she got confused, saw gold and ran with it?' asked Kai,

'Perhaps, but we need to find her. There is a town just the other side of these trees,'

Laura convinced John to follow along with them through the trees and overgrow. They came to what they assumed was a town. It reminded Kai of a pirate village but dropped in the middle of the jungle. The town radiated from a central building which the people used as a place to socialise. It was calm and the people were getting on with life as anyone would assume. But Kai knew better that something was going on and a story to unfold.

'Terry, what's the story then?' asked Kai,

'I don't know Kai, this isn't one of ours,' said Terry, 'we have had stories of jungles, we have had stories of pirates. But a pirate town in a jungle well, I can't remember such a tale,'

'So if we don't know the story, the hero, we won't know how to escape,'

'That is correct. I'm afraid,' said Terry.

He spent some time looking around taking in the sights of old oak cabins standing alone in their own spaces between trees.

'We're going to have to mingle, speak to the villagers and try and get an idea of where we are and they might give us a hint of what could be about to happen,' said Terry,

'Is it Karen who chooses where you will be sent?' said Kai.

He looked down at his bracelet realising he hadn't checked it for some time but it hadn't changed. It still showed no sign of working any time soon.

'I don't know Kai, this was a plan out of desperation, to be honest, I would like to think Karen would bring us home. I hope nothing has happened to her.'

Terry was worried about Karen, he had created or helped create her from his old mentor's machine. But he had become close friends with his digital companion in the time that family had been missing. Karen was after all the closest thing to a friend he had for all these years and all of a sudden she can not be contacted. Kai continued to question Terry on the unknown location where they were now stuck, but Terry didn't create it nor did his kids to his knowledge. He told Kai to lead the way into the town whilst he ciphers through his memories trying to remember where this story had come from. He could not remember Karen ever being able to imagine random stories and worlds.

The deeper into the villages they walked, the more crowded the public areas became. The pirate culture was as clear as the sky itself. Groups of men walked through the tight streets eyeing a confrontation. Villagers stayed in their tree houses watching the gangs march through, parting the crowds with the smallest of eye contact. Occasionally two pirate gangs from different lands would unintentionally collide. Few witness much of what happened after as they would have already retreated or not left alive for long enough to tell the tale.

'So who do we start with Terry? It's packed here,' said Kai,

'I have some gold, there is a tavern over there, seems like a good place to start,'

Kai smiled at what Terry assumed was him accepting his idea. Although the town was surrounded by forest, the tavern was placed in between two huge trees, dwarfing the log building. They cast the tavern in deep shadow. On entering they managed to silence the whole room with turning heads the minute each of them had both feet within.

'Perhaps not one of your best ideas,' whispered Kai,

Terry didn't let that faze him. He smiled and gestured in a way to say calm, or I come in peace. Two men stood up. Each with ripped vests and biceps that could fit Terry's and Kai within them with room for more. Terry stopped and began to lean back to Kai and say,

'I think you're right.'

Before he was interrupted by a tankard hurling from one man towards the other and the shouting and yelling commenced. No eyes were on them anymore and began to assume this was the norm for a pirate tavern. The dark room was only lit by candlelight glowing from a grand chandelier hanging from a wooded beam extruding from the depths of the framework. Artwork covered the walls showing pirates from history or maybe a more civilised age.

'We may struggle for a quick chat not alone a serious conversation,' said Kai,

'Somebody will come forward be patient,' said Laura, digging her elbow into Kai's side,

'My kids and I visited a pirate fleet out at sea once,' said Terry,

'It was George's story. He loved pirates, I was never so keen. But what we did find is with these pirate settlements and crews, for every five or six, troubled souls you will find one more than capable leader.

They looked around the room again and started to wonder where these one in six leaders were. Kai had decided that this room must be full of all the six and the sensible ones stayed at home. If they squinted, the room changed from a tavern full of grown men and women to a house they would see at the local zoo back home.
The crowd opened like a sea separating after a huge growling voice echoed over the shouting and drunken shenanigans going on around them.

'Henry!' everyone froze, 'another ale!'

The man sat at a small table, alone. The tables around him are also empty instantly telling them he is a feared local. He had long black messy hair, framing his old sagging round face. His large build filled the chair that he sat in and his shoulders were covered in a long throw like what his mum would cover their settee in. Terry waited for Henry the barman to return and gestured to get his attention.

'Look you two sit yourselves down on a table down there and I'll get us some drinks,'

The request didn't impress Kai and Laura, but after giving Terry disapproving looks they did as they were told. The Pirate's beady eyes followed them both as they pulled their stools away for their table as quietly as they could in a hope not to attract attention.

'I don't like it in here Kai, he's only just taken his eyes off us,' said Laura,

'Just ignore him, I think I know what Terry has in mind,'

'You not from round here are you,' said the pirate.

It was a gruff voice but to their surprise, it didn't have that traditional pirate slang as they would first assume.

'Err... no we're not, just visiting, er... family,' said Kai,

'Huh, I could tell, look what you're wearing, stand out like a sore thumb,'

They didn't even think about the clothes they still had on from when they first left the real world.

'We're never going to be taken seriously here looking like this. It made sense at Casemore because, well it was modern times,' said Laura,

'What you saying? were going to play dress up now?'

'If we want to get out of here then yeah I guess we will,'

'Christ,' said Kai quietly,

'He won't help you,' said the pirate laughing to himself, 'You religious lot, you can only rely on one person to get anywhere in this life and that's yourself. You pray to your god and be ignored, join a crew and be treated like scum by the captain or maybe become captain but then you only get betrayed by the crew. You're best off on your own, you don't need to look after anybody else, or follow anybody else's fantasies,' The man downed the rest of his drink and slammed the tankard onto the table, 'Henry!'

This time he only had to shout the name and Henry the barman scurried around the tavern dodging stumbling pirates until he reached the pirate's table.

'That's your fifth drink now Spike,' said Henry as he placed the tankard down nervously,

'What of it? I'm not drunk,'

'Well, Spike the gold you owe is adding up,' Said Henry,

'Here,' said Terry dropping a couple of gold coins in Henry's hand, 'That should cover it,'

Henry nodded and scurried back to the bar.

'Why did you do that?' said Spike, 'I don't need my drinks paid for,'

Terry placed his hands on the Spike's table and leaned into the pirate.

'I know, I can tell you're not poor,'

'Then what do you want?' asked Spike as he also leaned forward to match Terry,

'Information, that is all,'

'Information? on what?'

'May I?' Terry gestured towards the chair opposite Spike.

'Help yourself,'

Terry sat, made himself comfortable and remade eye contact with Spike.

'You know this town very well I can tell, we have been hired-,'

'By who?' interrupted Spike,

'I'm afraid I can't give out that information,'

Spike looked unnerved as he gulped on his drink, but gestured Terry to continue,

'I want to know everything you know about this town, the who's who, anybody who is worth knowing about,'

'You don't know where you are, do ya,' laughed Spike, 'These people are pirates, they just want to earn as much gold as they can, spend as much gold as they can and drink as much as they can. These pirates aren't the ones people write home about and tell stories of. If that's what you are looking for you want Port Royale, not Whitwall Forest,'

'What about the Harbour? There must be something interesting going wrong,' said Kai,

Spike gave Kai a short glance and laughed.

'So, you're together are you? should have guessed. Look at you, what are you? Royal Navy in a shoddy disguise? Nah, you would know all about the harbour if you were. I have never been there. It's more of an old town before the old pirates ventured out into the forest. They had had enough of the posh folk telling them what they could and couldn't do, how much to drink and how to spend their gold. They have no power over us out here, we land our boats and come straight to the forest. We have our fights but no real trouble, If you want to be left alone, you will be,'

'How far to the harbour?' asked Terry,

'Follow the old path beyond the archway to the bottom of the hill, you will see it. You will smell the arrogance of the people,'

'So if we visit the harbour were likely to find something?' asked Terry,

'Aye,' Spike laughed, 'You will find something there you will, visit Madame Nishe for a change of clothes, tell her Spike sent you, and she will dress you all,'

They all clinked their glasses together and drank. Non drinking as much as Spike who finished the rest of his tankard.

'Who wants another?' shouted Spike,

Laura, who started to see the new drunk manner of Spike pushed for Kai to get up so they could move on,

'I think we should move on now spike. But thank you for your help anyway, all the best,' said Terry as they collected all their things and tried dodging the rowdy pirates to find the way out.

'So what do you think?' asked Laura after leaving successfully,

'He could tell us anything, to be honest, but the harbour is our best bet, after visiting this Madame Nishe,' said Terry,

'What about John?' asked Laura remembering the confused man they brought with them that they left on the beach.

'I don't think he will be much use,' said Kai causing an upset response from Laura.

'We can't just leave him there Kai,'

'I'm more worried about Tianna, If she has our gold we need to find her whether she has her memory or not,' said Terry, 'look, I think we need to split up and move quicker because we don't know when, whoever the hero is, will complete their story and we are done for. I will go back to the beach and pick John up, you're right we can't just leave him there but I can't promise we can save him once we move on from here. Laura, find us a base, somewhere we can stay and plan our movements then go visit Madame Nishe, sort us out something to wear. We got lucky with a drunk Spike, but dressed like this the folk at the harbour may not be so accepting. Kai have a look around and see if you can find Tianna. Don't go too far and get lost. If you have no luck or you do see enough of her to learn what she's up to, then join Laura at Nishes and we will meet at the arches, to head to the harbour.'

Kai was once again about to head out to an unknown place, risking his life for something he didn't even know would work. His parents are out in the real world, maybe dead, maybe alive, captured? Who knows, but the longer he stays here the less likely he can save them. He knew his frustration was starting to show and now Laura was also going out alone. The worry of losing Laura as well as not being able to save his parents turned into stress that he wasn't sure for how much longer he would be able to control.

Chapter Twelve

Whitwall Harbour Royalty

The sun started to set turning the sky over Whitwall Forest a marble green. Kai followed the directions Spike had given him and eventually made it to the edge of the hill decline, looking over the vast harbour. It looked like a traditional pirate harbour. Dirty cemented buildings and wooden piers led out to sea where many ships had landed for their stay at Whitwall.

Kai didn't feel much for Tianna and a part of him wanted to turn around and claim she couldn't be found. He didn't thank Terry for giving him this responsibility, he would have much preferred to find John. Every decision he made or something difficult he knew he had to do, always came back to why he was doing it and that was to find his parents. He didn't know how or where they were. Has Bullet Brown taken them or have they given up and fled like Laura's parents? Kai hadn't spoken to Laura since about her parents, it was awkward for him and it's not a conversation he was ever very good at. He also couldn't decide if it was something Laura expected him to talk to her about or if she would rather not talk about it at all. He knew

that she was helping him so he should show her a bit more love. Does he love her? Or is it too early to say that? There wasn't a shop he could just go and buy flowers from to say 'I appreciate what you are doing for me.'
Kai managed to let the thoughts go to the back of his mind for now as he has got a job to do but with a huge note attached saying, 'You MUST come back to this later.'

The idea of pretending Tianna couldn't be found was finally discarded by Kai. But remember what Terry had said he needs to be inconspicuous so just strolling into the harbour was not going to end well for him. He found a patch of land halfway up the hill which gave him a good vantage spot to see what was going on in the harbour, but also it kept him out of sight.
The outskirts of the harbour were very quiet. There were a few men loading crates into horse carts to take off to the village or the other way towards the ships. As Kai looked further towards the centre he saw much more movement. In the middle of the harbour, stood a building that was vast in size. It resembled an old gothic church, similar to the cathedral he had seen on an old trip to York as a child. He watched as the crowd moved around entering and leaving the building but he didn't see anybody who resembled Tianna.

After a couple of hours of staring at people coming and going, Kai decided his luck was out until finally he thought he saw something. Was his mind now playing tricks on him because of the monotony of staring at groups of people for so long? He chose to have a closer look as he decided he couldn't go back without anything.

Just outside the cathedral, stood a person who looked Suspiciously like Tianna. Like himself, Terry and Laura, she was not dressed like the locals and although she had made much more of an effort to mix in she still stood out like a saw thumb. She wore an old black knee-length dress with a black overcoat reaching her leather boots. Her oversized black pirate-style hat would be perfect if her hair didn't look so immaculate. Even though she must have landed hard on arrival like the rest of them. She had a suspicious, confused look to her.

'What are you looking for?' Kai asked himself.

The gathering of people opened a path as horse-pulled carts arrived at the cathedral. Each cart was surrounded by four guards dressed all in black, with spears in one hand and the other holding on to a pistol clipped to the side of their belt. Seven carts rolled past and stopped at the entrance. In tandem, the drivers opened the door of the carts followed by what Kai assumed were important people to the harbour.

Kai once again searched for Tianna and when he spotted her she was staring at one of the carts. She didn't take her eyes off it. After all, it was a fancy cart with gold trimmings and ruby finish. A cart that would interest a woman of Tianna's interest. The man who got out was dressed very elegantly. He had a long royal blue jacket and shiny black boots a woman would envy. Long black curly hair fell from under his hat down to his shoulders. When Kai looked back to find Tianna she had gone. He decided he had seen enough and now needed to get back to Laura.

After a short search around Whitwall Forest, he came across a shack which had colourful ribbons stretching from the surrounding trees. Kai had a good assumption that this was the home of a dressmaker. He approached slowly and poked his head through the doorway that was covered with a beaded curtain. The multi-coloured beads hung from brown leather laces. Kai only saw Laura in the corner of the room, nobody else was anywhere to be seen. Laura was facing the wall, stroking her hand gently over two initials that were a part of many that filled the wall.

'Here you are,' said Kai,

Laura turned with a jump,

'Oh Kai, it's you.?'

'Where's Mrs…'

'Nishe?' said Laura, 'she's in the back somewhere looking for styles for three outsiders. Did you see Tianna?'

'Yeah, well I think so,' said Kai.

He continued to tell Laura what he believed he saw at the cathedral. The carts, the posh people coming out and how Tianna was staring relentlessly towards them,

'She must know something then?' asked Laura,

'I don't know, one minute I thought she looked suspicious but then other times she looked out of it and was a little confused. So we're not much better off other than we know she's in the harbour,'

'Well, that's something Kai, anyway Nishe will want to measure you to get you looking a bit more swashbuckling,' Laura giggled as she put her arms around Kai.

His body warmed up all of a sudden, he held her tighter and she returned the gesture. The feelings he thought up from a simple hug reminded him of being back outside his pub when they agreed to be boyfriend and girlfriend. Do these feelings happen through any hug? He wasn't a hugger usually so it's not a comparison he could make. This feeling was amazing so maybe he does need to tell her how he feels about her.

'Ah, you must be Kai,' A course woman's voice echoed through the hut making Kai jump letting go of Laura. They both turned to look at Mrs Nishe. She had cloaks and woollen tops folded over her large arms. Laura looked mildly excited but Kai was the complete opposite. The clothing looked as though he was about to go back in time to when he was at primary school and about to walk out onto the stage as a shepherd.

'Mrs Niche, what are the letters on the wall here?' asked Laura,

'Oh they are lost souls, most of them. They were here once upon a time, just like you getting a new set of clothing so they can fit in. But most have now moved on to different lands,' said Nishe,

'So they are initials? I wonder who they are?'

'Mrs Niche,' said Kai curiously, 'What is happening down at the harbour today and who are the people arriving?'

'Oh, have you had an invite, my boy?' Kai nodded tentatively, 'I would say you lucky boy but it's not my scene, that is why we all left to come up here. They never forgave the posh lot, these old pirates,'

'Spike?' asked Kai,

'Yes, he has a good soul does that Spike. He claims to be a captain but his boat still sits underwater at the dock. They still charge him silver to dock, I don't know where he gets his money from. He was an influence to encourage us all up here. But now he is just an old drunk, but il always be thankful to be up here rather than down there at the harbour. It stinks and it's dirty. The pompous twerps think they are better than us, and then all these pirates turn up and make us look bad. Anyway, if you're going to see them at the Whitwall Palace you're going to need much better clothing than these wait here,'

'You have an invite?' asked Laura,

'Nope,' said Kai,

'Ha you mean you thought on your feet, not like you Kai. So what's your invite for?' asked Laura with a smile glaring at Kai,

'I don't know Laura, it's fine, Mrs Niche won't know,'

'She knows, she just doesn't care, these 'posh' clothes are going to cost a fortune, she's getting gold in her pocket. We're going to have to ask what the occasion is,'

Laura wasn't wrong, but the style wasn't over the top. The material looked smart but Kai had the thought that they would look like a rich pirate more than a high flyer around the harbour. Mrs Niche started to show them the trimmed leather.

'Now pick your styles and I will put you something together, but these leathers are harder to come by so they will cost you more gold,' said Niche,

'Terry will sort that, what have I got to look forward to then Mrs Niche at this gathering?'

'A gathering?' Niche shrieked she then broke out in a cheeky giggle, 'this is more than just a gathering boy, this is the first time a meeting of pirate royalty has met outside Port Royale,'

'If the pirates have left the harbour why would they meet there?' asked Laura,

'They are still pirates deep down, and they can't resist the company that comes with it. There is going to be a lot of gold, a lot of pirates and a lot of beer,'

'So what are they meeting for?' asked Laura.

Mrs Niche walked over to her old crooked bookshelf which held hundreds of old books. She looked over the spines with her old fingers until she came upon a black-coloured book with golden trimmings. She gently pulled the book out and turned to show Kai and Laura,

'There are four ancient pirate families which consider themselves in line for the throne. But once the monarch is killed or dies, it doesn't go to an heir like a child because that creates war. So they all agreed that with death the throne would be voted for by the other families,'

They all gathered around the table that Niche placed the book on open at a page with family crests on.

'I saw seven carts arriving this morning?'

'Yes, but these are the four major families,' said Niche, pointing to the four large crests on the left of the open page. She moved her finger and gaze to the other page that had three smaller crests on it.

'These families, Emsworth, Fillmore and Grace. They are not respected enough to ever take the throne, they never have. So it's common knowledge that they arrive purely to make the votes more… what's the word?'

'Conclusive?' said Laura,

'Yes, conclusive,'

'Who do you think will be elected?' asked Kai,

'Be what? You mean picked?' asked Niche confused, kai nodded, 'well King Darrel Hornstem the second has just died. Now he has a son called Peter and we all think he killed him. King Darrel was the most loved King for hundreds of years, he has been on the throne for forty-five years. Peter thinks his father's popularity will win him the day but we're not so sure. But I do know he will do anything to win that vote, even murder!'

Kai and Laura looked at each other as if a lightbulb appeared over both of them.

'So we should look out for this Peter Hornstem then?' asked Laura,

'The night before the challenges begin, they hold the funeral down at the docks where they see the king out to the open sea. Perhaps if you're looking for anything that is what will be a good place to start.'

After leaving Mrs Niche's hut, Kai and Laura awaited Terry and John's arrival at the arches as requested. The knowledge of there being a potential plan calmed their nervousness somewhat. Although dealing with pirate royalty wasn't a fight they were looking forward to. The sun had passed the midday height before they spotted Terry and John walking out of the forest towards them.

'Laura, did you find a place to stay?' Asked Kai,

'Ohh yeah I did, just a small cabin in the forest, it'll do for us I'm sure, sleeps three people,' said Laura,

Sleeps three people? What does that mean? this echoed in Kai's mind several times before he realised that he hadn't responded,

'You ok Kai?'

'Oh yeah great, nice one,' said Kai, really meaning yea I am but are we okay? He assumed a more suitable situation would arise to discuss this issue further. That's if it is an issue or just a problem Kai's mind is creating because she hasn't said it for a while. That is, I love you, boyfriend or girlfriend. Kai wondered again if Laura questioned the position of their relationship.

'Not sure you will be able to watch the footy there though Kai,' smiled Laura attempted to lighten Kai's clear off-putting mood.

Kai replied with a small smile and looked back to Terry and John who were close by,

'Yeah, found him,' shouted Terry, 'halfway up a tree,'

'What were you doing up there John?' asked Laura softly,

'I dunno, where are we then?' said John,

'Whitwall Forest John,' said Kai,

John shrugged back at Kai and continued to look around clearly confused.

'Still doesn't know what planet he's on,' said Terry,

'He can join the club,' said Kai, 'he doesn't remember anything then?'

Terry shook his head and took a sip from his new hip flask.

'Did you find her Kai?'

Kai and Laura explained their conversation with Mrs Niche and Kai's spotting of Tianna.

'So does she know who and where she is then?'

'Well, she wasn't climbing trees, Terry,' said Kai, 'she was mingling as you would expect any person would I suppose, but that doesn't mean anything does it? Her new character might just have a better level of common sense than Johns, unfortunate new persona,'

'We need to get into that vote. Or even just as a guest, come on let's get these clothes on and get to the harbour.

Whitwall Harbour still looked very quiet for a location of a royal funeral and vote. Many of the people Kai saw earlier in the day had retreated to their homes. The cathedral stood tall over the square, looming them in shadow as the sun started to set behind it. Many market stalls started to put items away from their shelves in preparation for returning home with any unsold goods. Today was different, they wouldn't go home, they would be joining the masses who would line the streets to see off their old King to rest out at sea. They spotted a tall man standing with parchment in his hands as if he were waiting for someone or something. His patience looked as though it was running out as he caught their eye several times before repeatedly looking away. Terry pulled at Kai's sleeve and approached the waiting man.

'Are you lost?' said the man in a high important voice,

'I could say the same to you, why do you keep looking at us?' said Kai, whilst taking a swift nudge in the side from Terry. The man's face tightened and turned a light red.

'Do you know who you are talking to boy?'

The man stepped into Kai and looked down into his eyes,

'We do apologise, my lord, he is young,' said Terry in a grovelling way, 'we were looking for whoever is in charge of the royal engagement tomorrow as we are currently out of work and would be very grateful for our next post,'

'Did you register?' said the man, sliding his finger down his parchment, 'what are your names?'

'Oh no we didn't register, we have only just arrived by chance,'

The man's eyes rolled from side to side, then remained on John for some time.

'What experience do you hold?'

'Well we are all competent guards, you could post us anywhere and you will have no worries.'

The man rolled up the parchment aggressively without taking his eyes off John, making him freeze to the spot. His beady eyes caught Johns who slowly swallowed like he was about to vomit. The man finally released John and looked back at Terry smiling.

'I don't believe you, I have space for you in the kitchens, but you do not come up from the kitchens and talk to anybody, do you understand? The guests will not want to be introduced to anybody who speaks as commonly as you, what pirate group are you from? Don't answer, I would have to hang you all,' The man turned to walk away, he stopped and looked back at them, 'that gate in the corner,' he said, pointing to a wooden gate attached to the cathedral, 'be there for dawn, it's going to be a busy day,'
He continued to walk away laughing to himself, 'guards? please, couldn't guard an old rotten pig.'

Chapter Thirteen

The Burning Funeral

The sun no longer lit any part of Whitwall Harbour. The streets were in darkness with the route of the coffin lit only by candlelight which led to the end of the dock. The people were congregating by the edge of the road, managed by royal guards dressed in their bright red jackets. They held long blunderbuss guns ready to put a stop to any trouble that could interrupt the funeral of the deceased king.

Kai, Terry, Laura and John walked down the route that had been made for the king which ran from the cathedral to the docks. The road was filled by excited townsfolk who were trying to get a view of the king and the families who will soon be voting to decide who would take the crown.

'It's like they're glad he's dead,' said Laura,
'It might be the only time these people see a royal alive or dead, not to mention the elected royal,' said Terry, looking for the end of the road.
They found a spot to stand near the pier so that they could see off the coffin. There was a perfect view up the

mountain to where Whitwall forest began and the old pirates took to escape the royal way of life taking over at Whitwall.

'So Terry, when we're working in the kitchens how are going to see anything?' asked Kai,

'We're not going to work in the kitchens, well we will start in the kitchens, but we will then merge in with the people in the royals,' said Terry,

Kai and Laura were surprised and a little annoyed by the confidence of Terry that they could mix in so easily,

'What makes you think it will be so simple?' asked Kai,

'Trust me, It will be fine.'

Two knights on horseback started marching towards them followed by a large cart. It held a wooden coffin with two swords crossing over the top. Men, women and children of all ages stood and watched in awe as the dead king passed by in front of their eyes. Behind the king, a member of the other families who would now contest for the throne followed. They were preceded by the King's son and the favourite to become the next King. His march, posture and arrogance showed his confidence in the real possibility that he would be successful. Many of the people lining the streets were locals to the harbour but scattered between were the odd old pirate from atop the hill. The King lost a lot of followers once the so-called new folk appeared at Whitwall. The old pirates believed they needed more support and shouldn't have to be pushed aside by invaders. But he was considered a good king all round which was enough for many to make the short trip down to pay their respects.

The coffin made it to the end of the road and the representatives from each family lifted the king up and lowered him down into a small boat. It had straw lining the bottom which the coffin sat on. A man dressed all in grey stepped forward from the group and addressed the gathering. His loud echoed voice rang around the harbour.

'King Darrel of House Hornstem second of his name, ruler of the free people, the seas, the high mountains above and the sands below. We hereby pass your body to the lords and ladies of our past, as you saw us to our future. I hereby declare the beginning of the royal selection. Let the gods help us find the next in line to continue the protection and strength of this great land. May the King rest in peace.'

He bowed down to the dead King as two men of the Guard pushed the boat, and it slowly followed the tide out to sea.

Now something happened that Kai wasn't expecting. One of the guards who pushed the boat picked up a bow and arrow, lit it and fired the flaming arrow which hit the straw lighting it and the King.

'What did you expect Kai, the coffin to bob around on the sea for the next god knows how many years,' said Laura, a little annoyed at Kai's stupid assumptions,

'Enough you two,' snapped Terry, 'These are the ones we need to watch, whatever is going to happen at that vote will involve these and we need to be ready to get close and get out of here.'

The family members started marching away from the docks as the flaming boat sailed away, the fire not yet causing enough damage to sink it. Slowly, the smoke darkened, burning away the remaining straw and eating great holes in the boat causing it to take on water. The King had passed the horizon and lost into the depths of the sea. The journey back from the harbour showed a different side to the houses. They were welcomed by excited crowds whilst travelling with the dead King, but the return journey showed emotion Kai didn't expect. Peter Hornstem, the son of King Darrel was getting most of the looks and attention. The crowds were still on the streets watching in silence. Peter Hornstem was a young handsome man. His prominent jawline wore fine black stubbled facial hair under a crooked hooked nose and for the first time since he first appeared behind his father's coffin a tear appeared in the corner of his eye. Then a second and third, until a glistening reflected from the prominent moonlight.

'Well, that doesn't look like a son who just killed his father,' said Laura,

'Are they tears of sorrow or regret?' said Kai,

'Why do you always assume the worst in people?' said Laura, her gentle whisper became more aggressive,

'At some point Laura, were going to have to look out for guilt, might as well start with the obvious,'

'The man is crying, Kai!' Laura snapped forgetting where she was,

'Regret,'

'Exactly how you will be feeling if you carry on, learn when to stop,' Terry warned,

They continued watching Peter silently sobbing, along with what seemed like everybody else except them, until they reached the cathedral steps,

'So now what?' asked Laura.

The others shrugged their shoulders as they were walking back down the route Peter had taken back to the cathedral. They noticed that as the cathedral doors opened many guards flowed out wearing different coloured armour and their house sigil. Each Knight carried a lit torch and stopped in front of the steps to the cathedral, stopping the Lords and ladies in their place.

'What is this?' Terry gasped, as they watched carefully.

The line of Knights opened a small path and ushered the Lords past as they were turning to look around for what the commotion was. Until they saw a house on the edge of the harbour town set alight. Flames rose above the closer buildings, sending smoke billowing into the darkened sky. The citizens who once stood in silence like soldiers standing at attention were now fleeing like chickens who had just lost their heads. The road that guided the King to the sea was now a chaotic stampede of people trying to find the best way to safety. Kai knew this moment would be pivotal to finding the answer to the story at hand but feared for their safety as an unknown threat was approaching.

The Knights locked the cathedral doors behind all the higher-ups of the families and marched as one towards the chaos. This did little to calm the townspeople down as they continued their panicked fleeing.

'You would have thought they would have prepared the town for this in advance,' said a passing knight,

He wore a red cloak with a black outline of a tiger of house Hornstern talking to a green cloak-wearing Knight of house Fillmore, who nodded in agreement,

'Should have been prepared? what does he mean by that?' said Kai as he overheard the knight,

'If this is a regular occurrence then there is little for us to find out tonight. I suggest we just get to safety and return for work at dawn,' said Terry as the others nodded in agreement.

Getting to safety was a whole other task The streets of Whitwall that surrounded the cathedral were thin and short so whoever caused the riots could be hiding away. They could attack again at any point or they have concealed themselves within the other terrified townsmen. Kai led the way as he knew getting to the hill that looked over the harbour town would be the answer to getting to safety. His memory of the streets around Whitwall was not concrete. His geographical memory wasn't any good at home not alone in a foreign, made-up town.

The blanket of smoke still rising from the burning building blocked any view of the hillside or the sea, making Kai's decisions on his route even harder. They pushed forward in whichever direction felt right but with each corner they turned, panicked people bumped into them. Laura continued to keep pace with Kai, the next corner however came too quickly and a woman the same size collided with Laura knocking her down. For a few seconds, her head was spinning after it bounced off the dirty floor. People continued to run around Laura as if she was not there. She lay holding her forehead until her vision steadied and she could no longer see foggy rings that outlined her view. As she sat up against the wall of a building, she let her head fall to her right shoulder and there she saw a man or a woman, she wasn't sure. They were dressed like a pirate, but they had their heads covered with a balaclava, swinging their sword at passing civilians. At each building, they passed a lit torch was thrown through the front windows until her eyes met theirs and all attention was now on Laura.

'Come on Laura let's go,' said Kai as he pulled her to her feet. The unknown man was approaching closer as flames seeped off the windows as they walked past, creating curtains of smoke as they came closer.

'Laura come on… we need to move,' Kai continued to tug on her arm, but she just stood staring at the attacker. No matter how close they appeared she was transfixed. The noises around her became echoes, her vision was tunnelled. Laura felt Kai's arms wrap around her as the attacker's sword rose to the sky. Kai braced for the Imminent strike. Kai didn't understand why it took so long for him to think about it, he had a gun! Dolmans gun! As quickly as he could, as steady as he could, he raised it toward the attacker but he had already stopped. The man had been knocked to the floor and quickly killed by a Knight wearing blue clothing underneath his armour. His cloak had a fox waiting to pounce as its sigil. He didn't remember seeing this coat of arms when Laura and Mrs Niche showed him the families in the book. That thought however left quickly as they rose and fled as quickly as they could.

'Terry! There you are!' shouted Kai, as they smashed through a cabin door halfway up the hill, 'thanks for your help back there,'

'I thought you were following us, besides what help is an old man like me against these attackers?' pleaded Terry,

'So you can march on a gangster's mansion but you can't help us escape some rogue pirates,'

Terry almost argued back but changed his mind once he saw Laura's face step from behind Kai. Terry sat down in the corner of the cabin which had a single candle lit in the middle of the room, leaving the edge in shadow,

'Do you know who they are Terry?' asked Laura,

'Well they're pirates that's obvious isn't it, who else would it be?' said Terry unconvinced in his assumptions,

'They must be after somebody, one of the candidates maybe?' suggested Kai,

'No, it seemed too random for that,' said Laura as she stood and looked out of the window out over the harbour below,

'What do you mean random?' asked Kai,

'They were burning houses, swinging swords at anybody who they approached. Kai, I think these are the people we need to protect one of those family members from. I guess that Peter Hornstem,'

'They have guards though you saw how quickly they appeared at any sign of trouble,'

'They just want to scare him,' said Terry quietly, 'remind the houses that they are still here,'

'Why would they forget, the council are there for the people aren't they,' said Laura,

'These old pirates left Whitwall and moved into the forest because of the council and what they stood for,' Terry got up and headed to the door, 'it's time we left now, get some rest. It should be safe, we can find out more in the morning,'

Kai didn't agree, he would happily rest and fall asleep in this abandoned cabin against the risk of going back outside. The suggestion of heading back into the forest to sleep among the people whom they have now accused of attacking the town is not what Kai felt to be safe. He waited as Terry, John and Laura left and looked down at the bracelet still around his wrist. He left it on in the hope it would suddenly and for some reason he could no longer think of, power up and take him back home. There were no signs of this, the bracelet remained as it had been for so long now, dark, lifeless and how he felt at the moment, useless.

The dark muddy pathway leading up to the forest didn't do anything to help improve Kai's mood. The top of the hill where the wooden archway marked the entrance to the old pirate village seemed unreachable. The darkness of night, deepened by the shade from the surrounding trees which transformed the pathway into a valley of doom. At the top of the hill was a sight Kai did not expect, a glowing candle-lit lamp started to brighten up the road. Holding up the lamp was the old pirate, Captain Spike. He looked down towards Kai and the others, he wasn't sure if Spike could see him or not but his eyes glared directly at him. An arrogant smile tightened Spike's cheeks. Kai froze, unable to move if he wanted to, what was he doing? Was he a part of the attack on the town or maybe he masterminded it? He couldn't be sure, but he wanted to find out. Kai found the strength return in his legs and pushed on, every step felt like progress as he scaled a cliff face.

Kai looked up in the hope the archway was close, it was, but Spike had gone. When he looked behind him, he hoped Terry and Laura would confirm he saw the old pirate but, Terry had his arm around Laura being pushed uphill.

'Why didn't you shout me?' asked Kai as he hurried to take Terry's arm of Laura,

'We did, you were in your little world again,' Laura replied as she strode up the hill away from them,

'You have a good one there Kai,' said Terry short of breath,

'Yeah, I can't help but feel like she's slipping away though,' Kai replied,

'How's that?'

'I don't know, ever since the bank job, something hasn't felt right,'

Terry stopped and placed his hands on Kais' shoulders,

'She will come around, you guys have been through a lot the past few days, just give her time.'

Kai nodded but wasn't sure if he believed that. He chose not to bring up the question of seeing Spike as nobody else had seen him. For now, he was ready to find the cabin Laura had ready for them and get some sleep.

Chapter Fourteen

The Council

The bells rang out from the cathedral, signalling not only a new day but the start of the royal gathering and council. The sun pierced its way through the moth-eaten curtains that were hanging from each window. This gave Kai the impression that he was waking up to a glorious hot morning yet the air was telling him something else. He shivered as he sat up making him rub his arms with his hands over his hairs that stood up like needles. He made it to a window where he pushed the curtain aside to see layers of thin ice glistening on the leaves and grass outside. He was sure that the day before felt more like a summer day so it surprised him to find it so cold. The small cabin they had found was in no way capable of keeping out such cold weather. It was a nice little cabin with a living area and three rooms for them to sleep individually. Which of course caused another crisis in Kai's mind on whether to join Laura in a room or go by himself. He did decide to give her more space and time and go with the latter. His single room comprised a bed, adequate wooded furnishings and very well-finished wooden trims. He wasn't sure if he got lucky with the bedroom and possibly left the other two with less of a standard room, which made him feel guilty for Laura again. Another conversation that needed to be had but Kai didn't have the heart to have it any time soon. Instead, he let her have space, time and her room. A decision he still hadn't had a reaction to, they were all very tired when they returned and she didn't come to find him which told him he made the correct one.

Kai left as soon he got dressed before everyone else woke up because there was somebody he wanted to see before the council started. After seeing the attack on the town the night before there was a high chance that the killer they were looking for wasn't a part of the royal council. Kai was sure he saw Spike at the top of the hill even if the others didn't, so he wanted to ask him what he was up to.

The search for Spike was a short one. Kai started at the saloon where they first met him and to his surprise or not, drinkers were already starting at this early hour. The vision of the landlord negotiating early hour licensing like his dad at home got shaken away as the thought of there being that authority here was absurd. Behind the building was a dense area of trees where a person had started swinging his axe at small logs he had cut down from the surrounding trees. It didn't take Kai long to realise this was Spike.

'Not where I expected to find you Spike,' said Kai as he approached him,

'Captain Spike,' said the pirate before looking up at Kai, 'oh it's you, what d'ya want?'

'I think you know, the others didn't see you at the top of the hill but I did, what are you up to?'

'OK,' Spike chuckled, 'can a man not go to look out at a commotion down the road?'

'A commotion? Pirates attacked the harbour, Spike!'

Kai wasn't sure where this courage to confront a man twice his size in height and width had come from but he wasn't ready to stand down,

'What makes you so sure they were pirates?' asked Spike,

It was a reasonable question after all and Kai knew this as it could have been anyone. His courage had faded a little bit but enough remained to continue the questioning. He figured any information he could get from Spike whilst he had his backup was a bonus after all.

'They had to be pirates, where else did they come from? And you, I think you know who they are,'

Spike straightened up and felt like he was ten feet tall dwarfing Kai.

'Look 'ere, I don't know what you are up to but you're meddling in the wrong places boy. I liked you and was considering helping you out, that's why I came to the harbour path to see if I could find you,'

And with that response, Kai already regretted his actions. Having the experienced captain on his side may have been useful. Now he had the dilemma of deciding if he should apologise and convince him to reconsider or show he had courage in his convictions and continue to lay into the man. He chose the latter.

'I don't believe you,' said Kai trying his best to match up to Spike, 'I think you were trying to trick us by sending us to the harbour when you're building some sort of rebellion up here,'

'No, like I said to you the other day, were up here by choice and were happy. Why would we want to attack a funeral for a King who most of us still respected?'

'Why weren't you there for it then?'

'Let's just say I have a reputation there,'

Spike slowly returned to his wood chopping, turning his back on Kai,'

'I bet you have,' Kai said under his breath,

Spike threw down his axe and opened up a small box lying on the floor next to him. He sighed as he looked at the contents and back up at Kai,

'I respect your courage little man,'

'Kai,' Kai corrected, but Spike ignored him and carried on,

'I have no interest in what is going on down there, and I would advise you to think the same,'

'I can't, we need to…' Kai paused, 'It doesn't matter.' Spike didn't push Kai for the truth and instead reached down and picked a long sword up. The blade glistened from the reflection of the ice around them. The grip of the sword was silver with thin gold spiralling up to the blade,

'I'm still going to help you, we're safe here from any trouble down there and even from over the seas. We have developed a weapon on our ship that will destroy anybody who approaches. I have been building weapons and if they try anything, they won't know what has hit them. The stern of my ship will be the last thing they ever see. I will do what I must, sacrifice who I need to, to remove my enemies. But of course that doesn't help you does it, here,' Spike reached down and passed Kai another sword from his box. This one wasn't as elegant as the other one Spike had kept himself, 'if you're going to get yourself into a fight, you need to learn how to fight. There isn't much I can teach you about your little pistol you have but a sword, I can teach you to defend yourself,'

Spike held his sword up at Kai before he could compute what was happening and raised his sword into a defensive stance. Spike swung slow swings at Kai who managed to defect each hit and Spike threw instructions at him on how he should stand and defend. The hits came quicker and stronger, some missing and others deflected by Kai. Kai listened and learned from Spike but he was amazed by the speed and accuracy of the huge man in front of him. Kai could now defend himself and he started his own attack on

Spike, making strike after strike that the pirate deflected. He blocked Kai's next swing which sent him backwards, but as Kai went for another strike, Spike held the huge axe behind his head. Kai shrank back into a defensive stance with panic on his face,

'You have picked up very quick,' Laughed Spike, as he lowered his axe and reached out his hand, 'I don't know what you are up to Kai but if you keep trouble away from these good people, we will keep away from you,' Kai nodded at Spike in response hoping it was a nice gesture, 'Hey boy, leave my sword there you can get your own.'

Laura, John and Terry were leaving the cabin when Kai arrived back, he chose not to bring up his visit to Spike,

'Here you are!' said Terry relieved, 'we thought you had gone on without us,'

'No, just a little walk as you two chose to sleep in,'

'A short walk?' said Laura not believing what Kai had told them,

'Yeah, well I couldn't get back to sleep and, well we have a big day ahead of us so I thought I would clear my head,'

'And have you?' asked Laura Suspiciously,

'*No*,' He thought to himself if anything he had added to his thoughts from an unsuccessful visit to Spike,

'Yes, I think so,' he lied,

'Well you are right about one thing Kai and that is we have a long day ahead so I suggest we move. The last thing we need to start the day with is that miserable jobsworth doing the recruitment on our case for being late,' said Terry as they led them away from the cabin, through the archway and down the road into Whitworth Harbour.

The harbour town was busy with workers trying to put the damaged buildings back together from the attack the night before. The grand cathedral stood tall above the rest of the harbour untouched with a queue of people winding from the side gate which they were to meet. The queue moved quickly after they joined and they noticed many were leaving the queue after getting to the front. They recognised the man waiting for them at the front of the line whilst he was speaking to the group ahead of them.

'You didn't register with the council I'm afraid there is no more room,' The man spat in annoyance as if he had been on repeat, 'you needed to be appointed before last night which you have not. Now it's unfortunate what happened in the town and I have sympathies about your property sir but this royal council is an important business! Not a charity or a way to make small gold on the side,'

'Please I'm a Baker I can work in the kitchens,'

'And so can the other fifteen men and women who registered before the deadline so please move aside,'

The official had lost his patience and clicked his fingers to a guard next to him to move the Baker on. He lifted him and carried away leaving Kai staring into the eyes of the official,

'Now then, I remember you four, the kitchens isn't it if my memory is correct, what's your names?'

'Kai Fox,'

'Ah yes!' he cut them off before anyone else could answer, 'it is the kitchens, all of you, through this gate down the steps to the left and follow the passageway. Now the cathedral is heavily guarded so please don't wander off, I'm not sure why, but you're giving me a strange feeling you might be up to no good,'

'What makes you think that?' said Kai cheerfully as the official move is very close to Kai,

'I have very reliable foresight, let's hope it's lost its edge, for your sake.' He then gave them a sudden jerk of his head to move them on, which they did quickly.

The passageway was lit only by candles on the walls but still very cold and gloomy. They walked very quickly to get out the other end but the kitchens were not much better.

Stoves lined one wall whilst two spits rotated very large pigs over fire pits in the middle. Laura started to go white at the sight of the pigs and the general atmosphere of the already bustling kitchen,

'What's up, Laura? It's cleaner than the Black Bull in here,' joked Kai, Laura just shook her head and Terry stared and Kai was concerned,

'I ate at that pub!'

'I'm joking Terry, well mostly,'

A large man walked towards them dressed in off-white greasy clothes, with a long apron down his front.

'My last recruits, let's have a look at you then,'

They stood in a line and waited for the chef to affront them. John caught his eye as although he had been very quiet since arriving at Whitwall, he was still very awkward in most situations. His eyes flew from side to side trying to capture everything and understand where he was and who he was.

'You can do the washing up, over there,' the chef said pushing John towards the back wall that had two huge sinks slowly filling with pots, 'the rest of you cutting up the vegetables, quickly Powell will tell you how I want them,'

Powell was a very gangly-looking man with two prominent front teeth and spoke with a lisp.

'You can do carrots, you can do the potatoes and you the cabbage, come on quickly!' said Powell pushing each one to a different part of the worktop and chopping board,

'where's the ve-...'

Before Kai could finish three crates landed in front of them.

'You're welcome,' grumbled a man with a hunchback as he strolled away,

'Well they are a friendly lot down here,' said Terry as they started chopping and peeling their given vegetables, 'now keep a look out for anything suspicious, dangerous place kitchens, with knives and whatnot, you know? killer in the kitchen?' Terry smiled waving his sharp knife,

'This isn't Cluedo Terry of course they would use a knife in the kitchen they won't scare them with a carrot,' said Kai concentrating back on his cabbages,

'He has a point though Kai, a murder weapon comes from somewhere,'

'Exactly, any one of these people could be our killer,' said Terry,

'John is looking sus,' said Kai,

'Don't be stupid Kai it can't be John,' said Laura almost angry that he would make such a silly suggestion,

'No, I know but look at him,'

They all looked around at the sinks and John was grappling with a young boy who was also allocated the pot-washing role. The boy had come down from the forest, a family member of the old pirates. This is why he had been given the pot-washing job rather than anything else with more responsibility. The young boy slapped John on the cheek which caused a retaliation from John by throwing him to the ground ready to throw a punch. Kai managed to catch his arm before it swung,

'Hey John come on now he's a young lad,' said Kai,

'He threatened me, so I had to show him,' said John, still clenching his fist over the boy,

'John you're twice his size now get up,' Kai continued to pull at his arm,

'What is going on here?' said the officer who registered them from behind the on-lookers,

'Officer Mullen,' said the chef sheepishly, 'how can I help?'

Mullen stared at John and the boy as they both got to their feet slowly,

'I have lost a member of my team for the council room, they haven't been seen since the attack on the town and I need a replacement, any suggestions?' Mullen then looked again at John and the pirate boy, 'you can keep those two, and I expect sufficient disciplinary action,'

'Of course sir, you can take any of these,' the chef waved towards Kai, Laura and Terry,

'Ah the self-proclaimed guards, you boy, you can come with me, prove your worth... as you were.'

Mullen led Kai back down the passageway and up the stairs and he was then out of any down-looking building into a grand Hall. A room that was the size of Blackpool Towers ballroom and the beauty of the inside of Buckingham Palace, he assumed anyway. The walls were painted a ruby red, and trimmed with gold and paintings of former kings lined the spaces in between,

'You will be stationed here, you deliver drinks and snacks when ordered. Until then you remain at your station, and you do not interact with anybody. I do not want you to make eye contact not alone make conversation. If anybody speaks to you, you may reply but I can assure you that the most that you will receive is an order for a refill. You complete the request efficiently and return here, do I make myself clear?'

'Yes, Mullen,'

'I did not permit you to use my name, I am officer or sir to you, and you must remember your place. A mistake like that with one of the royal families, well, you could be hanged, what a shame that would be.'

Mullen scurried away to the other side of the hall where guards started to line up either side of huge wooden doors. Many people lined the wall where the portraits hung. These were also important people, but not important enough to make the council itself, but enough to boast about it afterwards. The doors swung open, and Knights marched in holding flags with their house's emblem. Each house had three officials, one being the nominated family member. The other two were usually personally picked assistants or maids. Kai recognised the crests of the first three,

Emsworth, Grace and Fillmore, from Mrs Niches' old book. But the next three were a mystery to him. Mrs Niche said there were four major families, one of which was the Hornstem family, but he hadn't seen Peter Hornstem yet and he assumed he would be last.

Six of the families had taken their seats leaving two empty. An awkward silence followed leaving impatient looks on the other families, but they didn't look surprised,

'Where is Peter Hornstem?' Kai asked whoever stood next to him. It was a young boy with light red coloured hair, who only reached his elbow in height,

'He will come last, my father always told me that the family of the crown always came last but the Hornstem family took it too far and made the others wait,' said the little boy,

'What's your name? you don't look very old,' said Kai softly.

'My name is Loki, my father used to help at councils all around the land, but he can't anymore so he sent me,'

'Loki? As in the god?' asked Kai,

'What God? I don't believe in a god, I make my way in life, and I work hard for everything I have,'

'I'm sure you do, maybe they need more like you in this council Loki,'

Loki looked down, suddenly shying away from his previous confident persona,

'I'm sure you will do your father proud Loki.'

Their attention was taken by the heavy clanking from armour as the infamous Horn Guards marched into the council chamber. They were followed by the son of the former King and favourite to be elected Peter Hornstem. The Horn Guards lined up along a wall as Peter took his seat at the head of the table, under the gaze of the others. One last man entered the room, he wore a long ruby robe and a huge black hat like one associated with a pirate. It had gold trims and looked as elegant as a King's crown. He had an old face and a serious frown as he looked around the table slowly stopped at Peter and sniggered to himself,

'Shall we begin?' he said in a coarse voice as he continued to stand waiting for the others to rise, 'I Sir Ivor Atencio Royal Chair of this great land hereby begin the council of succession. Do we have the permission and support of the family of the deceased King?'

The room was silent as everyone turned and waited for a response from Peter Hornstem who sat very casually in his chair not paying any attention. His aid nudged him slightly until he realised the attention was all on him. Atencio did not repeat himself and did little more than raise his sharp eyebrow at him. The lack of respect from each party to the other was obvious for all to see. Peter sat up and leant towards his aid for his next move. The aid whispered in his ear before he finally spoke,

'Royal Chair I give my support and permission to commence this royal council of succession,' he nodded and smirked towards Atencio and lifted his empty glass towards him,

'Thank you, master Hornstem. We all sit here as equals with the best interest of this great land in mind, Let's begin.'

Chapter Fifteen

The Lost Initials

'Master Scotlin Grace you may begin your case,' said Ivor Atencio,

Scotlin Grace was a young man of twenty-six years, he had a pointed chin and was dressed with a thin goatee beard.

'My fellow council members, the Hornstem family have ruled with grace and humility, I offer my condolences to Peter, son of Darrel. He was a good king, one my parents couldn't think twice about voting for. Unfortunately, Peter does not hold his father's attributes which is why I call for a much-needed change,'

'The Grace family, to bring the real change that this land needs? Please boy sit down and leave the speaking time for the families who have the backbone and respect to lead!'

'Mr Watson that will do. I will decide who speaks and when. So please hold your tongue,' Atencio barked after Scotlin had been abruptly interrupted by Franklin, the head of the Watson family. Franklin had been on the council for forty years due to Darrel's long reign. This was his first chance like the other leaders to challenge for the crown.

Franklin frowned disapprovingly at Atencio. He sat back and pushed some of his long silver hair over his shoulder. Peter Hornstem smiled at Franklin contently, he hadn't seemed to be offended by Scotlin's comments,

'Please Master Grace continue,' said Atencio,

'Yes, do go on,' said Peter.

Atencio unsheathed his long sword and slammed it on the table.

'I don't want to hear another word coming from anyone other than who I have invited to talk, do I make myself clear,'

Silence followed Atencio's outburst, and he gestured once again for Scotlin to continue,

'Does he not have a point though?' whispered Kai hoping Loki could hear him, 'Surely to get this done quickly you should just hear from who is more likely to win?'

'Master Grace is a very clever man. They are interrupting him because Grace, Emsworth and Fillmore have never had a leader that shows any kind of sophistication. Scotlin might change all that,' said Loki,

'So these other families who I was told were the major families who are they?' asked Kai,

'Well you know Hornstem and you have just been introduced to the Watson family. There is also the Balliol family, they are a fierce group, quiet, but you wouldn't go to war with them. That is Danzen Balliol the oldest son of the leader Carl. I have heard he is sick but no one is sure. The other family is the Canmores. They have held the throne almost as long as the Hornstem family, a huge family tree. I couldn't tell you who would be next in line, it all gets a bit confusing,'

'How do you know all this Loki?'

'My father teaches me the family history all the time he is obsessed with it. As long as the Canmore family don't win, he will be happy,'

They all snapped upright when Mullen suddenly reappeared from behind them,

'Why hasn't anyone served any drinks yet? move yourselves!' he snapped as quietly but aggressively as he could.

All seven of the servers ran with jugs of water and wine to the table and started pouring to anyone who held a glass up. Kai didn't have a clue where he should go first or any of the planned procedures, so awkwardly followed Loki as much as he could. Once they were sufficiently watered, the discussion continued,

'Danzen Balliol, here representing his father Carl Balliol. Please state your case,' said Atencio,

Danzen Balliol stood and towered over all who sat around the table. His muscles were mighty, and his strong jaw was covered with jet-black facial hair,

'The Balliol family are strong, well respected. We have long been fighting for our opportunity to prove that we can make this land prosper once again. The Hornstem rule has faltered near the end and the arrogance of this boy who wants to continue any legacy his father had.'

Each leader had their say in turn and Peter sat in amusement as each speech used him and his family as a reason not to vote for the Hornstems but to vote for them. Ivor Atencio continued the council until finally, Peter Hornstem had his turn to have his say,

'Thank you Mr Atencio for finally letting me stand up for myself,' said Peter as he got up and started pacing around the table, 'you have all beaten my family and me even though my father governed this land for over forty years! I didn't hear many people complaining. My father had been ill for many years before his death. I picked up more of the role than people may think so the legacy is far from tarnished,'

'So you killed him to take the position full-time?' snarled Franklin,

'Watson!' shouted Atencio, 'that is enough of that, you have had your time,'

'I opened the doors to the outer communities to enter our realm which led to the council being other than Port Royale. They will prosper under a continuation of the Hornstem ruling with me as the new King. I would like to remind the Grace and Emsworth family representatives of the negotiation and treaty we have in place, you do remember that don't you?' they both nodded shyly but highly embarrassed, 'I would confidently say that without the treaty you would no longer be at this table... Balliol!' he snapped, 'remember what our family did for your forces during the Nixon campaign? Perhaps we should have left you all to die, and you would have I might add! you hardly controlled a competent regiment,'

'We are stronger now! And our people are being reminded of the times of our unbeatable defence,' said Danzen Balliol,

'Yes perhaps, but memory is a funny thing Danzen! Glory days may come back in their mind but not before one of you and your father are on your knees in front of me, not my father, me! Begging for aid to save the house of Belliol, the great house of the west.'

Peter sat back in his chair after easily silencing the other leaders, especially Danzen Belliol. The pretentious look of victory already slapped on Peter's face as the quiet fed its growth. For the first time during the opening of the council, Atencio didn't have to shout to regain order. Instead after looking around the table at the family leaders all he saw were men who had been beaten by a clever young man.

The council meeting continued for the rest of the day. This time there were few arguments, and much more politics than Kai could understand. Loki however stood and listened intensively until Atencio called time on the meeting for the day. After finishing a few cleaning jobs and reorganisation the hall, Loki waited with Kai until Laura, Terry and John finished their work.

'You enjoyed that didn't you Loki?'

Loki was sitting on the steps of the cathedral looking carefully around the square,

'Yes I did, it was interesting, what did you think?'

'Well, they can be a fiery bunch at times,' replied Kai, although he was looking for clues more then perhaps he should listened,

'Who do you think is going to win?' asked Kai,

'I think it's too early to tell, Peter has the obvious upper hand but all it takes is one of the other families to find some courage and they will earn support. After all Peter Hornstem is relying on fear to win, one of the other families just needs respect and they will win the votes,'

Kai was still impressed by the way Loki had such an interest in the council and could see him growing up to be a clever leader himself. They said their goodbyes and Loki ran off towards the edge of the square and leapt onto a cart being pulled away.

The misty evening air rolled through the forest, small candles lit the small area around them leaving the rest as a frightening unknown. Kai had been left by himself in the cabin as Laura had left some time ago and Terry went for a drink with Spike. Kai had no interest in sharing his oxygen with those pirates not alone a couple of drinks and conversation. So, he decided to go out and find Laura as it had been a while with no word of where she was.

The search did not take long. Laura was stood outside an old hut that belonged to Mrs Niche, she leaned against a windowsill to look inside,

'What you doing?'

Laura jumped in shock after Kai had to sneak up behind her,

'Kai, what is wrong with you?'

'Me?' said Kai still laughing, 'you're the one standing outside an old woman's house in the dark,' laura pushed Kai away and turned back to the window, 'what are you looking for?' Kai joined Laura bent over looking through the window into the darkness of Mrs Niche's front room.

Laura ignored him and went for the front door,

'Laura she's not in, what are you doing?'

Laura tried the front door, which was locked, so she tried a window round the side which swung open easily. She climbed up through the small window then misplaced her hand, fell forward taking plant pots with her and landed with a crash,

'Laura!'

Kai looked around before leaning into the house to find her,

'Where are you?'

'I'm down here,' said Laura, not worried about the volume of her voice, 'why are you whispering? we're hardly being subtle now are we, get in here,'

Kai fumbled his way through the window into the dark, cold room, where they had been talking to Mrs Niche a couple of nights before. Laura lit three candles on a candelabra which barely lit the room. Instead of lighting the room, it made the cobwebs glisten and the dust that had settled on the bookshelf and its library of books show itself. This didn't surprise Kai as the way of life these pirates lived was far different from the rich people of Casemore. What did surprise him was Mrs Niche's absence, she didn't drink with the likes of Spike or venture out into the wilderness. Tonight her house was empty and cold.

The room went dark again as Laura walked off into the other rooms. Kai followed kicking several items as he passed. Once Kai caught up they were standing in front of a wall made of stone. It looked clean and brushed. There was no moss growing over it or any damage apart from letters carved into it. Laura stood staring at the letters and let her fingers follow the grooves making the shapes.

'I saw this when we got fitted for our clothes,' said Laura,

'I remember you asked Niche about it and she said something about lost souls,' said Kai.

He continued to look around not realising Laura was still touching the wall. She didn't reply immediately but continued to gaze intrigued. Kai stopped and looked at Laura, and tried to read her thoughts as she was now quiet. It occurred to him that this was the first time they had been alone and managed to have a form of conversation. Although it was very mixed in terms of success, how that would be judged? he didn't know. Kai was conflicted at this very moment and the reason for the conflict was right in front of him. He missed his parents and needed to save them His thoughts on his relationship with Laura clouded his concentration and his desire to rescue them. Was the frostiness between them a sign that he needed to concentrate on helping his family? Or is it a warning that the people around him who want to help need his gratitude and attention? Laura needed his help and attention; he was sure of it, but knew it wasn't as easy as just putting his hand on her shoulder,

Laura was still looking at the same place for a while and ran her fingers through the carved letters many times,

'Are you ok?' asked Kai, 'you have been looking at those letters for ages,'

'I don't know, these are letters, well I think they are,'

She was interrupted by a crash in the front room. It sounded like a window was hit by a stone the size of a fist,

'What do you think that was?' gasped Laura,

'I don't know, wait here," said Kai, trying his best to find his courage again.

He kept himself low and crawled around the corner into the front room, but it was empty. Or so he thought. A purring noise emerged as he started to turn away. Kai zoned in on a shadow behind the bookcase as two amber dots appeared to float along the wall towards him.

'What the hell?'

'What is it?' whispered Laura,

'I don't know, wait.'

Laura did just that and so did he as the two golden orbs came closer. Kai started to lean towards them to get a closer look until small sharp teeth appeared beneath making Kai jump back,

'Woahh!'

Laura pulled Kai away from harm until the object went through the moonlight revealing a soft black-furred bo'dy and long tail trailing behind. Laura slapped Kai on the arm in frustration.

'God's sake Kai it's a cat!' she walked back towards the wall she was inspecting whilst Kai stared at the cat shaking his head,

'You gave us a scare there little guy,' he said as he stroked the back of the cat, 'you're cute aren't you,'

Kai had always wanted a pet but living above a pub restaurant had its issues when it came to cats who wanted to explore. The closest response to a yes, he ever got for his father was 'I guess it will keep the rats away.' But that never got him down to the cattery or rescue centre to pick up a pet. He held the cat for a bit continuing to stroke him,

'Hey, do you think it's Mrs Niches? asked Kai, but received no reply, 'I don't think it gets much attention, or he's very needy… Laura,'

'Yeah, I guess,' said Laura, not knowing what she was responding to,

'What is it with that wall that is interesting you so much?'

'Look, is it not obvious? In these letters, there are some individual ones, some in couples and even triples. Remember what Terry has said about his worlds before we came, think about it,'

'Some sort of equation?' said Kai,

'No, these people are simple pirates Kai I don't think any of them have learned algebra, do you?'

Kai agreed, but this obvious conclusion that Laura had figured out didn't come to him as easily. He chose to not pursue this, instead, he went a different path. Enough was enough, they were alone, and it was time to find out for sure where they both stood with each other. He chose to go and embrace Laura by putting his arm around her and turning her body around to face him. Laura's eyes looked directly into Kais, he looked down at her, and the sight of her dark blue eyes, a small round nose was new to him. Was this a bad sign, did he not know Laura at all? To decide this and possibly their future as a couple, he went in for a kiss.

Before he made a connection, a crack shot down the centre of the wall. The floor beneath them shook, throwing them both to the floor,

'Laura, where are you?' shouted Kai, not realising she was behind him crawling back towards the engraved wall.

Cracks climbed up the wall like tree roots tunnelling into the ground. Many of the letters and shapes shattered into pieces as they fell to the floor. Laura covered her head as parts crumbled and fell on her.

'Laura stop, come on!' shouted Kai as he waved his arms trying to grasp Laura's leg to pull her back.

Dust rose from the floor as the vibrations intensified, stopping Kai from getting to his feet. He could no longer see or hear Laura, debris was falling from the roof and books were being thrown from the shelves.

'This must be it, it's over!' said Kai to himself, 'but how?'

He couldn't leave Laura, the front door was in sight and he felt he could make it.

'Laura!' he shouted in vain, but nothing, there was no response just more dust and rumbles.

He thought he must be crazy but he left his corner and crawled towards the place he last saw Laura. He climbed over fallen beams and ducked under tumbled bookcases, but she was nowhere to be seen. Has she got herself out? Or is she stuck under something? He had to find out,

'Laura! Where are you?' he shouted again, and again,

He heard a sound that could have been someone coming towards him but he wasn't sure. Before he could find out he felt a weight hit the top of his head knocking him to the floor. Kai lay on his back, staring at what was left of the ceiling, or so he assumed. His vision was blurred and he couldn't move. A shadow appeared above him, but before he could look close enough to see who or what it was, his eyes closed.

Chapter Sixteen

Miss Gold

'Do you think we should wake him?' said Terry,

'Nah! Leave him he will wake up in time, Mrs Niche has looked after him so now enjoy your sausages man,' said Spike,

Spike was sat turning sausages and bacon on a small man-made fire pit, excitedly ready to dish out more food. Smoke rose from the fire and crackling meat through the fresh morning air. Spike and Terry were tired as they had very little sleep after helping as many people as they could from the earthquake the past evening. Many cabins and other buildings within Whitwall Forest had been destroyed or at best seriously damaged. Terry's stomach rumbled as his sausages were passed to him along with an old metal fork. There wasn't any bread or rolls to eat as a hotdog like he was used to at home.

Kai was still lying down covered in a thick fur throw. He hadn't been disturbed since Mrs Niche had bandaged his head following his nasty bump from the wooden beam. Once his bandage had been fitted he has since been allowed to sleep, although Spike's last batch of sausages had made his nose twitch. He stroked his head grumbling as he started to sit up and open his eyes,

'Sausages?' he said quietly,

'Ah, you're alive, just in time for breakfast boy,' said Spike, picking up a metal tray and placing a couple of sausages on and passing them to Kai,

'What happened?' asked Kai to whoever was listening,

'It was an earthquake Kai, how are you feeling?' asked Terry, placing a hand on Kai's shoulder,

'An earthquake? I thought the world was ending,'

'Ha! It isn't bad kid, not yet,' laughed Spike, he quickly took a bite of another sausage but still let out another chuckle,

'So did I, but we are still here and it seems to have been just an earthquake. The mountain and forest seem to have been hit worse but the harbour has taken a little bit of damage.'

Kai stood up and he could see some of the harbour in the distance. Most buildings remained upright but glass windows had shattered and cracks appeared up some walls,

'Where's Laura?' asked Kai suddenly,'

'She was seen last with you,' replied Terry,

'Yeah she was, we were at Mrs Niches, and she was obsessing about that wall she has. Well she had, that had loads of carvings on it, initials of lost souls or something. She must have pulled me away from the house though, after I got hit,'

Terry didn't answer immediately but considered what Kai had said before giving a reply,

'If she did recover you, it means she dropped you outside and left, but to where?'

'Oh god,' said Kai holding his head, 'she could be anywhere, she could be hurt, we need to go and look for her,'

'Yes we do I agree, there's a lot of space to search I'm not sure where to start. She is not down near the beach as I just found John sleeping down there,'

'Sleeping on the beach?' replied Kai, unsurprised,

'Yea, he will be fine, come on let's go to the harbour it's the best place to start,' said Terry turning to lead the way then found him self staring into to eyes of a huge brown horse,

'Going somewhere gentlemen?'

Kai looked up and Ivor Atencio looked down on them. His face had an unimpressed scowl to it. Similar to someone who has eaten something foul,

'Mr Atencio,' Kai said quickly, remembering Terry wouldn't know who this man was, 'we're heading to the harbour, sir,'

'Hmm, timely,' said Atencio slowly, 'the council is about to begin and your presence has been requested,'

'Wow, and you came to find me out yourself, I am honoured,' said Kai nervously,

"Time is limited boy, and sometimes some things are easier being done yourself. Please don't get some idea that you are special. I have other reasons to be here as well,' Kai and Terry waited looking at Ivor for a reason,'I'm not going to share that information with you two, you will however need to be swift as you have been selected to assist Miss Gold at the council,'

'Who is Miss Gold?' asked Kai, Atencio rolled his eyes, turned his horse and moved on, 'who is Miss Gold?' Kai repeated, but Terry shrugged his shoulders,

'You had better move, Kai, I will look for Laura, I am sure she is OK and won't be too far away.'

Kai nodded at Terry and headed back to their cabin to try and smarten himself up.

The walk down to the cathedral was a very lonely one. It wasn't until he saw little Loki, the boy he spent the day with at the last meeting, waiting by the gates.

'Hey Loki, how are you?' asked Kai pleasantly,

'I don't know, I have been told to wait here. I hope I haven't done anything wrong,' replied Loki in a whisper,

'Well, is there anything you can think of that you might have done?'

Loki shook his head quickly. This was the first time Kai had noticed Loki show his young age, something he hid very well. Kai tried to comfort him by crouching to Loki's eye line and he placed his hand on his shoulder,

'It's probably something to do with the earthquake last night, nothing to worry about,' his words didn't do much to relax Loki, 'tell you what il wait here with you, ok?'

That did the trick. Loki was instantly back to his usual self and his confidence in his knowledge was unquestionable,

'Look Kai, the cracks in the buildings there weren't actually from the earthquake,' he said pointing to an old schoolhouse on the edge of the plaza. It looked as though it had been hit pretty hard, 'it is thousands of years old, the building I mean and the builders weren't very good and it nearly collapsed on top of all the children in the school... Look! the sails passing behind the building. I can see the flag, it's the Gold family!'

The gold flag with ruby rose in the centre flew high above the mast, and its sails dominated the harbour skyline like low clouds had been blown in.

The Gold family! Kai forgot that Loki is the know-it-all in this world, maybe he could now get his answers,

'Look Loki,' said Kai quietly, 'I have been selected to assist Miss Gold in today's council, what do you know about the family and why are they here?'

'Oh wow, you're so lucky! Miss Gold is an amazing person. She has been pushing for her family to be considered for the council for years, but the other families wouldn't have it. She visited here when the council was announced and helped people in the harbour and even negotiated peace when the pirates threatened the town,'

'Why should her family be considered as a position of royalty?' asked Kai,

'Family history, her ancestors once fought for the throne, but the line was then rumoured to have ended. Then ever since they have not been able to prove her bloodline,'

Kai was still amazed about the knowledge this young boy had, keeping him nearby could help him,

'Stay with me Loki, you may be more helpful to Miss Gold than me.'

The leaders of each family sat around the council table patiently waiting to begin. There were of course a couple of empty chairs. Ivor Atencio was yet to arrive to take the chair at the head of the table. The chair to his right was still empty like in the meeting the previous day and more to everyone's suspicions, Peter Hornstems's chair was also empty. Kai stood with Loki where he started the last council meeting watching as the leaders sat staring at each other in complete silence,

'That is preposterous!' screamed Atencio as he barged through the double doors, 'the ship is here, I saw the golden flag, and she begged to join this council, I give her that opportunity and she can't be here on time,' Atencio eyeballed Kai as he walked past towards his chair, 'you, stand behind that seat next to me, come on!'

'Loki come with me,' said Kai holding on to his shoulder, 'he is with me, I can't leave him alone,'

Atencio scowled at Kai but nodded sharply in approval, but to also get moving into position,

'Are you going to tell us what's going on Ivor?' said Danzen Balliol, 'where is Hornstem? Has he finally decided to give up,'

Atencio looked at each leader who all watched intently, then Peter's empty chair and lastly the double doors into the hall.

'Peter Hornstem won't be joining us today; I can't tell you why yet because our latest member of the council has not yet arrived.'

Kai looked down at the floor as he felt the burning eyes glaring towards him from every other member of the council. He was relieved of this pressure as two horns blew and the doors opened. This moved the centre of gaze onto a tall blonde-haired woman dressed in a long golden dress,

'Kai! That's her!' said Loki excitedly, 'that's Miss Gold,'

'Yes, it is,' said Kai, staring into the eyes of Miss Gold,

'Put your eyes back in your sockets young man,' said Atencio impatiently, 'Miss Gold, it's nice that you have finally decided to join us,'

'Thank you, Ivor,' she replied, 'I see you managed to fulfil my request, and one extra, what is your name?'

'Loki Ma'am,'

'They seemed to come as a package Miss Gold,' said Atencio,

'Kai Fox, isn't it?' Miss Gold asked,

'Yes Miss,' replied Kai feeling like he was in school answering his teacher,

'Excellent, we have a lot to talk about.'

What would someone from a world of imagination want to talk to him about? Laura? John? Terry? He didn't know and he wasn't sure that he was looking forward to finding out,

'Miss Gold, would I be asking too much for us to be able to begin?' said Asensio,

'Of course, Ivor,'

Kai admired Miss Gold's confidence and how she demanded respect in the council. It is clear that none of the other leaders was used to or appreciated having a female on the council. Miss Gold sat in her chair leaving Kai and Loki to stand either side of her,

'OK, let's begin. I officially declare today's council in order,' said Atencio, 'as I'm sure you can see we are missing Mr Hornstem,'

'Oh, has Peter got himself stuck in that earthquake?' joked Scotlin Grace,

'Well Mr Grace you are not too far off,' said Ivor, breaking the sniggers and laughter from around the table, 'Peter Hornstem, he has been found dead, Murdered!' The silence became reoccurring gasps and whispering, which became louder and angrier. Loki stood in complete shock, not taking his eyes off Atencio as he continued to wait for the opportunity to continue, 'the council must push on in its attempt to find a new leader, however, it will also run simultaneously with a murder investigation. We are all suspects and expect to be questioned on your whereabouts over the past evening. The only proven innocent member of this council is Miss Gold. She only arrived this morning after being summoned by myself once I was informed of the news,'

'Why would we kill another leader during a council it would be far too obvious, are you sure he wasn't killed during the earthquake?' Balliol asked,

'He was found minutes before the earthquake struck,' Atensio added, 'he was found wounded by what looked like a blade through his chest,'

'Mr Atencio that will do!' a loud voice interrupted. It came a man in armour followed by a dozen guards, 'No more information must be given at this time,'

'And who are you to interrupt a royal council? Let alone tell me what I can and can't say. Nobody holds my tongue,' scowled Atencio.

The situation became increasingly tense, Loki stepped closer to Kai who then placed his arm around his shoulder,

'I am Captain Hawkins of the royal guard, and I am now investigating Mr Hornstem's death. Usually, this would fall on to the family to begin however as I'm sure you're aware Peter was the last in the Hornstems line. Killing him would be an easy way to remove a family from the council and must now be dealt with. You will all be interviewed one by one which is why no more information can be given at this time. The cathedral staff have already been questioned and been made aware if they are of interest or not,'

'This isn't good,' said Kai under his breath,

'Let me remind you,' continued Hawkins, 'if found guilty, the punishment is hanging! You will be called when we are ready.'

The Council ended without completing any significant dealings, creating more questions than answers. The family leaders left the hall to await an investigation interview in their separate chambers. Kai and Loki were placed in a well-furnished room with Miss Gold, the room looked like a suite for royalty. Kai and Loki sat at a table watching Miss Gold pacing from one side of the room to the other with her hand clasping her forehead in clear stress,

'What's wrong with you?' asked Kai,

Miss Gold stopped and looked at Kai,

'What do you mean, what's wrong? Have you seen what is about to happen?' said Miss Gold,

'Well, yeah but Atencio said himself your not guilty,'

'Yes me, but not you,' Miss Gold looked terrified of this problem, but Kai didn't understand why,

'Why do you care what happens to us? Why did you go out of your way to make sure you had us by your side?'

Miss Gold fell into her chair and let her head fall into her hands,

'You are of interest to us. What happened to Peter handed us an opportunity to get to you,'

Kai stood slowly, not taking his eyes off Miss Gold. His hands were shaking in what he wasn't sure was fear or anger,

'Who are you? And why do you need me?' asked Kai, he was now stepping backwards until he nearly slipped on the long ruby curtains that slumped on the floor,

'I am Eleanor Gold...'

'Wait!' interrupted Kai, 'you know where I have come from don't you, Brown sent you, you know where my parents are!'

'No Kai wait, well yes actually I do know where you have come from, you're right I do. And I know who Mr Brown is, but I don't work for him, and I don't know where your parents are,'

'Then why me?'

'We knew you would be here after you got picked to be in the council hall and you are best positioned to help us,'

'Who is us?' asked Kai,

'Come and sit here and I'll explain.' Eleanor signalled to a chair on the other side of her desk, 'I don't know who killed Peter, it wasn't a part of any kind of plan. I'm not here alone and you weren't our original target. On my ship at the dock are three people very important to Terry, and you know where he is,'

'Terry is in the forest; he was with me when Atencio summoned me here, why didn't you just summon him?' asked Kai,

'Terry is too emotional; he has been searching for his family for decades. They found me and asked for help, along with many others who came to Terry for help and refuge from this Mr Brown. Some came alone, some as a family and some left family members behind. Do you know where he is now?'

Kai tried to take all the information in as well as thinking about Terry and Laura, his parents, Loki and now who Eleanor Gold is,

'Kai, do you know where Terry is?' asked Eleanor,

'No,' replied Kai, he didn't know where Terry was, 'The last time I saw him he went looking for Laura, my friend,'

'Laura who?'

'Laura Cassidy, why?' Eleanor exhaled after a moment of thought and continued, 'I…it doesn't matter. The most important thing is that I can keep you away from the guards and any accusations so I can find Terry and get his family back to him and get them home,'

'Are you from the real world?' asked Kai,

Eleanor's demeanour changed and was upset by the question Kai had asked,

'What is the real world, Kai? This one? Yours? If you were to die here your fate would still be the same. The things that make you scared here are the same as your world, the things you enjoy. I have lived on Potter Island a couple of miles off this coast all my life. My parents brought me up like any other family, I was loved, encouraged and disciplined when I stepped out of line. I have spoken to many people who have escaped to these worlds of imagination as Terry's family refers to them and your world doesn't sound like paradise. We all have wars and people who live for power and money. Controlled by governments we don't all believe in and people who feel they can control what we enjoy and say. Your world is no more real than mine,'

'I mean there's a big red button on Karen that would say otherwise, said Kai under his breath,

Eleanor looked accusingly at Kai who shook his head innocently,

'Come on, we can't just wait here, you know the truth now so let's get Terry and get you home,'

'So, we're leaving?' said Loki, he clearly didn't understand the conversation they had just had,

'Stay with us Loki,' said Kai,

He put his arm around him, and they headed to the door. They opened it to find a familiar face on the other side. It was Captain Hawkins and his men,

'Going somewhere, Miss Gold?'

Chapter Seventeen

Guilty without Trial

Kai, Eleanor and Loki were marshalled into a very small room, reminding Kai of a police interview room. The guards shut the door behind them and stood guard with two outside the door as well as two inside,

'Just answer the questions honestly Kai and you will be fine,' Eleanor whispered,

Kai nodded and was then pushed into a chair at a small table with Hawkins sitting on the other side,

'I was called after the murder was committed so why am I in here Captain?' asked Eleanor with confident authority,

'Because I find your acceptance into the council by Ivor Atencio a little convenient Miss Gold,' said Hawkins,

'And what does that mean? I am a family leader and will be shown more respect,'

'You will find our timing was opportune. Meaning we got to you and your council before you were made a fully committed leader, so no Miss Gold, I shall not show you any more respect. However, you are right about you not being here during that time so I will give the respect of having a guarded escort back to your ship,'

'I appreciate the escort Hawkins and the acknowledgement that I am innocent, but I am still very committed to winning the vote to rule this land,' replied Eleanor trying her best to stay composed but with every word her composure weaned,

'Oh no Miss Gold, I didn't say you were innocent,' Hawkins laughed, 'I still believe you have some sort of involvement and with respect, I want you out of the way whilst I talk to the boy. I think your influence could change the outcome of this investigation. This child would be incapable of killing so he can go with you, Miss Gold. Now on your way,'

The captain's guards pushed Eleanor and Loki out of the room leaving Kai alone with Hawkins. The captain was smiling and satisfied like he had had an early win,

'I didn't kill Peter Hornstem,' said Kai, feeling he should be more forward if he's going to get out of this,

'Is that right, well answer me this, where were you around two hours before the earthquake?' asked Hawkins,

'I don't know, in the forest I guess,'

'You got up the mountain that quickly, didn't you? Because you were serving for the first council session am I correct?'

'Yes, I was. And yes, I did,' replied Kai,

Kai did his best not to give anything away, but also felt much more comfortable now Captain Hawkins was alone,

'Can I call you Mr Fox?'

Kai nodded.

'Good, Mr Fox I have been told that you were seen in the location of the murder, and then later you were seen breaking into a cabin up in the forest. Not that I particularly care for the pirates it just looks bad on your case,'

Who had seen him in Mrs Niches? That means they must have seen Laura. He began to wonder if that meant they had caught Laura as well and if she was in trouble,

'I don't think you're going to have any proof of that captain,' said Kai,

He felt very confident about this as it's not like there are any CCTV cameras dotted around the cathedral,

'We have the word of a very reliable source,' Said Hawkins, who then began the wave his hand behind him,

Kai took a gasp as a lady with long brown hair walked in and stood behind the captain,

'It's you! Why?' said Kai as Tianna smiled back at him,

'You don't have to reply, Tianna,' Hawkins said, 'Mr fox you're here to answer to me only and Tianna is only here to give evidence.

Tianna rounded the table and leaned into Kai,

'You have a lot to answer for Kai Fox, this isn't the first murder you have committed is it, remember Casemore? Claxton? Dolman?'

Kai didn't deny these allegations,

'There you go, Captain. Even if there isn't enough proof of Hornstem's murder, he has enough to be punished for, he also works with Terry Toone who is also on my client's wanted list,'

'Ok, I have heard enough, Kai Fox I am sentencing you to death, you are to be hung by the neck until dead,'

'What! That wasn't even a trial, you have just listened to some accusations and assumed them to be true,'

'Mr Fox, thanks to you we have no ruler, no monarchy. I am the captain and must assume control of this situation before chaos ensues,'

'At least give me a chance to get some proof together to show some sort of jury,'

Tianna shook her head at the captain who turned back to Kai.

'Unfortunately, Mr Fox the decision is made,'

'The council and courts will see what is happening here and will come and find me and Miss Gold,' said Kai desperately,

'We are the courts, Kai! What do you not understand!' screamed Tianna, pushing the captain out of the way.

Tianna's outburst frit Kai. It was at this point as he looked into Tianna's frightening bloodshot eyes, that he believed he was in a mess that nobody would be able to rescue him from. He had no way of contacting Terry. Eleanor and Loki had been taken away to who knows where and Laura? Has she been captured, gotten lost or just left? He was alone now, facing a different danger than he had ever faced. He missed his parents, his pub and the town of Havelock. Southampton now sounds desirable, he even wondered for a second whether his parents had just run off to Southampton. Maybe they left a note, and he has just missed it.

'We're not the council yet, Tianna.' said a calm low voice. Kai looked up and couldn't believe his eyes.

'Bullet?' said Kai,

He had to blink repeatedly to believe his eyes that Mr Brown was standing in front of him and not just another vision.

'You remember me then?' said Brown, smiling as he moved Tianna and the captain out of the way so he could sit opposite Kai,

'Where are my parents?'

Kai wasn't scared, his anger began to boil within him. Only this time he was chained down so he couldn't let his rage take over.

Mr Brown didn't react to Kai. He didn't rise to the anger or try in any way to confront Kai. He sat and looked into Kai's eyes. The way he stroked his stubbled chin with a small grin showing that the anger in Kai pleased him.

'Your parents are alive and well,' said Brown before gulping the ruby-coloured wine, 'They will be staying at my place for a while until things sort themselves out,'

Kai took a deep breath to lower his voice before replying

'Why don't you take the pub? It's empty, I'm here and you have my parents. Let us go and we will move away and never see us again,'

'This was never about the pub, Kai. It was never about your parents; well, your father owes me some substantial money but that's for another time. It didn't have to be about you, but you then got yourself involved,'

'You took my parents!'

'Yes, I did, but if you didn't get yourself close to that Terry Toone, you wouldn't be in this position. Your father isn't a bad bloke, but he owes me money. Otherwise, you and your parents are nothing to me, completely irrelevant,'

'Let us go then!' Kai rose as far as he could out of his chair until his chains held him back. A guard then pushed Kai back into his seat.

Mr Brown waited until Kai looked back up at him and regained eye contact,

'You are now relevant Kai; you are the only person in this room who knows where Terry is,'

'What do you want with Terry? What has he done to you?'

Brown paused again, taking a sip of his wine,

'Terry Toone has been harbouring people who are of interest to me. I spotted him near your parents' pub, and it was a great coincidence that your dad needed a loan. I knew that he would try and look after them and get them into his worlds to protect them,'

'So my parents were scapegoats for you to get to Terry,'

'You became that scapegoat Kai. You led me to Terry's studio where I learned how all the machinery worked,'

Brown glanced pleasingly at the bracelet on Kai's wrist, which was still blacked out, and completely unresponsive,

'Wait, you blocked the communication so we couldn't get back,' said Kai, making Brown smile in response, 'but why? Why didn't you just wait for us to return? Why risk coming here?'

'I needed to see this world for myself, to see what I was inheriting. People have left our real world for this synthetic, fake world because they think it is freedom,' said Brown with a short laugh.

'But you saw what happened to Casemore right? You must have if you were blocking our connection,' said Kai, 'the story ended, that world is no longer there. You want to risk everything by being in here when you could have waited for us,'

'It shows that Terry doesn't know what he has control of if that is your belief. Casemore does still exist. The story doesn't just end. The destruction, the fear. Yes, that was me playing with the power that the technology has and it shows that with someone like me in control of the machinery and these worlds, well, the prison system may suddenly become a hell of a lot cheaper.'

Kai looked at Tianna and saw her face drop at the new knowledge that she was almost killed by Mr Brown playing with his new toy. He also looked at the Captain, who in contrast was as blank as a confused child, completely oblivious to what they were discussing,

'Playing with your new power?' shouted Tianna, 'do you know how close I came to being killed in that place?'

Brown turned round to Tianna and looked her up and down with annoyance,

'You're right Tianna I could have killed you, but I got you out didn't I?'

'To play longer with Fox and Toone I suppose. Maybe I should have run to a different world like all the others that have tried to escape you,' said Tianna,

'Let's not pretend we don't know what you are capable of Tianna, the Hornstem family no longer exists because of you,'

Kai lifted his head in interest, as well as the Captain,

'Wait a minute, you're saying he is innocent and you killed Peter?' the Captain's face lost its colour as he took

steps back against the wall, 'this is wrong, I need to inform-
...'

'Don't take another step captain,' said Brown,

He didn't need to be told twice as he was stopped by a dozen men at the door, who had already dealt with the Captain's guards,

'This execution will go ahead with you leading the event captain. This needs to look official I don't need to deal with a local uprising. First captain make sure that Miss Gold and that boy are back on their ship,' the captain scurried away so Brown could return his attention to Kai, 'I do sympathise that you have been caught up in all of this Kai, but before I go I could make this all go away,'

'I doubt that,' said Kai, he wasn't looking up at Brown by this point. He was just staring at his old leather shoes that he had been given by Mrs Niche. This pantomime that he has been a part of, thinking he was doing it to help Terry find his family and find a way to save his parents. But the person he was about to fight with was pulling every string in Terry's world. How could Terry not know that Brown was in control? He had something so powerful, but neither of them realised the power it had until now they too later and are about to see the destruction of their lives,

'Neither of us want this to happen, Kai,' said Brown, 'you're a young lad, who is a part of a good family and has been mixed up in a dispute between myself and Terry Toone. It isn't fair, I see that now. Look I will cancel this whole thing I will take you back to my ship where I have the equipment to send you back home. I will even release your family and leave you to run your pub, consider the loan payment a gift,'

'What do you want from me?' asked Kai, suspicious of Brown's sudden change of heart,

'Something so simple all it will cost you is a location. Where is Terry Toone?'

The evening sky over Whitewall Harbour bled a Ruby red as crowds began to gather within the courtyard of the grand cathedral. Workers were finishing the construction of a structure that would stage the hanging execution. The mood was solemn within the crowd, some not showing confidence in the charges given and who had been charged. Captain Hawkins led his men onto the new structure in a sign that the proceedings were about to begin.

Ivor Atencio stormed out of the cathedral and approached the stage. He was no longer well dressed and well finished. He looked tired, his skin was white as winter snow and dark purple bags hung under each eye. He still strode with purpose as he approached the captain and his men,

'Captain Hawkins, this is a disgrace and unjust,' he shouted with vigour, 'You know better than to punish a man without a real trial, high born or not,' Hawkins didn't respond, he barely gave Atencio eye contact, 'you're better than this Hawkins, these people know this is not proper. If a conviction was just, the crowd's voice would reflect it. Their silence is telling, you know it yourself Hawkins that this is wrong,'

Hawkins broke his stern stature to address Atencio,

'Please return to the council chambers with the family leaders, that is your place and where you will remain,'

'I shall not, I don't know who this man is that you have decided to bow down to Hawkins but he has no power here!'

'Men please escort Ivor Atencio back to the cathedral, he is not to be harmed just escorted,'

His guards stepped off the platform and circled Atencio but he resisted,

'You're a coward Hawkins! It is your job to protect the people and fight for them. Not bow to the first man with a big ship and some muscles,'

Hawkins's persona weakened visibly from his facial expression. He bit his lip and strengthened his stance,

'Use necessary force, get him back to that cathedral. I can protect you Ivor, but you have to stay in line,'

'You need to stay in line Captain!' Atencio's voice lowered as he was taken away by the captain's guards.

The guards returned to Hawkins on the platform as they waited patiently for the execution to begin. A further hour passed before Mr Brown appeared and strode onto the platform,

'People of Whitwall, you may not know who I am. My name is Amon Brown, your leaders of this isle have been significantly weakened, that is before the sad passing of Peter Hornstem. I am here to ease this new transition into the new era. By ruling with confidence and conviction. Yet, the man you have come to see be punished for murder is no longer our main suspect as new information has been given. I can assure you that my men are currently working to locate and deliver the culprit to us. So you can have confidence that punishment will be given to the correct person,'

'Bullet,' said one of his guards from behind him,

Bullet stopped talking and leaned in to listen to what his guard had to say,

'The team are back, Toone isn't there and there is no evidence he ever was. Also, they got attacked by some wild beast so we assume it was planned,'

'So he lied,' Bullet said under his breath as he turned back to the crowd, 'of course he did, a change of plan. New information has once again come in, we are going to commence with the original punishment,' He announced and turned back to his guard, 'bring me the boy.'

Kai was waiting in a small passageway surrounded by two of Captain Hawkins's guards. Six men dressed in all black like modern-day marines were led by Amon Brown. The silence in the passage was echoed by sewage water dripping from the walls drop by drop. Captain Hawkins was no more than a silhouette at the end of the tunnel, walking towards them,

'It is time Mr Fox,'

'Captain you know this is wrong, why are you going along with it?' asked Kai,

'I have been overruled,'

'Overpowered more like. You're the captain here, why are you letting this imposter tell you who to punish and how,' said Kai,

'Hawkins you have had your orders,' a guard dressed in black warned.

Hawkins nodded at Brown's men and signalled to Kai to continue moving. Gunshots then echoed hitting three of Brown's guards and killing them instantly. The others stood alert, looking for where they came from,

'Show yourself, whoever you are!' shouted Hawkins,

Two of Brown's men suddenly started wrestling with two people who had jumped out from a small gap in the wall. The guards made quick work of the pair and kneeled them down in front of them,

'Drop your weapons in front of you, now!' said the guard,

Kai locked up and realised who they were,

'Laura? Terry?'

'We will take these out with the boy,' said Browns guard, 'we will have a triple execution,'

Hawkins stood in front of the guards blocking his path,

'Move aside captain, bullet is waiting,'

'Mr Brown isn't in charge, the boy is right, not doing my duty as Captain to allow an imposter to take control of the town. Ivor Atencio told me I need to stay in line, to do that I need to put the safety of the town and it's peoples lives before mine. Now let them go.'

Captain Hawkins and his men drew their swords and stood in an attacking stance. Brown's guards looked at each other and pulled their guns out at the captain,

'Run!' shouted Hawkins as he swung his sword at the guns.

Terry grabbed Kai and pulled him back down the small tunnel as quickly as he could, leaving behind a dying sound of gunshots and clashing of metal.

Chapter Eighteen

Unexpected Reunion

The tunnel came to an end as the sun began to set behind the buildings. They continued running away as Whitwall guards split up in groups to search the town.

'Stay here I'll go on ahead,' said Laura,

Terry and Kai watched her jog cautiously around the corner. The setting sun and huge walls around Whitwall harbour made it easy to hide but harder to know what was around corners.

'Terry, where are we heading?'

'I don't know, we were told where you were and agreed to meet just round the corner,' said Terry,

'Wait, who?'

'I don't know, Laura sorted it,'

Kai looked around and started to climb up to the top of a wall and saw huge sails dominate the skyline. Several ships sat in the harbour, many owned by the families who attended the council. One ship he didn't recognise, had a sinister look to it. Painted completely black, with gothic trimmings and woodwork across its body. Engraved letters on the bow read 'Shadow of the seas'.

'Terry, does Bullet have a ship?'

Terry shrugged his shoulders and replied,

'Why?'

'Well, there is a typical bad guy ship in the harbour,'

Terry climbed up the wall the best he could although it was a struggle, he could tell his age was starting to catch up with him. Terry gasped at the sight of the huge ship and the others that had also anchored at the port,

'Terry, Kai!' shouted Laura, as she leant around the corner, 'come on!'

Kai let himself drop to the ground and then helped Terry down and caught up with Laura who was standing with Loki. Kai was relieved to see him and it became clear who had helped Laura and Terry find him,

'Loki where is Miss Gold?' asked Kai,

'She is on her ship with the others,' replied Loki,

'Others?'

'We will find out when we get there Kai come on,' said Laura who led the way to the ships,

The streets began to fill with soldiers, guards and Browns men who all seemed to be under Bullet's command. The group were spotted and began to run, every corner they turned, they seemed to have been blocked. Every window had archers raining arrows down on them, forcing them to get cover,

'This is impossible,' said Terry, panting heavily, '"why are we going to the ships, let's surprise them and go to the pirates they might just protect us,'

'No Terry we need to get to Eleanor's ship,' said Kai,

'Why? wait you spent too much time with her Kai,' Terry began to whisper, 'I know I told you to give Laura some space, but not to go find another woman!'

Laura shock her head hearing every word,

'Terry, Eleanor was never here for me. She was after you the whole time,'

'What did she want me for?,' said Terry before everyone paused,

'She's with your family, she searched me out because she knew I was in the council room and saw that as an opportunity to get to you. I think they will be with her on her ship,'

Terry opened his mouth to reply but nothing came out, as his mind thought about what Kai had just told him,

'You mean my family could be on that ship?'

Yes, Terry but we need to go now.'

The paths around Whitwall harbour became a maze full of guards hunting them down as they found the way out to get to the ships. They could see the sails, but high walls and buildings hid the correct paths for them to take.

They began to run as arrows started to rain over them once again. Kai held Loki by his arm and pulled him along with him until the cover of a blacksmith's store gave them protection. Arrow bolts thudded into the wooden trimmings of the blacksmiths and gunshots for Brown's men started to echo through the streets,

'Where's Terry?' asked Laura,

Kai began to look around with panicked urgency for Terry but the dark misty streets made it impossible for him to see. He hesitated for a second and then pushed himself out into the street. His senses became a mess of blurred images and muffled sounds. The shouts of guards were plain followed closely by the feeling of an incoming arrow blowing past him. He had tunnel vision concentrating solely on spotting his friend. He knew he must have been seen and these were not just random shots fired into the foggy streets, it must only be a matter of time until he was hit. His bravery started to wane. He wanted to find Terry desperately, but he had put himself in great danger and felt a sense of obligation to make sure Loki and Laura were safe. Just as he started to give up, there he was. Terry was leaning up against a wall wincing in pain,

'Terry, are you ok? we need to go,'

'You came back for me. I thought you had gone,' said Terry breathlessly.

Kai threw Terry's arm over his shoulder and lifted him away from the wall,

'Put your weight on me and just keep walking,'

Kai couldn't know his way back, he tried to picture the way he came and retake his steps,

'My shoulder, I can't hold on to you,' said Terry painfully.

Kai held on firmly and carried on, trying to ignore the risk of being hit or getting lost. The former was becoming more true than he wanted to believe. The fog had risen somewhat and the barrage of arrows stopped but Kai didn't recognise where he was.

Bright flames appeared ahead of them, shadows were moving in front of it waving. Kai didn't think twice and headed straight for it. Kai knew this could have been a trap or something he couldn't trust but his options were short. They were currently a lying duck for when the barrage was to continue.

The streets started to become recognisable to Kai. This fire which was lit started showing its surroundings although the shadows were still shadows. The fire however was a blacksmith's forge,

'The blacksmith shop!' said Kai in relief,

The shadows became clear as Laura and Loki ran out to help Kai lift Terry inside,

'Good thinking lighting the forge!' said Kai,

'It was Loki's idea,' said Laura smiling, 'although we need to move as I'm sure they have seen it too,'

'Terry is hurt, and they know we are here, they have stopped shooting for a reason and I think we need to go before we find out why,' said Kai,

He looked at Terry's shoulder and he saw a broken Arrow piercing through. Kai showed Laura and agreed to move now to get to Eleanor's ship.

The streets were empty which made the journey quicker as they arrived and climbed aboard as Eleanor's guards helped lift Terry over. They stood watching as Miss Gold's crew surrounded them. Kai's eyes searched the desk for Eleanor but she couldn't be seen. The crew stood in silence as the group nervously waited, Loki held on to Laura's leg. Just as Kai was about to speak, the crew's circle opened and Eleanor Gold stepped forward,

'Eleanor…' said Kai before being interrupted by her first mate,

'Miss Gold!'

'It's OK, this is Kai Fox who we were helping, and I'm assuming this is Terry Toone, are you hurt?' asked Eleanor,

'Er yes, he is,' said Kai,

'That's OK we can help him, we have been looking for you for some time Mr Toone. With your regular entering and leaving of this world has made it difficult,' said Eleanor,

'Where's my family?' demanded Terry,

'You're family… are waiting to see you,'

Eleanor stepped to the side and three people dashed past her,

'Charlotte! Emma! George!'

Terry grabbed both his children and held on to them as tightly as he could. It was a moment he hadn't been able to feel for many years and he was going to make the most of it,

'That was some ghost story hey Emma?' said Terry with a tear starting to fall down his cheek. Terry could see Emma looking him up and down, 'I know I look a lot older the last time I saw you darling but I'm still the same daddy I was then and will be forever more I promise,'

Emma's smile stretched from ear to ear, and George being older than Emma was more awkward but threw his arms around Terry,

'I've missed you kiddo,' said Terry,

The kids stepped aside to let Charlotte get to Terry, she helped him up and gently gave him a kiss and a loving but soft hug,

'I still see the man I married all those years ago. A man who hasn't given up on us, when many would have,' said Charlotte,

'Never,' said Terry quietly,

Kai looked at Laura awkwardly who shook her head,

'Let me help you inside Terry we need to sort your shoulder out,'

'Ah... yes thank you, Laura. Charlotte, kids, this is Laura, Kai and Loki. They have helped me on this journey,'

George and Emma both shied away but Charlotte acknowledged and thanked them all before helping Laura move Terry inside.

Once they passed the group of crew mates Laura stopped motionless, staring at a couple looking out to the sea,

'Laura? Are you okay?' asked Kai,

'Yeah,' she replied nervously without looking at him. 'can you take Terry please?'

Kai nodded and took Terry's arm as he glanced over to the couple, before helping Terry inside. Laura approached the couple shyly, the man and woman turned to see her before the woman began to tear up,

'Mum? Dad?'

They nodded emotionally and Laura threw her arms around her parents. The reunion she had dreamed of since finishing school that day years ago.

Kai stood at the doorway of the ship deck and watched Laura as they continued to have a teary embrace.

'Kai, we need to go they are going to follow us,' said Eleanor as she started to rouse her crew, 'lift the anchor, drop the sails!'

Eleanor joined Kai looking at the harbour as Brown's men and the other guards who had joined his cause, ran towards their ships,

'We won't get out of here quick enough,' said Kai,

They watched as the anchor was lifted into place and the sails blew in the wind, pushing the ship away from the harbour,

'Do you have ores?' asked Kai uninterested as he continued to look over towards Laura and her parents,

Eleanor grasped at his arm and smiled as she dragged him below deck bringing as many abled crew as possible,

Long ores flew out and immediately started pushing the ship away from the harbour and other ships that started to prepare to chase. The manpower increased the speed of their ship. The ores slapped the surface and dragged them away faster and faster. Kai could only watch as half a dozen ships twice the size as their own, released their large white sails and were soon out of the harbour,

'They're going to be soon caught up with us Eleanor,' warned Kai,

Eleanor nodded in agreement,

'We have just given ourselves some time to plan a response,'

'A response?' said Kai in disbelief, 'Eleanor they have six ships with three times the battle capabilities that we have,'

'Don't underestimate my ship, Kai,' she turned and faced the crew who remained on deck, 'prepare the canons,'

Eleanor's ship had canons on the deck and the lower level, they were all being pushed into position,

Kai could only see a warrior in Eleanor now who had picked up a thirst for battle. Half of the ores were pulled back aboard and replaced with canons,

'Eleanor this isn't a battle we can win,' said Kai, she didn't listen to him or at least she didn't react. The ship slowed significantly, allowing the already-closing ships to gain more ground, 'Eleanor!'

'If you don't want to be a part of this battle Kai then take yourself below deck and hide. Otherwise, pull yourself together and be the person I believe I have picked up not the coward.'

Kai froze and watched Eleanor walk away from him. She was right, but he believed he was as well. All the crew aboard were preparing themselves for war. He spotted Laura getting last-minute tips from her father with a sword and then archery with her mother. Terry was below deck with his family, as they helped heal his wound, but importantly, with his family. Kai had started this journey to save his parents, to find gold to pay off Bullet. The gold was gone, or to his knowledge anyway. He imagines Captain Spike spending it on ale in the bar of the pirate forest. How did it go from his mission in Casemore Town to a battle that the odds weighed heavily against him at sea against Mr Brown?

The battle was inevitable along with his participation in that fight. He needed to come to terms with that if he stood any chance of surviving. This journey wasn't just about him and his parents. It was about all the people who had been affected by Mr Brown's actions. Laura and her parents, Terry and his family. Kai wondered to himself whether his parents ever thought about looking for Terry, or if they knew about him. How would someone find Terry for respite from Bullet's constant threats? Surely he didn't really search for everyone. It's going to be a tough battle, but he has a chance to stop Mr Brown and save his parents without the gold.

Kai found Terry, who was still being treated but had regained his usual energy. Loki was also there playing with Emma and George.

'We're preparing to fight Terry,' said Kai, 'you should stay here though and continue to rest,'

This was an obvious statement but was a sign of Kai's nerves and feelings towards the situation. Or maybe it made him feel like he was ready and confident to up arms in battle,

'I would fight alongside you Kai but my shoulder, and wife are telling me otherwise,' said Terry smiling,

'Terry, you have your family back you need to enjoy any minute you get with them. Make the most of it,'

Kai could feel tears building in his eyes, he doesn't cry often and he can now feel the heavy weight this adventure has had on him,

'You think you have failed, don't you,' said Terry,

'Haven't I? I mean the gold's gone, so even if I get out of this I'm not going to be able to buy my parents freedom,'

'Mr Brown doesn't want money Kai, he is here for me because of the sanctuary I have given his victims. Maybe the gold you thought you were looking for isn't the gold you need,'

Kai sat confused,

'What do mean?'

'Come on Kai, I'm not speaking in difficult riddles here, think about it,' said Terry and then glanced towards the door. Standing in the doorway was Eleanor Gold, 'I don't mean in a way you probably thinking but she will win this fight, if there is no Mr Brown there is no problem. Help her win and she will help you,'

Kai knew Terry was right and Eleanor had the determination and confidence to maybe pull this off.

George approached Kai and handed him a sheathed sword and a pistol,

'You can have these, that sword is from Atlantis. It was given to me when I visited with my dad, it will help you win,' said George,

'Atlantis?' said Kai,

He felt the hilt which was gold and crafted with a Royal Blue gem sitting between two crossed horse heads at the end,

'My stories of Atlantis were his favourite before I lost them, the people loved the kids. Remember Kai you're not just fighting people from this world, Browns men are from our world but this doesn't mean they are stronger. They will be easily confused and not used to these surroundings, you can do this,'

The thought of killing actual people from the real world wasn't a pleasant thought for Kai. He shuddered at the realisation that it was going to be different or worse than the mission at Casemore. They were all storybook characters, although since meeting Loki and Eleanor, he had found there was so much more to these people. They had backstories, family and even a purpose. That was more than what Kai felt at times when working at the pub. He turned up for work when his parents told him to, serving arrogant and entitled customers. He came on this journey to save his parents, was that his purpose or his dad's bad decision-making? Whatever the answer was to that question was irrelevant, as at this moment his purpose was clearer than ever. His friends have been reunited with lost families and they need him to step up and protect them to bring them home,

'This is a beautiful sword, George. I can see how much it means to you so I will look after it and return it to you, I promise. When this is all over you need to take me to Atlantis, deal?'

'Deal!"

Terry shook Kai's hand and wished him good luck, before taking a seat and holding his injured shoulder,

Kai nodded at George and his family and left the room with Eleanor after giving Loki a wink who returned a shy smile.

<u>Chapter Nineteen</u>

The Kingdom Portal

Whitehall harbour was now a horizon being overshadowed by the sails of Mr Brown's newly acquired fleet. Eleanor's ship slowed considerably as the rowing had stopped and the crew waited. Kai stood next to Eleanor staring at their oncoming enemy, before being joined by Laura and her dad. They stood next to Kai and watched making Kai's curiosity rise as he looked at them then to the boats and back again,

'You ok?' asked Kai,

Laura smiled and replied,

'Yeah, are you?'

Kai returned the smile and nodded a little awkwardly,

'Oh Dad this is Kai, Kai this is Ted, my dad,' said Laura, breaking the silence that became uncomfortable,

'Nice to meet you Kai, Laura has told us a lot about you,' said Ted as he reached out to shake Kai's hand,

Kai returned the gesture but didn't reply immediately. He couldn't help but look into Ted's eyes and pass judgment on him. He and his wife left their young daughter to flee from Mr Brown, and he was curious as to why. Why didn't they take her with them? It made him also wonder if his parents would have done the same in their situation. Or even if they found Terry before being taken by Brown. He then questioned whether Southampton was just a code word they used instead of Terry's weird imagination, they had packed after all. He had felt anger when his parents told him about moving and even more so when he saw their suitcases in the pub. He was amazed how Laura seemed to have forgiven and forgotten quickly after reuniting with her mum and dad. Kai missed his parents terribly, and although he was on his journey to save them he hadn't been hit with this realisation of how much he missed them,

The enemy was fast approaching and this was not the time to pass any judgements on crew mates, he replied simply with,

'Nice to meet you too,'

Brown's fleet no longer sailed straight at them but tactically turned to obstruct any means of escape. They were faster and more determined to get into position than it looked like Eleanor was to flee. Eleanor watched closely but was quiet. She didn't show any sign of nerves, but she didn't give any signs of confidence either. Her crew seemed to trust her word and respect her orders enough to complete them without argument. They had fear in their faces but their willingness to fight for the flag was apparent,

'Are you ready for this?' Kai asked Eleanor,

'What? A fight to the death at sea? Yeah of course,'

Mr Brown's ships had now surrounded Eleanor's, every available canon had two crewmen behind it. They dropped the anchor and chose to stand their ground against Brown. The sea was silent, the seagulls had avoided the ships and stayed ashore. The flag which was slapping in the wind was the only sound on deck. Eleanor waited and watched Brown's fleet slowly sail around them, she found Mr Brown's flagship. It was painted solid black with golden trims from bow to stern. It was sat head-on with Eleanor's, whilst the rest of the fleet sat idle,

'Whilst he's directly ahead he isn't a threat,' said Kai,

'I'm not waiting any more, Fire!' shouted Eleanor.

The ship shuddered as smoke billowed out of the many cannons down each side. Shards of wood, smoke and fire flew from Brown's ships as many of the shots made direct hits,

'Again!' shouted Eleanor,

'We're sitting ducks if we don't move,' said Kai, 'they will fire back!'

This was obvious to Kai as he was sure it was to Eleanor but he felt he needed to be some form of voice of reason. Eleanor stared at Brown's ship and ordered for some ores to be used as they were about to sail ahead. The anchor rose as they started to move forward directly for the flagship. Brown's fleet had turned side on to Eleanor and prepared to fire, some with more significant damage than others,

'Fire!,

On Eleanor's command, another wave of ammo crashed into the surrounding fleet. More smoke and wood filled the skies,

'She's got balls that one,' said Ted as he gestured towards Eleanor,

Kai looked at Eleanor before responding,

'She's got something, let's just hope a plan is in there as well,'

The wind was starting to blow ferociously driving them faster as they approached Brown's ship. The other ships were unable to get more than one unsuccessful round of shots off at them as they were too close to brown,

'Eleanor we're coming in hot!" shouted Kai, 'Eleanor!'

Eleanor was looking over her shoulder instead, as a smile grew bigger,

"What? We don't need to worry about the rest of the fleet anymore,' she said,

Kai took a look for himself and gasped at what he saw. Behind the surrounding ships belonging to Brown sat another fleet of ships, but these were different. At the tip of the masts waved a familiar flag, a skull and crossbones sat on a backdrop of trees.

'Spike!' said Kai in relief, 'we have hope, well assuming he's on our...'

Kai got cut off by thunderous bangs as they fired at Brown's ships causing chaos and destruction. Holes the size of bowling balls were blown into the side of the vessels, causing many to take on water. Many had been damaged beyond repair and the few that were able attempted to flee back towards the harbour. This was before the second round of fire which finished off the fleet. Mast fell to the deck below, sailors chose to abandon the ships into the sea which was made rough by the winds coming in stronger and more fierce. The once intimidating fleet was sinking deeper into the sea and through the wreckage, flames and smoke came the ship leading the fleet,

'We should slow down now Eleanor!' said Kai after watching the fall of Brown's fleet,

Eleanor agreed and immediately ordered action to slow the ship, however, it was too late. Their ship had been travelling at such speed towards Mr Brown that any chance of slowing or turning was impossible,

'We're going to hit them!' a crewman shouted,

'Why aren't they moving? It's like they want us to hit them,' said Kai,

'Brown knows it will disable us, and he can then pick us off one by one,' said Eleanor,

'But that would be suicide for him surely?' said Kai,

The shining gold trimmings of Brown's ship started to blind the crew as the sunlight hit and reflected,

'Unless he has an escape route? Kai on that ship he must have a way of getting back to your world,'

If Eleanor was right, Kai faced a true dilemma. Does he get back to his parents and somehow win this battle or is it more important to keep Brown from returning? After all his parents will be safe if Brown is no longer around to terrorism them,

'Hit them, as hard as we can,' said Kai, to a concerned-looking Eleanor, 'If we are going down, we need to take him down and stop him from returning,'

Eleanor nodded and looked around at the ship that she had had all her life which was soon to be destroyed by her orders,

'Full ahead! everything that we have got, let's take them down with us!' Eleanor shouted as a true leader would,

They could feel their speed increasing and Brown's ship starting to turn after realising what was heading towards him,

'Brace yourselves!'

The waves between the ships crashed into each hull before Eleanor and Brown's ships collided. Eleanor hit the side of Brown, lifting out of the sea taking most of Brown's ship with it. Brown's side was scattered in the sea as shards flew from the ship's body in a devastating crash. The ships interlocked and were keeping each other afloat. Sailors were flung from the deck from the impact as others chose to jump to save themselves,

'Are you all OK?' Laura shouted after pushing her way back out onto the deck along with her family,

'Well, it's nice to see familiar faces,' They looked over to Brown's ship to see the man himself holding tightly to the wooden railings of his ship. His forehead had been gashed causing a line of blood to run down the side of his head, 'you need to choose very carefully now, join back with me or stay and die with your daughter and friends,'

'We have left Laura once, we will not make that mistake again even if it does mean our lives,'

Laura stepped in front of Ted in a sign of solidarity,

'Aww bless, love that. OK, I believe you, so let me try something else. I will let you live, however, in return, I want Terry Toone! You can keep his family, how's that?'

No one answered Brown and just looked at each other searching for a reply,

'We're not going to give you Terry,' said Eleanor, she looked to her side for backup but Kai was not there,

'Looking for Mr Fox,' Brown chuckled, 'he must have jumped overboard with the other cowards. Bring Mr Toone to me,'

Kai hadn't fled overboard like Brown had suggested. He had made his way below deck to find Terry and his family. He called out to Terry but had no reply and found himself going deeper and deeper within the ship's damaged hull. It wasn't long before Kai heard the whimpers of scared children,

'Terry!' shouted Kai,

He worked his way through the obstacles made by damaged wooden planks to get to Terry and his family,

'Your alive, where are Laura and the others?' asked Terry,

'They are OK for now, they are on the deck with Brown,'

'We need to go and help them!'

'No, no, Terry I have an idea,' said Kai as he helped Terry up to his feet, 'on Brown's ship we think he has a machine similar to Karen and I need to find it.'

Terry agreed and followed Kai along with his wife and kids. The path ahead was horrific. The wooden hull of the ships had tangled like two spider webs, that much so that the crossing from one ship to the other was two beams three inches thick,

'Kai, the kids won't be able to do this,'

'Those kids have survived here for fifty-odd years Terry! I think they will be fine crossing a plank two metres max,'

Kai stood at the edge of the boat and looked down. The waves between both ships raged like a pack of wild dogs jumping up at him, the rain started pounding down from above. This wasn't as easy as he originally sold it to Terry,

'I'll go first,' said Kai, trying to boost his confidence,

The boats were locked holding the planks stable as he placed his right foot out first,

'You can do this, you can do this!'

The strong wind blowing between the ships was not helping him as he tried to edge along. A final leap got him across, he gestured for Charlotte to come next, and then George. Their experience in these worlds was showing as they made very short work of it,

'OK Emma, your turn sweetheart,' said Terry as he helped her onto the plank holding her hand for as long as possible.

She was two steps away from the other side when a huge wave crashed into the side of the boat, loosening the plank. Emma lost her balance and fell,

'Emma, no!' screamed Terry and Charlotte together,

She fell from the plank trying to grab anything she couldn't but stopped suddenly. Emma opened her eyes slowly and looked up and clinging on tightly to her wrist was Kai. He was desperately trying to hold on, as his feet and knees were slipping along the damp wooden floor. Every time Kai slipped or tried to move, Emma lowered closer and closer to the raging waves which were crashing between the two ships,

Charlotte and George held on to Kai, one by his shoulders and the other by his ankles, pulling him back in. When Kai slipped, however, so did they. Charlotte managed to anchor herself against the inside of the boat whilst still holding on to Kai easing the pressure. But Kai couldn't hold Emma's wrist for much longer. Her thin wrists were slipping from the water splashing around them, Kai dared not readjust his grip in case he lost it completely,

'Grab my wrists Emma!' shouted Kai, desperately trying to help his grip,

The more she tried, the more it felt like Kai's grip was loosening,

'I can't, I can't hold on!' shouted Emma,

'I have you Emma!' Terry's voice echoed from above, Kai looked up to see Terry balancing the two beams, one of which was very loose,

'Terry, what are you doing? Are you mad!'

The planks wobbled, Terry held on to Emma's left arm whilst Kai had her right. They continued to pull together. Emma's head was now above the ledge, she was almost there. Terry's strength weekend as he slumped a little when a sharp pain shot across his shoulder from his wound.

They continued to pull. Waves still battered the ships and now to nobody's knowledge, cracks started to appear in the planks that Terry was standing on. They pulled and were so close to getting Emma back on board, that Terry felt the board bulk but continued to help get his daughter to safety,

'Terry get off the plank now!' shouted Kai as he saw the planks begin the snap,

'No, I'm OK we're nearly there!'

Emma got her knees onto the ledge and was safely on board as the planks broke apart and fell. Luckily before they went Charlotte and George had helped Terry and saved him from falling,

'Kai I will never be able to thank you enough for that,' said Terry,

'Just help get me home and to my parents,' Kai replied,

The inside of Brown's ship was a mess. Pictures of Brown, painted like he was an important historical figure were hung awkwardly on the wall. Some were damaged after being flung from their hangers after the collision. Other items were scattered around adding to the obvious signs of the battle,

'Brown must still be on deck, let's keep looking,' said Kai as he started opening any door he found, most of which were cupboards or small break rooms,

'Dad, Mr Fox. What about here?' said Emma, standing in front of yet another door but his one had a huge padlock on,

'Terry, I think this is it. Well done Emma,'

Kai tried to use his strength to break away the lock from the wooden door but failed,

'There must be a key, somewhere. Over there in the desk,'

Kai pointed at an old desk in the corner which appeared to belong to Brown. It was covered in old maps and watches.

Charlotte and Terry rifled through the draws and the papers but couldn't find a key,

'He will have it on him at all times I bet,' said Terry,

Kai growled in frustration and started to kick out at anything that was on the floor around him, but mostly at the door that seemed to have defeated him. He was ready to give up, but once again after time and time again, hope seemed to have been lost. He looked up at George and Emma who had backed themselves into the corner of the room frit by his little outburst. He then looked up at Terry and Charlotte who to his amazement were holding the desk ready to ram the door down,

'We're not giving up yet Kai, and neither are you,' said Terry,

'You have brought us this far and I'm ready to get my family home. So you can have your tantrum, or you can move aside so we can get through this door,'

'We don't even know for sure if anything is behind this door,' said Kai,

'If not, then we are in the same place we were two minutes ago. But if what you think is behind that door then we can get home, my family can get home and you save yours,'

'But we don't have the money, so I'm no better off,'

'Yes but we know Brown is here, we get out and delete the memory from Karen's database, and then he is gone for good. Leaving you free to find your parents,' Kai pondered this for a few seconds, 'now this desk is bloody heavy so move out the damn way,'

Kai smiled and stepped aside as Terry and Charlotte rammed the door. The first one left cracks in the wood, the second cracked the boards. Kai saw something inside that picked up his mood,

'Terry wait,' Kai Joined them and stood at the back of the desk, 'on three, one, two, three!'

They all pushed together the desk flew through the door followed by Terry, Charlotte and Kai, who landed on top of them. And there it was. Not Karen, nor anything that looked like Karen. But Terry instantly knew what he was looking at. In the centre of the room was a podium, holding a sphere with clouds floating around inside. Surrounding the globe were golden wings creating a nest,

'It's marvellous,' he gasped, 'look Charlotte, this has to be the best I have ever seen,'

'What is it?' asked Kai,

'Not what you were expecting Kai?' Terry smiled,

'Well, it's no Karen is it,'

Terry chuckled and stood back up after investigating closely,

'No, that it is not, however, what this is Kai, is a Kingdom portal. They are very rare but very handy to get home if our bracelets stop working like now,'

'How does it work?' asked Kai,

Terry placed one hand around the sphere and held his arm with his bracelet on close on the other side. His bracelet lit up, just like it did when they first travelled. Kai could barely hold his excitement, he was very close to going home.

Chapter Twenty

The Secret Weapon

'Terry, this is it, you can go home!' said Kai, with a tear starting to grow in his eye,

Terry looked down at the cloudy sphere, which started to show an image of his studio inside the whirls of cloud. He then looked at his family who smiled back at him and Charlotte nodded,

'No,' said Terry quietly, 'no Kai, you go first, I brought you here, you deserve to go,'

'I…I can't go. Terry Laura is up there, fighting, I can't leave her,'

'Then we stay,' Terry removed his hands from the sphere and took a step back, 'this is all our battle, Brown is after me, I won't allow anyone to lose their life because of me,'

'Terry your family have been here for too long! They don't deserve to have to put up with this place any longer!'

The Toone family stood in silence and looked up at their father. Charlotte and the kids stepped further away from the sphere,

'We're not going, it doesn't feel right,' said Charlotte,

'Putting the kids at further risk doesn't feel right,' said Kai.

They continued to stare at Kai who reluctantly agreed and led them back into the office, they were greeted by two huge men.

Both were dressed in black marine gear. One had tattoos covering each arm, which were both the same width as one of the kids. The other was smaller but his scars over his face and lack of front teeth were enough to tell Kai that they were from his world,

'Well what do we have here,' said the tattooed man, 'Terry Toone and you must be Kai Fox. I do recognise you, Brown said I would know your face from that disgrace of a pub in town,'

Terry took a step closer and looked carefully at the men,

'Brian? Joshua?' he said, Brian had the tattoos and Joshua had the scars and lack of teeth, 'what are you doing here? You work at the fair,'

'No, we work for Brown,' replied Brian,

'Yeah, we have been watching you, Terry, for longer than you know,' said Joshua in an odd screechy voice.

Kai stood in front of Terry making Brian's beady eyes follow him and tense up,

'We don't need to start being brave here young man, you're all coming with us, don't start playing hero,' Kai didn't move and stared back silently, 'look fellas you can come with us or we lock the doors and let you go down with the ships. Your odds aren't great either way but at least come listen to Brown, he has all your friends secured on deck so you fighting a losing battle anyway,'

Kai tried to weigh up his options, which were slim to none. Although if he was to be locked in he and Terry could go home, but he couldn't leave Laura. He had to carry on and at least try to save Laura, he had an idea,

'Just take me, leave Terry and his family here,'

'Nice try kid, Brown wants Terry, you're just in the way,'

Brian stepped forward spun Kai around and tied his hands behind his back,

'Please leave him I will come up please,' pleaded Terry.

Kai fell to his knees, he felt the room spinning around him. The waves continued to bob the ship around and mixed this with his dizziness made him feel nauseous,

'You're all coming up with us, move over there,' spat Joshua, waving a small pistol towards the doorway,

Kai remained down trying to regain his senses and to quickly think of a plan,

'Josh il take these up you bring the boy once he's up,' said Brian as he pushed Terry and the others out of the room and onto the deck,

Josh pulled at Kai's arm to pull him up but Kai struggled,

'Come on, get up and stand up, your not getting out of this,'

Kai sensed an opportunity. Out of the two soldiers, if that is what they called themselves, Joshua was the one he felt he could overpower. Although at the moment Kai was still on his knees as Josh stood over him with a pistol to his head, so the odds were not in his favour. He needed to act quickly before Brian returned, so he raised himself to his feet. Joshua let go of him, allowing him a bit of freedom. He took a step back and charged shoulder-first into Josh forcing him into the wall. His head swung back as he hit, and it bounced off a wooded shelf instantly knocking him out. Kai stood in shock at what he had just done, a trickle of blood started running from the back of Joshua's head,

'Come on Kai, it's fine you have done and seen worse,' he said to himself,

Kai battled with the ropes that tied his wrists but couldn't wriggle them loose. The ropes were burning as he tried to loosen them,

'Aggh there must be something!'

Kai looked around frantically and then he saw something that just might work. Above the desk nailed to the wall was a blue shield with two swords crossed behind it. He stood on the chair and used his arm to knock the shield to the floor. It fell with a clank and the swords fell away. Kai knelt and began to rub the ropes against the blade like a saw,

'Joshua!' shouted Brian from outside, 'What you doing? Is he causing you trouble? come on,'

'Oh come on,' said Kai, thrusting his arms quicker, nearly getting through the rope,

'Joshua?' said Brian, he entered the room and ran over to Josh who was still lying where he fell, 'what the hell happened?'

The ropes tying Kai's wrists became loose enough for him to release himself and sat against the desk as quietly as he could. The room went quiet until he heard a click of Brian's pistol,

'I know you in here Fox, come out and face me like the man you think you are,'

Kai didn't have a weapon and Brian had a gun what chance did he have at all? He knew he would be captured if he stayed still as the only thing covering the noises he was making was the bouncing of the ship on the waves.

One wrong movement and he was dead, what can he do? The sword and shield in front of him glistened as if it were a sign. He remembered the sparring sessions he had with Spike,

'That might just work,' he whispered to himself,
He had to be quick and use the element of surprise, if he still had it, that is. His palms began to sweat as he reached for the sword. Brian continued to stride around the room not looking carefully but had an angered hatred for revenge in his eyes. The heavy sword scraped the wooden floor alerting Brian who glared at the desk,

'Hiding are we, you should have jumped me when you had the chance,'

Brian aimed his gun at the desk and fired multiple shots but as quickly as he pulled the trigger the bright red shield bounded from behind it. Bullets ricocheted off the shield and the sword was thrusted into his stomach. Brian went limp and absently looked into Kai's eyes.

'You won't win Kai,' mumbled Brian painfully, 'Brown won't go away, perhaps death is the best way to escape.'

Kai's attack face fell to a softer look at Brian, almost sympathetic. Brian dropped the gun on the floor as Kai's sword was what was holding him up,

'Josh and I have been trying for years we just didn't know it, we had been corrupted and followed him, to get out of his prison. Your parents are there, you need to keep fighting or you will be too late, take the keys out of my pocket,'

'Where is it? Please where is it!'

Brian closed his eyes and his head fell back. Kai let go of the sword and Brian fell to the floor, in anger Kai swung his leg and kicked the desk. Were all these people with Brown, parents, husbands and wives who had fallen for his lies and felt the only way out was to fight for him?

Kai picked up both Brian and Joshua's pistols and the sword and shield, the one that wasn't impaling Brian. With the sword tucked into his belt armed with a shield and pistol, he found the keys in Brians pocket and left the room, heading to the deck. He stepped out onto the deck with his shield raised. Terry, Charlotte, Emma and George were still on Brown's ship and held at gunpoint, whilst Brown was on Eleanor's holding her at gunpoint,

'You continue to surprise me, Kai,' shouted Brown, 'But now it ends, who do you save?' he pushes Eleanor to the floor, then grabs Laura by the scruff and pulls her to the front, 'you can try and save the Toones but if you're feeling really brave you can try and save the one you love,' now the pistol was pointing to Laura's temple, 'or, I will be very generous and allow you to leave, right now and you can go and save you, parents. You have seen the sphere, you know how to use it, get yourself home, collect your parents and I will leave you in peace,'

'Kai, go to your parents, that's what you came for!' Shouted Laura,

'Sounds like there is a little bit of guilt there missy, you didn't come here for Kai's parents did you? You used him as a reason to come and find your own. Didn't you!' Laura couldn't respond, not how she wanted to, 'silence, you see Kai!' chortled Brown, 'run along Kai, it's for the best. Go and collect your parents. I mean look, even your pirate friends are abandoning you.'

The pirate fleet was all facing away from them and towards the harbour. He was right, his odds were worsening by the second. He had a decision to make, everyone was staring at him waiting for him to make a move or to just walk away. But Kai couldn't take his eyes off Spikes' boat, why stage an attack and then just sail back at the last minute? His last conversation with Spike came back to his mind,

'I have been building weapons and if they try anything, they won't know what has hit them. The stern of my ship will be the last thing they ever see,'

'The stern of his ship,' Kai said to himself still staring and then he saw it,

A wooden trap door opened and a three-barrelled Canon was rolled to position. Then above up on the deck out stepped Spike and at that point, Kai knew he was going to fire to wipe out whatever the case,

'I will do what I must, sacrifice who I need to, to remove my enemies,'

'Oh no,' said Kai as he looked around at Terry, Laura and Eleanor, 'get cover!' Kai ducked down under his shield,

'What are you doing boy!' said Brown, 'if these are some sort of delay tactics they won't work,'

Seconds later it happened, smoke and fire erupted from the canons and before anyone could move, both ships jolted. The crewman flew overboard. The explosion was so severe, that the masts and wooden planks were thrown metres into the air if they hadn't already been vaporised. The hulls separated and each ship started taking on gallons of water. Kai tried his best to keep his balance on the deck of Brown's ship which was bobbing desperately trying to stay afloat. He looked for his friends but couldn't see anything. Smoke filled the air and clouded everything. Through the smoke, he saw the stern of Eleanor's ship standing upright slowly sinking. Flames billowed from the inside until they vanished below the sea. Kai could only watch not knowing whether his friends were aboard or even still alive.

There was one man he could see, he stood towering a few meters before him. His shallow eerie voice threatened him for the last time.

'This is over now Fox! Get out of my way! Your parents will pay for your meddling!'

Kai didn't realise he was leaning up against the broken door frame to Brown's office and way out. Kai saw Brown had a nasty gash on his forehead, making blood run down to his cheek. This made Kai check his head as he started to feel a sharp pain and he had also been cut open in a similar place. He knew he couldn't sit and allow Brown to leave. He looked around and found the weapons that he had collected,

'Move now!' shouted Brown raising his pistol,

Kai didn't hesitate and picked the pistols up and dived for cover shooting in Brown's direction. It happened so quickly he didn't know if he hit Brown or how many bullets he had shot, all he knew was he had emptied his cartridge. His answer was standing above him. Brown with a smile on his face looked down at a now helpless Kai Fox,

'Pathetic' he snarled, 'just like your helpless father, I'm looking forward to telling your parents how you failed to save them,'

Brown raised his pistol, aimed it at Kai and pulled the trigger,

Click. Nothing. Without wasting time wandering what had happened he reached out to his sword and swung it catching Brown's hand, making him drop the empty pistol. Kai held the sword ready to attack making Brown step away before he pulled a metal bar away from his ruined ship.

'You will never scare me, Kai, You will not stop me from getting back home,'

Kai watched the bar in Brown's hand and imagined it being swung around causing incredible damage to whatever it touched,

'Ah Mr Toone, your still alive?'

Kai turned back and saw Terry and his family beat up but alive,

'Terry, get yourselves home now, I'll hold him off here. GO!' shouted Kai before Terry could argue,

Terry guided his family back inside towards the sphere,

'You will hold me off will you?' laughed Brown,

His laugh was loud and hit a nerve inside of Kai,

'You told me that I don't scare you, well the truth is Brown, the way you look now with blood running your face, you don't scare anybody,'

Kai gripped his sword with his two hands and prepared himself. Brown's eyes filled with anger as if all his blood met behind his pupils. Like a raging bull, he charged at Kai, swinging his bar, destroying anything in his path. Unfortunately for Kai, he was stuck in his path and the sole target. Kai dodged each heavy swing, he blocked some with his sword trying desperately to hit back any kind of blow.

The sun began to sink below the horizon, and only the flames eating the destroyed ships lit the small deck they were battling. Another strong swing from Brown tested Kai's strength and grip. Until a last swing caught Kai on his knuckle making him drop the sword which hit the deck and slid away, off the side into the water.

He dropped to the floor grasping his hand in agony,

'Such a waste,' said Brown as he pattered his head wounds with his sleeve and stood over Kai, 'you have heart kid, brave. But like I said this was not your battle, I gave you the chance to leave and take your parents. Now you leave me no choice, you allowed Terry to escape me,' Brown lifted Kai's face to look him in the eye, 'it is over for you and your friends. I will finish you and go and find Terry, destroy him, his family and anybody who has aided him or stood in my way. I will burn your beloved pub to the ground and because of you that means your parents as well,'

Once Brown released his head he looked back to the deck and closed his eyes. How does he get out of this one? His parents aren't here, Terry isn't here, and he hasn't a clue where Eleanor and Laura are, even if they are still alive. Maybe this was his time, he had failed this time. Not only his parents but all the others as well.

'Kai move!'

He looked up, on Eleanor's wrecked ship, she and Laura stood behind a Canon with sparks sizzling from behind it. Kai froze, as did Brown. His arms were above his head holding the metal bar seconds before slamming it down. They had his attention,

'Don't do it!' Brown shouted, 'it will kill him as well as me,' he dropped the bar and grabbed Kai in a headlock and held him in front of him as a human shield, 'defuse it now!'

The girls looked at the fuse as it reached the end. They looked at each other, covered their ears and ducked. Smoke billowed from within following a thunderous crash. Brown released Kai flinching in fear, however, nothing followed other thick black clouds filling the air,

'Don't try and hide boy!'

Kai wasn't hiding, he wasn't looking for Brown either. He was looking for his friends but the smoke created a dusty wall between the two shipwrecks,

'I will find you, Kai, it will take more than a small diversion, to stop me and save your friends,'

'I don't need a diversion,'

The soot had started to settle, covering Brown's ship and all that stood on it. From behind a crate, Kai stepped out, plastered head to toe like he was camouflaged ready for battle. Before Brown could move to collect his weapon, Kai charged at him shoulder first, which dug deep into Brown's stomach. What came next happened completely in slow motion. Kai felt like he had hit a brick wall but the force with which he ran was enough to destabilise Brown. He stumbled and reached out to grab anything he could. But in vain he took his last desperate step before falling backwards off the side of his boat.

Kai didn't move, he couldn't help but think that he would be back, it wasn't over. Until he heard the splash of Brown hitting the water below.

Chapter Twenty-One

Somewhere In-between

White noise sounded around Kai's head as he couldn't stop staring at the place Brown had tumbled off the deck. His clothes were heavy and sodden from the sea splashing over the sides of the sinking ship. The heat from the fires burning on the wooden ships kept him warm. He still felt empty yet heavy. Soulless. It felt like nothing could lift him from the deck or find any energy to bring him back to the small sphere,

'Come on, we're going home!'

Kai was deaf to this until four hands grabbed his arms and pulled him to his feet,

'Are we in hell?' he asked,

Eleanor, Laura and her parents stood and looked around at the burning ship covered in fire a soot,

'It feels like hell,' Laura replied, 'but there is a way out Kai,'

She held his hand and encouraged him back towards the sphere, but Eleanor stayed still,

'It is hell, I'll miss that ship,'

Eleanor's ship only appeared above water with its mast and flag, which sank leaving no remains. Until the flag rose back up and settled on the surface,

'And there she goes, the last memory of my family I had is now gone,'

Ted held out a piece of wood and managed to rescue the flag from the sea,

'Here, Eleanor. It's the least we could do. You sacrificed more than I know you intended for us and we will never forget it,'

Eleanor smiled back at Ted and took the flag in her arms and held it to her chest,

'Thank you, Ted, although we're not out of the woods yet. We need to get you home,'

'What about you? You're coming with us aren't you,' asked Kai,

'Kai you don't belong here, just like I don't belong in your world,'

'But you will be alone at sea,' Kai laughed awkwardly,

'I'm sure Captain Spike will come and pillage sooner rather than later and take me back to land, I have work to do. There is no Monarch after all, perhaps it's my time to honour my family name and take the throne.'

Kai smiled, a little disappointed and surprised. Eleanor was one of the most incredible people he had met. Strong, in mind and body. Not many people could win a debate with her. She showed him and all the others that if now was the time, she could rule for a long time and be very successful and respected, even by the pirates.

Kai entered the cabin where the sphere was located and saw Terry inspecting it very carefully,

'Ah Kai, I thought you weren't coming,'

He tried an encouraging laugh towards his family but it wasn't returned,

'I thought you would be long gone by now,' said Kai,

'Oh god no. I was about to come and help you,' Terry lied, 'anyway, I think I have figured this thing out.'

Terry continued looking at the sphere whilst everyone started waiting,

'Well?' asked Laura,

'Oh yes well with this particular device, you cannot just go to any world like you can with Karen and return with our trusty bracelets,'

Kai scoffed at that, then received a sharp elbow in his side from Laura, which hurt a lot more then her other jabs,

'Carry on Terry,'

'This device will take you back from where it was last transported from. I would guess that Brown used Karen to get here so this one will take us back home,'

'So you think it's one of many that are scattered around different worlds that can be used as a portal as such?' said Kai,

'Well more like less permanent portals. Where you find them however is a mystery to me,'

'OK less talking now then,' interrupted Laura, 'Terry, Charlotte take the kids and get yourselves home we will follow Kai afterwards,'

Kai shook his head determinedly,

'No way, you and your parents can go before me I'll wait to make sure Brown doesn't reappear. Terry come on get out of here.'

Terry obliged Kai's request, he placed his hand over the sphere and his other arm around his family. A white mist started swirling from out of the sphere like a galaxy of stars. The others stepped back and once Terry, Charlotte and the kids were within its reach they started to glisten brightly. It felt like slow motion, but then instantaneously they were taken into the sphere and they were gone,

'Well, I hope that does go home and not to some other far-off land,' said Kai,

'I'm willing to take that chance,' said Ted as he gestured to the boat wreck that was slowly going down and would meet the same fate as Eleanor's,

'Laura you're up,'

Laura smiled but didn't move,

'Well,' said Ted awkwardly, 'thanks Kai, we wouldn't have made it here without you I suppose,' he held his hand out,

Kai was looking at Laura waiting for a reply that didn't seem like it was coming. Instead of waiting Ted found Kai's hand and shook it. Kai was still looking at Laura but broke the eye contact to give Ted a friendly nod,

'We will meet on the other side,' said Kai, 'That isn't the risk here, I'm here waiting to see if Brown gets back on board he is my problem. You have your parents now just go, and I'll bring Eleanor along with me,'

Laura finally accepted what Kai was telling her and joined her parents around the sphere,'

'You had better be right behind us Kai!'

'Sure thing, just make sure you get that kettle on,' said Kai,

They closed their eyes and the white ring shot out around them,

'Kai just go, with them,' said Eleanor,

'I can't, we don't know how powerful this thing is we might not make it back, like I said I will be right behind them,'

'When I first met you Kai it was all about your parents, I'm impressed how it's now about the other families as well,' said Eleanor,

The sphere was almost at the point of transfer, it lit up the whole room with its power,

'I may not have my gold, but I have gotten rid of Brown so that will have to do,'

'What if you took home another type of Gold?'

Kai looked at Eleanor speechless for a few seconds. He didn't know what to say. Was he still in a relationship? Did he feel that way for Eleanor? Or is this the time for this decision?

'You would be risking everything to come with me. You could just seize to exist when the sphere knows you not from my world.'

'It brought you to my world, why would it be any different?'

Kai put his arm around Eleanor and nodded as they waited for the sphere to complete sending Laura and her family home,

'Kai ' shouted Eleanor, as he fell to the floor after a gunshot,

'Nobody is going anywhere,' shouted Brown as he pulled himself onto the half-submerged ship, 'step away from the sphere or I shoot him again!'

Laura quickly moved away and her parents followed,

'Kai!' Laura shouted as she tried to comfort him,

'It's just his ankle, he'll be fine. I can't say he will be fine for long, that goes for all of you. Especially if you're still thinking about joining him in stopping me,' Kai continued to reach for his ankle in agony, Laura and Eleanor tried to comfort him but were then shooed away by Brown. He pointed The gun at them, lifted Kai by his arm and easily threw him over his shoulders, 'I'm done playing with you, this is what will happen now. Mr Fox and I will go back to our world and not one of you will try and follow. The minute I land back in that disgusting studio I'm going to delete the memory and that is all you will be, a memory,' Brown chortled, 'oh and don't worry, I'll kill Mr Fox when I arrive. I want Mr Toone to witness the damage he has done, and then I guess I'll kill him too and his family and then Kai's family. It's too easy all in one place, and you thought you had dealt with me ha! How unfortunate,'

Mr Brown stood in the doorway to the sphere and pointed his gun at them,

'Now get on your knees, anyone move I will shoot them. This ship will be gone soon and you with it. Your pirate friends didn't come through did they? They're pirates, after all, another tip, don't trust them ha ha!'

They all kneeled, but Laura remained standing staring into Brown's eyes,

'Laura, come on get down,' said Ted,

'No,'

Kai opened his eyes for the first time and saw Laura standing alone,

'Brave girl,'

'You said yourself we will go down with this ship, so I will drown or you will shoot me. They both sound like they will end the same way and to be honest, maybe I'll take the quick death,'

'Fair enough,' said Brown as he pointed his gun at Laura,

Kai then watched the rest of them stand up before him, they were standing up for him,

'Oh and Kai,' said Laura, 'it's just your damn ankle!'

She was right. Kai swung and dug his knee into Brown's side as hard as he could. They both fell to the floor and Kai stretched to kick the gun out of Brown's reach.

Laura's parents both jumped on to Brown to hold him back from Kai. This was a difficult task as he still towered over them,

'Laura get him and yourself out of here now!' ordered Eleanor, who then picked up a piece of wooden debris and clattered it around Brown's chin knocking him back down,

'Ouch,' said Kai,

Laura helped Kai up and limped him to the sphere,

'Come on now Kai it's time to go, hold on!'

They both placed their hands on the sphere, which lit up brilliantly. Both bracelets came to life suddenly making the starry ring surround them. Kai held himself up on one leg, balancing precariously. Laura couldn't concentrate, she looked at Kai and then back at her parents and back at Kai,

'Laura, what are you doing?' shouted Kai,

Laura tried to concentrate by closing her eyes but then she couldn't keep it back any more,

'I'm sorry Kai, I can't lose my parents again,'

'No Laura wait!'

Kai tried to grab her but lost his balance and fell to the floor and the sphere went dark.

Although outnumbered Brown continued to battle on. Ted at one point managed to tie his hands around the remains of a mast but this didn't keep him back. His size pushed his way through knocking Ted to the floor, but with another hit round the head from Eleanor he fell to the floor face first. This allowed Laura to help her parents and Eleanor went to help Kai,

'Kai come on get up, let's try again,' said Eleanor as she lifted him and placed his hand on the sphere,

'Where's Laura, she needs to come too,'

'She's getting her parents, she will be here,' reassured Eleanor,

Just as Kai had calmed and accepted the situation, Brown lifted his hand grabbed Ted's ankle and pulled him down,

'No Dad!' shouted Laura, desperately trying to help,

Kai's bracelet lit up and white rings shot out once again, but Kai was not prepared to go,

'We have to wait for Laura, we can't leave her with Brown,' said Kai,

They continued to wrestle Brown, who had blood pouring down his face from the blow from Eleanor. His eyes met with Kai's and he roared at him, making sure Kai knew he wasn't getting away that easily,

'Kai go we will be right behind you, go!'

Kai could not concentrate on the sphere, or where and how it will transport him,

'Why is this damn thing not doing anything?' said Eleanor in frustration,

Kai stayed quiet and tried to close his eyes like he saw Terry do before him,

'Are we going? I think I can feel something,' he shouted,

'No,' replied Eleanor, 'and you're imagining it,'

'Is that not the point, this is all my imagination, right?'

Kai then opened his eyes after feeling a slap across his face,

'Ouch, what was that for?'

'You didn't imagine that then Kai, no? Come on pull yourself together,' said Eleanor,

They both put their hands back on the sphere. The rings came out once again, this time his bracelet lit up and attracted the rings to travel through it.

'Wait what is it doing?' said Kai, but then Eleanor pulled back her hand, 'what are you doing?' he said as he flinched,

This time she slammed her hand down on top of the bracelet and they both lit up. Kai felt weightless, drunk almost. It didn't feel the same as when he returned to his world before. He was in darkness. Apart from occasional misty shapes that flew past like meteors followed by terrifying lightning bolts,

'Eleanor? Eleanor, where are you?' there was no reply. He didn't understand why she had followed, she knew the risks and now, she could well be dead, 'Eleanor!'

He didn't get a reply but in the distance, he saw someone floating in mid-air. It was Eleanor, she was lying flat and was not moving. Kai called her again, but once again received no answer. He wanted to get to her but after looking down he noticed he was standing on a boat deck that was also just floating,

'Where am I?' he shouted to anybody who could hear him,

'*Kai,*' A soft voice echoed around him. He looked up at Eleanor but she was still not moving, 'Kai!' the same voice but it was more panicked,

'Hello!' he called back desperately looking around, but there was nobody,

'Kai I don't know if you can hear me.'

'Laura!'

This time it was clearer and he knew who it was, but this time a different voice echoed,

'Dad, where do you think they are? Where is Kai?'

'George?'

He was sure he was dreaming, he looked at his leg and he could walk. This must be a dream. He inspected his leg closet and there was no bullet hole, no pain,

'Kai!' this time Kai knew it was Laura, it was her voice but it was pained and desperate, 'Kai if you can hear me, or Eleanor If your there! You need to delete the memory we won't be making it back. Don't wait, don't hesitate or think about it. Kai, I'm with my parents I need to help them now,'

This could be heard in the background, muffled angry shouts and Laura's voice continued,

'Kai, you brought me to my parents, if it wasn't for you I would have never seen them again. Now look after Eleanor she won't know what's going on I don't know what world will be harder for her,' Laura sobbed as she tried to give a single laugh, 'I need to go, he will break through soon. It took a long time to know what I wanted Kai, I always thought it was just my parents I needed, but now that I'm not with you, I know that I need you too. But don't wait for me, just remember me, delete Karen's memory. It's the only way we will stop Brown. I'm going now, please do it, Kai. Remember don't hesitate and look after Eleanor,' the echo stops leaving silence.

All Kai could hear was the sizzling of the meteor-like object flying around in the distance,

'I love you, Kai,' the echo was quiet as if it was far away, distant voices were just audible,

'Laura come on, help hold this door. Wait destroy the sphere,'

'Wait Laura, no I can't do it. Take me back I should have stayed to help you. We could have left together,' Kai fell to his knees and hit the deck with his fists, 'I love you, Laura,' he sobbed, as he calmed and sat on the wooden deck.

As hard as he knew it was going to be, he knew what it was he needed to do, but first, he needed to get back. But how? He didn't know where he was, only that it seemed to be some sort of space between the real world and the imaginary. Laura was sacrificing her life to save his and many others and there wasn't time, he had to move quickly.

He looked back at Eleanor who was still floating nearby but out of reach,

'OK, how do I do this without floating away?' he looked around the deck of the ship for something to help him, but there was nothing. He wasn't any better off on the deck than he would be floating around, 'right here we go, Eleanor I'm coming, hopefully,'

He stepped up onto the wooden side of the deck and jumped. He didn't fall, he started to float up, and he moved his arms like he was doing the front crawl in a swimming pool. Then he could reach out and grab hold of Eleanor's clothing.

'Eleanor, it's me, can you hear me?'

She didn't answer but he could feel what he thought was her breath against his cheek, so he held her tight,

'Come on wake up Eleanor, we're just floating together until we find a way out of here,' his bracelet lit up again, so he tried to free his other hand to press it without letting go of her. When he did, nothing happened, 'why won't you work!'

He held Eleanor closer and wrapped his arms tightly around her. He could feel her heart beating against his and her breathing was becoming heavier until her eyes shot open and she inhaled deeply. The black space around them turned bright white. The boat deck he was standing on rose past him and out of sight. Other objects, guns, swords, clocks and bells also flew past them like they were falling. But they weren't they were completely stationary. The objects stopped and beneath them was a black hole. It is closer and closer. Eleanor had her eyes open still but wasn't communicating or seemingly oblivious to her surroundings. Kai watched the black hole approach and didn't panic, he just closed his eyes and waited.

Chapter Twenty-Two

Just Use Your Imagination

Kai's body went cold as the darkness surrounded him and Eleanor. The cool feeling remained as the weightlessness disappeared and he fell face-first on the hard studio floor. He was no longer holding Eleanor and was suddenly in a lot of pain. He scrambled around a little delirious until he heard a recognisable voice,

'Kai, are you OK? You took long enough,'

Kai looked up at Terry and took a huge sigh of relief,

'Ah, Terry it's you, am I home?' said Kai,

'You're home alright, and I see you have brought a guest.'

They both looked over at Eleanor, who was curled in the fetal position not talking or moving, only breathing. She was been comforted by Charlotte and the kids,

'Eleanor?' said Kai, as he crawled over to her, 'hey, you ok?'

Kai nudged her arm, which only made her eyes blink but no big reaction,

'Kai, why did it take so long for you guys, to follow us?'

Kai explained how Brown returned and was stuck in the purgatory-like space, but then stopped,

'Oh no,' he whispered,

'what is it? Where is Laura and her parents?'

Kai didn't answer and hobbled zombie-like over to Karen's console,

'No Kai, what are you doing?'

'She told me what to do before we left and then even spoke to me afterwards, I need to delete the memory,'

The kids gasped and stepped away from Eleanor as she started to sit up and look at her new surroundings,

'She told you to what?'

'Ye I know, and I'm wasting time,' Kai started to panic a little as he searched for what he hoped would be a big red button that said delete, but it was never going to be that easy,

'Kai you know what that means don't you,' warned Terry,

'Yes Terry, I know!'

Kai continued to search the panel, but in his hurry, all the words under each button merged.

'Why did she tell you to do that, what happened?'

Kai stopped and took a deep breath,

'She sacrificed herself so we could get out. Do you think this is what I want to do? I'm killing my best friend,' a tear rolled down his cheek and a realisation of what he just said. He tried so hard to make a relationship work but It never felt right. He did love her, but not as he was so desperate to, 'she is my best friend,' Kai finished,

A big flash and gut-wrenching crackle came from the platform. Terry could see and understood what he had to do, so he leaned over the console and unclipped a small plastic cover which revealed three switches. Terry then held down a button to the side which lit three lights below,

'I'll hold this button, and you can flick these switches starting with the one on the left. This will delete the memory,'

Kai didn't hesitate and flicked the first switch, then the second,

'Dad, there must be another way?' shouted Emma,

Terry looked at Charlotte for help as he couldn't release the button. She held Emma by the shoulders,

'Sweetheart,' said Charlotte softly, 'there isn't another way without risking Brown re-entering our world and causing more pain to others,'

'But Laura is in there and she has just found her parents,' said Emma,

'I know, but that is exactly it Emma. She has found her parents, remember how long it has been since we saw your dad and the feelings you had when he found us? Laura has wanted that since she was your age and she did not want to go through that again. So she stayed with them and with that sacrificed herself for all of us,'

Kai listened intently and after a nudge from Terry, he flicked the last switch,

The room went eerily quiet, Karen and all her parts were silent and just sat in darkness. Kai didn't move, he closed his eyes and pictured Laura standing on the deck of Brown's ship. Her parents and Brown were fighting around them like they were in fast-forward. The water level rose, slowly swallowing the ship and Laura, closed her eyes and body part by body part sank into the depths of the dark blackness of the sea.

Nobody spoke for a while as they let each other try to comprehend what had just happened. Eventually, George tugged at Kai's t-shirt waiting for him to turn around,

'We think you should have this,' George said,

He handed Kai a piece of paper and ran back to his mother. Kai opened the folded paper, which he discovered was full of addresses that were scribbled out,

'What is this?' asked Kai,

'It's mine,' said Terry as he re-joined his family who was still caring for Eleanor, 'in between the time of looking for my family, I have also been hunting for Brown's prison, or where he holds people imprisoned. Most of the leads I got turned out to be wrong, but the last one I have yet to check as I came about it just before I found you. I'm more confident than any of the others that is the correct location,'

'Why are only telling me this now?' said Kai, he wanted to show anger but his exhausted expression just showed his sorrow,

'I wasn't so sure and Brown and his cronies would have been there. Well, they won't now, the security would be minimal,' Reassured Terry,

Eleanor stood up with Kai and looked at the letter. She had been very confused but she started to look and sound like the Eleanor Gold Kai was used to,

'Let me see, Parsonwood Hill Farm, Parsons Road, Lei..... ses....ter....shire,'

'Leicestershire,' corrected Kai,

'Right,' said Eleanor, 'I will go with you, you will still need help against whoever is there, it won't be completely deserted,'

'Well, I suppose I better find my parents then,' said Kai awkwardly as he walked towards the door mistakenly leaving Eleanor behind,

'Thank you for what you have done for us Kai, we will never forget it,' said Terry.

He stood with his family, his arms around his wife and son as if they were posing for a recent family photo. Kai was happy for them. But he hadn't quite found a way to understand how after entering Terry's world, he had left without his girlfriend but with another girl he barely knew. They were both going to be alien to this world he thought he knew.

Kai nodded back to Terry and smiled as although a strange situation this is for him, this has gotten rid of Brown. He also in a way got Laura what she wanted and gained him an address for a possible location of his parents,

'I wish you all the best for the future Terry, but do us a favour,' the smile fell off Terry's face, 'don't turn that bloody machine on again.'

Kai left with a smile on his face and received one from Terry and each of his family. But after shutting the door of the studio and telling Terry not to turn Karen's power back on was like leaving Laura to her fate for good.

Almost a week had gone by before Kai had left the Black Bull in search of Parsonwood Hill Farm. Eleanor had put on a brave face after living with Kai at the pub. She struggled to get used to the different foods that Kai saw as normal but was completely foreign to her. The tap water made her sick but Kai didn't tell her the pub had been unoccupied for some time and had panicked he had risked that legionnaires made her ill.

Kai contracted a company to come and clean the pub and called Kevin an old assistant manager who hadn't found another job yet to come and recruit a new team.

'If a man called Dean calls for a head chef's job, bloody say no,' Kai said over the phone. Kevin who worked with the old head chef laughed and agreed.

Kai found the location of the farm after putting the address in his phone and borrowed his parent's car to make the journey. It had a long gravel drive which led them to a large wooden barn, which was surrounded by empty fields which hadn't held any type of animals for years,

'What is this place?' asked Eleanor,

'It isn't our idea of a farm,'

The place had been deserted for some time. A house sat behind the farm, it was old and it was a single-level home. This was also abandoned as wildlife and nature had overtook it. So much so that nettle branches were crawling out of the smashed windows and up onto the roof,

'We'll check the barn then,' said Kai as he tried to lift the wooden bar that locked the huge doors together, 'here, you get that side and we will go together. 1, 2.'

They both pushed up and slowly the bar moved out of its place. Once removed the doors open slightly on their own as if they had been held shut for some time. The barn was thick with dust, every footstep created a storm of particles in front of them. Windows high up near the ceiling allowed the sunlight to pierce the room leaving the corners in shadows,

'This doesn't feel like the place Eleanor,' said Kai, 'why would it be completely deserted if my parents were here somewhere,'

'Maybe Brown took all his people with him, maybe he underestimated you,' said Eleanor,

He nodded to show it may be true but didn't believe it. Brown would be smarter than to leave his farms unattended when there are prisoners,

'Or Kai, they have just left, as Brown has been away for some time now.'
That he did believe could be true, but the farm had no signs of life anywhere. Kai knew there would be something to show that people were working here or doing something.

'There must be a reason why Terry was looking at this place as a possible prison, he wouldn't just guess, it means too much to him,' said Kai,

'Well we look harder then!' said Eleanor determined.

Box after box they pushed aside for evidence of Brown's occupation or clues to where it could be. Old blankets covered farming equipment which was scattered around the room. When they pulled away the blankets they discovered more rakes and cobwebs filled with curled-up spiders.

The search inside the barn proved unsuccessful. There was just no sign of any life not alone his family. Before they left, Kai circled the barn on the outside and found hatch doors that led down some steps below ground. Kai hesitated but was also pushed by Eleanor to carry on and together lifted the old wooden doors.

The steps were shrouded in darkness and unknowns. It filled their hearts with fear and unease, but these were steps Kai had to take. No matter what he met along the way, what was at the end, it had to be a light. At the bottom of the steps Kai could turn the torch of his phone off because as he hoped, a light shined at the end of the passageway. The source of the light was an old lamp standing on a small four-legged table, behind the bars of a jail cell. Kai's heart stopped, he took one huge deep breath as he stepped into the light and exhaled at the sight of two people sitting on a wooded bench. He barely recognised them, their skin was bruised, and their hair was rough and broken. But it was them, it was his parents.

Len Fox was the first to look up and make eye contact with Kai. He moved slowly and his eyelids pinched slightly as he concentrated, trying to focus. He stood up, Kai was taken aback by how thin Len was. He wasn't ever a big guy but his imprisonment and lack of available food was evident. Kai couldn't move or say anything, and Eleanor stayed back and allowed Kai to greet his dad.
Len raised his hand and placed it on Kai's cheek. Kai froze and let him do it, he didn't know how to react. In his mind, it had only been a few days since he last saw his parents but when he thought about what he had been through since, it had felt a long time,

'Kai, you're here?' said Len in a rasp,

'Eleanor please can you get the water from the car,' said Kai as held the car keys out.

He didn't look at Eleanor, he didn't take his eyes off his dad who looked like he hadn't had a drink in about six months. Lens movement made Jen Fox stand and approach the bars. She didn't say a word instead she threw her arms around Kai and held him as close as she could. She didn't think about how she pulled him against the bars which separated them,

'Kai you found us, how?' Jen asked,

'I have found you, that is all that matters now,' said Kai, trying his best to keep composed,

'But Mr Brown, he will be here soon he will find you,'

'He won't, I promise,' replied Kai. 'Mr Brown is gone, he won't hurt us anymore. He has taken enough, but now I have found you we can go home. Which is still standing, by the way, Dennis and all,' smiled Kai.

Tears started to fall from Jen's face and along with a smile made her look much more alive than when he first saw her,

'How did you do it Kai?' asked Len, who had a very inquisitive look on his face,

'We outsmarted him, Dad, it's a long story but one I will tell you once we're home. But for now, all you need to know is Brown won't hurt us anymore,'

'That's great Kai, what I meant was how did you keep Dennis alive without the pub?'

Kai laughed along with Jen. Len was being serious but without pushing the issue chose to smile and chuckle as if the joke was intended. Eleanor returned water bottles from the car and handed them to Len and Jen.

'Ah thank you, Laura,' Len said, after taking the bottle. The smile that Eleanor arrived with faded and looked disappointingly at Kai. Who shook his head and gestured to Eleanor to leave it and that he would introduce them. For now, he let them drink, Jen took little sips when Len finished his bottle within a minute,

'Mum, Dad, this is Eleanor, she helped me find you,' they both looked at Eleanor and smiled pleasantly, and both awkwardly reintroduced themselves, 'we need to find a way to get you guys out of here,' Said Kai as he shook the padlock as if it would just fall off.

Kai looked for anything he could use to hit the lock with but the passageway was clear and tidier than he would have expected. Before he finished looking he heard a click and a clank and saw the padlock slide across the floor. He turned to face Eleanor who was holding the ring of keys, which he recognised as the ones they had taken from Brown's bouncer Brian.

'It would seem she did more than help you find us Kai,' said Jen, who threw her arms around Eleanor, who in turn took the embrace like it was her mother. Something she had been without for as long as she could remember.

Kai was a little disappointed that he didn't think of this but was able to put that aside to just be thankful he had Eleanor with him,

'So, you didn't kill Mr Brown, Kai? Did you?' asked Len as they walked up the steps back out to the outside world,

'No Dad,' said Kai, 'but trust me he is worlds away from us now,'

'Yeah, but how, he was the most dangerous man I have ever seen,'

'Hey, I'm stronger than I look you know,'

'We both are,' Said Eleanor, interrupting the conversation.

The sun started to rise creating a flame-like horizon, as the night sky became a morning blue,

'Ah you came in my car as well, I'll drive,' said Len,

'No! No, you won't dad,' Kai had to slap his hand onto the car door to stop Len, 'I will drive you just sit in the back with mum, relax and enjoy the ride,'

After getting his parents into the back seats of his car, Kai spent a minute looking at the barn that had held his parents captive,

'When did they all leave?' asked Kai,

'We don't know,' said Jen, 'We haven't seen the outside of that basement for days,'

'Wait Jen, can you not remember what that boy said when the guard asked for Brown,'
Everyone waited in silence,
'He's gone to the studio to change the world,'
'Oh, but Len that was a while ago.' said Jen,
'Yes, but they only came back once more to give us food and water, and he did not look happy,'
'What do you mean?' interrupted Eleanor,
Len smiled at them like he was about to tell them a joke,
'He had the face like our waitresses when Kai was manager, like his manager had gone AWOL,' chuckled Len,
Jen slapped Len on his arm,
'Len!'
'Sorry, all I meant is that they looked leaderless or they no longer had a reason to be doing what they were doing. And so they left,'
Kai started the car and began to head down the stone driveway, leaving the abandoned farm behind them,
'How do you think they knew he wasn't coming back?' said Eleanor,
She had asked louder than she had intended as Len's ears had pricked up. Kai answered before his dad could interrupt,
'I don't know unless someone had got a message out somehow.'
They were on the road now and on the way to get their lives back to somewhat normal, or as normal as it ever was in the fox's household or working at the Black Bull,
'Anyway Kai, you never told me how you defeated Brown,' said Len,
Kai looked at Eleanor and rolled his eyes, then replied,
'Do you know what dad, use your imagination!'

Printed in Great Britain
by Amazon